# POSSESSION

Possession Duet
#1

THE REDEMPTION SERIES

*USA TODAY* BESTSELLING AUTHOR

# T.K. LEIGH

# POSSESSION

Published by Carpe Per Diem, Inc. / Tracy Kellam, 25852 McBean Parkway # 806, Santa Clarita, CA 91355

Edited by: Kim Young, Kim's Editing Services

Image Permission:

Geber86 Copyright 2020

Used under license from iStock Photo

# BOOKS BY T.K. LEIGH

## CONTEMPORARY ROMANCE
### *The Redemption Series*
Promise: A Redemption Duet Prologue
Commitment (Redemption Duet #1)
Redemption (Redemption Duet #2)
Possession (Possession Duet #1)
Atonement (Possession Duet #2)

### *The Dating Games Series*
Dating Games
Wicked Games
Mind Games
Dangerous Games
Royal Games
Tangled Games

## ROMANTIC COMEDY
### *The Book Boyfriend Chronicles*
The Other Side of Someday
Writing Mr. Right

## ROMANTIC SUSPENSE

### *The Inferno Saga*
Part One: Spark
Part Two: Smoke
Part Three: Flame
Part Four: Burn

For more information on any of these titles and upcoming releases, please visit T.K.'s website:
www.tkleighauthor.com

*To the great RBG.*
*Thank you for paving the way.*

Dear Reader,

Thank you so much for picking up Possession. I can't tell you what your support means to me.

This is a bit of an interesting book. I've been planning this story for nearly two years now. Unfortunately, other projects kept getting in the way, but when I finished up my last release, Royal Games, I said I was going to finally take the time to write what I knew would be a very challenging book.

Then the race riots started happening, and I nearly canceled the project altogether. All along, I knew this would be an interracial romance, and that it would address subjects that may make people uncomfortable or angry, and rightly so. Because of this, I started to question whether the time was right, given the current state of violence in our country.

Thankfully, a dear friend and reader I respect very much, who also happens to be a black woman, told me to just write the dang book. So that's what I did. I wrote the dang book. And I can't tell you how proud of this book I am. I've never been one to shy away from difficult subjects, but I didn't know if I was the right person to tell this story. I'm still not sure I am, but I've learned so much about myself during this process.

It goes without saying that I absolutely love this story. I love these characters. And I love the love that comes off the pages. Like I mentioned, this isn't an easy story to read or experience. You will get angry. You will question things. But at the end of the day, you will feel this incredible love between the characters.

With that being said, I'd be remiss if I didn't mention there are a few scenes which may trigger extremely sensitive readers. As with all my books, I approach sensitive subjects with care and respect, and don't glorify or write certain things with unnecessary detail just for the shock factor. That's never been my style. Sometimes what the camera doesn't show you is more poignant than what it does. And this is the approach I take here.

Again, thank you for picking up a copy of Possession. I adore this story. I hope you do, too. I hope it makes you think.

Makes you angry. But most of all, I hope it makes you feel love.

Peace and love,
~ T.K.

"What do you need me to do? I want to help while I'm here. Want me to reach out to some of these designers for you?"

"Sure. There are a bunch of business cards on the desk in my office if you want to check some of them out."

"Can do."

It's no surprise she wants a say in who we hire to work on our grandparents' old house. Despite Julia being adopted, because my mother needed something else to brag about to all her society friends, my sister formed an incredible bond with Meemaw and Gampy. For all intents and purposes, they raised her. Not my parents.

I suppose the same could be said of me, too.

"Thanks, Jules." Spying the time on the stove, I exhale deeply. "Well, I'm off to play golf." I feign enthusiasm over the prospect.

While I don't mind the sport, I have no desire to play in this tournament. Unfortunately, I don't have a choice. It's something my father started years ago as a way to flaunt his wealth in front of clients and friends. According to him, in order to make money, you need to act like you have money. And now that I've taken over the day-to-day running of the firm, I can't skip out on the annual display of wealth and privilege.

"I'll never understand why men like playing a game where they whack balls across grass," Julia retorts.

"It's more a game of focus than whacking balls, but I see your point."

"And an excuse to see who has the biggest balls. Or at least bank account."

I shrug. "It is what it is."

"I suppose." Julia reaches up, messing up my hair so it's no longer slicked back and perfect. That's the good thing about her staying with me. She keeps me grounded. She doesn't let the people I have no choice but to associate with influence me.

Leaning down, I kiss her forehead, then walk to Imogene, giving her a quick peck on the cheek. "Love you, sweet pea. You be good for your mama, okay?"

"Yes, sir."

19

Then I turn, steeling myself to spend the next several hours surrounded by people who think happiness is measured in terms of stock portfolios and love is a sign of weakness.

needed, so they abandoned the project. It sat vacant for years. Until just a week ago when it returned to the rightful owners." A smile lights up her face as she soaks in her surroundings, almost in disbelief. "Come on. I'll show you what used to be the dining room." She gestures to a set of double doors and slides them open.

"Holy crap," I breathe, trying to hide my excitement. "Double pocket doors?" I run my hand along the frame. "You don't see these much anymore."

"They're original, too. It's amazing what a little WD-40 can do."

"They started constructing houses with these around the time this was built," I offer, hoping to impress her with my knowledge of history of design.

I'll do whatever I need in order to get this job. I've only seen one room and am already in love. I have no idea how this woman found me, but that doesn't matter. All that does is the feeling inside me that this is kismet, fate, destiny. I can't explain it. Almost like that same electricity I experienced the first time I peered into Weston's eyes. But it's more than that. Like this is the day I take that first step toward achieving what I've always wanted but never had the guts to pursue — my own historic restoration and design business.

"My brother and I used to mess around with them when we were younger. Meemaw loved cooking. I would sit with her for hours, trying to learn everything I could. When it was time to eat, I'd open these doors and announce to my brother and Gampy that 'Dinner was served'," she mimics in a proper British accent as she leads me into the formal dining room.

A chandelier hangs from the high ceiling, and I can almost picture the dinner parties that were held within these walls. There's a fireplace here, as well. This one with a more formal design than the one in the living room. Whereas some designers would probably want to tear down the wall between the living and dining rooms, I refuse to do that here. It's more important to maintain the original integrity of the house. And tearing down the wall would mean destroying the pocket doors, and I firmly believe there's a special place in hell for people who would commit such a travesty without cause.

"What's through here?" I gesture toward a small door on the far side of the room.

"Butler's pantry." Julia reaches for what I suspect to be the original knob and opens the door. "Of course, when we were kids, we called it Meemaw's pantry."

"I like that." I smile, following her into a small room with a window overlooking the side of the property, shelves filling the walls on either side. As with every other room, it needs some love. But unlike the others, a huge section of the wall between the pantry and kitchen is missing. "What happened here?"

"Previous owners were probably hoping to open up the kitchen."

"Idiots," I mumble, unable to stop myself.

She nods. "I agree wholeheartedly."

"I'd like to fix the wall. I understand why they did it. These days, it seems every interior designer is all about knocking down every wall possible, but I don't want to do that here. It'll destroy this place's character. I'd like to keep this Meemaw's pantry. Find a vintage desk for below the window. Put some photos of Meemaw on it."

"I love that idea." A gleam in her eyes, she reaches for my hand and squeezes. "Better yet, Meemaw would like it."

"Good."

"Come on. There's still lots more to see." She walks out of the pantry, continuing her tour.

As she leads me through the rest of the house, I listen to her reminisce about her childhood here and offer the occasional suggestion about how to bring this place back to life, constantly snapping photos so I don't forget a single detail.

After touring the bedrooms on the upper level and the enormous covered rear porch just off the kitchen that I can picture as the perfect entertaining area, we head back toward the front door.

Julia turns to me. "So what do you think?"

"It may be an old house, but it has great bones. Based on what you told me about wanting to update the electrical, plumbing, and HVAC, the interior will need to be taken down to just its frame. I know some great contractors who will be able to rewire this place and not destroy its character. We'll need to test for asbestos, but since it was built in the 1850s, I doubt we'll find any. That wasn't really commercially available until later in the century, and not used regularly until the 1900s, so that definitely works to our advantage."

"Guess it's a good thing we bought an ancient house instead of one that's just really old." Julia laughs.

I smile. "Always good to look on the bright side, especially with historic renovations. You have to go in with the mindset that anything can go wrong, and probably will. With all that said, I have no desire to completely redo this house. Like I mentioned, I'm not interested in tearing down the walls. I want to keep as much of the original ceiling, flooring, and hardware as I can. And definitely the fireplaces and the stained glass throughout. Where you see walls right now, you'll see walls when I'm finished. The kitchen will be updated and modernized, but it will still have a historic feel to it. I've seen state-of-the-art stoves and refrigerators that have a more antique style. I don't enter into a historic remodel to destroy. I do it to preserve. So I'd like to save everything I can. Maybe recycle some of the broken fixtures into art pieces."

The more I speak, the more animated my voice becomes, idea after idea popping into my head. There's so much potential here. It's an interior designer's wet dream. At least it's *my* wet dream.

"This is an incredible house that's filled with history. The last thing I want to do is erase that history. In fact, I want to weave its history throughout the renovation."

Julia exhales a long breath, almost out of relief. Then she grabs my hands in hers, squeezing them. "You're the first designer I've spoken to who gets it."

"I hope so. And if you hire me, I promise to treat your baby with the care and attention she deserves. With the care and attention necessary to preserve your memories of spending summers here with your grandparents. This is a stunning house, and I promise to make it stunning again. Will make it somewhere you can create new memories."

"That's it. You're hired. When can you start?" She laughs, and I join in. Then she levels her gaze on me. "But seriously. Do you have other pressing projects, or can you get started right away?"

I furrow my brow. "You're serious?"

"Absolutely. When you know, you know. And with you, I know."

I blink, caught off guard. I didn't expect to get hired on the spot, especially without drawing up any sort of budget. "I didn't even tell you what it's going to cost."

She waves me off. "Doesn't matter. You can't put a price on history. Plus, my brother has more money than he knows what to do with, and I don't mind spending it."

"But I really should—"

Before I can finish my statement, the sound of barking cuts through, followed by a rambunctious dog flying through the now-broken screen door and jumping on me, panting and tail wagging.

"Oh god." Julia's expression turns horrified as she peels the Pointer mix off me. "No, Zeus. Down, boy."

I inhale a sharp breath at the name. Most people wouldn't think twice about a dog being named Zeus. It's a common name for dogs. But most people weren't betrayed by a man obsessed with Greek mythology. I wonder if this is a sign I shouldn't be here.

"Your dog's name is Zeus?" I ask in a small voice, telling myself it's just a coincidence, that I can't allow the memory of *him* to destroy one of the first good things to happen to me in years. If I avoided everyone who named their pet Zeus, or some other character from Greek mythology, I doubt I'd have many acquaintances.

She struggles to hold the dog back from jumping up on me again. "A Greek god he is not, I'm afraid."

"Well, he seems just as promiscuous as Zeus. He couldn't keep it in his pants, either."

"Zeus!" a deep voice calls out, followed by heavy footsteps on the front porch. "Get back here, you obedience school dropout!"

Every muscle in my body stiffens and I whip my head up, a rush of adrenaline filling me when I see a man stride purposefully into the house, a beautiful little girl with golden curls in his arms. I blink, convinced I must be imagining this. But there's no mistaking the buzz of electricity filling me.

The same buzz that coursed through me a week ago.

The same buzz that grows even more intense when I peer into Weston's blue eyes once more.

# CHAPTER FIVE

Mouth agape, eyes wide, I stare at Londyn, dumbfounded. How did this happen?

When Julia told me she thought she found a good fit for a designer, never once did I expect it would be Londyn. I want to pinch myself, make sure this is actually happening and not the result of my subconscious playing a trick on me.

"Glad you made it back," Julia says, yanking me back to the present. "Wes, this is—"

"Londyn…" I lower Imogene to her feet and extend my hand toward her.

With slow motions, she allows me to take her hand in mine, inhaling a barely noticeable breath when our skin touches. My pulse steadily increases, a pulling sensation settling low in my stomach.

Over the past week, I'd convinced myself I imagined the magnetism I experienced when we met. Convinced myself it was simply from the adrenaline rush of putting my own life at risk to save hers.

But now that I'm here, that *she's* here, I realize that's not the case. This pull toward her is real, palpable…powerful.

"Yes…" Julia's analytical gaze ping-pongs between us. "Londyn, this is my brother, Wes."

Londyn briefly closes her eyes, her shoulders seeming to relax. "He's your brother," she states more for herself than anyone else.

"Yes. My brother." Julia scrunches her brow. "Why?"

"No reason." Londyn pulls her hand from mine. "I thought maybe he was your husband or something."

"Definitely not." Julia grimaces. "No offense, Wes."

"None taken." I chuckle, then face Londyn, gesturing to the little blonde at my side. "And this is Julia's daughter,

Imogene."

Londyn crouches down to be eye level with my niece, a brilliant smile lighting up her face. "Hi, Imogene. That's such a pretty name."

"Thank you, ma'am," she says with all the manners my sister has ingrained into her. "Mama says I'm named after Meemaw. She used to live here, but I never got to meet her. She went up to heaven before I was born."

She offers Imogene a sincere look. "I'm sorry to hear that, but I promise to help your mama and uncle bring this house back to life so you'll have a piece of your meemaw. Okay?"

Imogene nods. "Okay." She cranes her head up toward Julia. "Can I go play outside with Zeus?"

"Of course, lovebug. Just be careful and stay out of the brush. There's no telling what kind of critters are out there."

"I will," Imogene promises, already running down the long hallway toward the back porch, Zeus following loyally behind her, barking.

"She's a beautiful little girl," Londyn offers as she stands.

"She is. But she's certainly a handful." Julia rolls her eyes in feigned annoyance, but no one can ignore the love and absolute wonder in her gaze as she looks out the open back door at Imogene and Zeus chasing each other, her giggles making their way into the house.

I shove my hands into my pockets, feeling awkward in Londyn's presence. I'm generally calm and confident around women. But with her, I seem to forget how to speak, my mind only able to focus on her addictive scent and glossy, heart-shaped lips.

"So...," Julia begins, her voice snapping me out of my trance yet again.

"Do you have any design experience?" I ask quickly, praying Julia didn't pick up on the fact I'd just been staring at Londyn's lips. Hoping Londyn didn't, either. "I know you refurbish old furniture, but there's a big difference between fixing up furniture and fixing up an entire house."

"I have a bachelor's in art history, where I specialized in architectural preservation, as well as a master's in interior

31

design from the Atlanta School of Design."

"You didn't know she was a designer?" Julia counters. "Why else would you leave her card for me?"

"To be honest, I didn't. Her card was…" I scrape my fingers through my hair, chewing on my lower lip. "Well, for me."

"Is that right?" Julia smirks, giving me a look reminiscent of one she gave me in our teenage years whenever I came home smelling of perfume.

"Yes." I narrow my eyes, silently telling her not to press the subject.

"Well…" She plasters a bright smile on her face. "I'm glad I found her card on your desk. I checked out her webpage and Instagram, loved what I saw, and reached out. When I learned she just got fired from Margo St. James due to staff reductions, I knew I had to swipe her up before someone else did."

I shoot my wide eyes to hers, stunned at this revelation. "You worked for Margo St. James?" I didn't know what I expected to learn about her design background, but never did I think she'd worked for one of the top interior designers in the state, perhaps the entire country.

While I had stalked her website and Instagram, I hadn't noticed any mention of the job she'd just gotten fired from the day we met. Probably because I was too focused on admiring her photos to look at anything else.

"You know who she is?" She arches a perfectly manicured brow.

"Our paths have crossed a time or two."

"Wes is an architect," Julia explains proudly.

"You are?" Londyn blinks repeatedly, just as taken aback by this revelation as I was about who she worked for.

I nod. "I am."

"You two have quite a lot in common," Julia encourages.

It doesn't take a genius to figure out what she's trying to do. Sometimes she's just as bad as my mother. As least I know Julia won't try to set me up with someone who's only interested in the size of my bank account. Still, I'm not sure I'm ready to put myself through another relationship. Not after the disaster and heartache of my last one. I have everything I need. The architecture firm. The charity work I do. And, occasionally, Julia and Imogene. They offer me love and companionship. That's enough for me.

After several moments of uncomfortable silence, Londyn looks at Julia. "Well, I should get back to the city. I have so many ideas floating in my head. I can't wait to get started. Like I said, I promise to honor the history and memories you have of this house." She glances in my direction. "Both of you."

My sister smiles appreciatively, taking her hand and squeezing. "Thank you."

"Of course." She holds her gaze another moment, then peers at me, an unexpected shyness about her. "It was nice to see you again, Wes."

I smile. It doesn't escape my notice that she's finally dropped the formality of Weston and called me Wes.

"Wonderful to see you again, Londyn," I say smoothly as I extend my hand toward her. She takes it, and I wrap my fingers around her, delicately brushing my thumb along her knuckles, causing a subtle shiver to roll through her. "Surprising, yet wonderful." I maintain my hold for a protracted moment, turning a simple handshake into something more, not caring Julia's witnessing our interaction.

"Thanks again for this opportunity."

"No problem at all." My sister smirks, a devilish glint in her eyes.

I reluctantly release Londyn's hand. She steps back, flashing a smile at Julia.

"I'll have Wes get in touch with you sometime over the next few days to talk about the next steps." Julia waves her hand around. "While I can make some mean macarons and other pastries, Wes is the expert when it comes to building stuff."

Londyn tilts her head, squinting at Julia. "*That's* why you look so familiar," she exclaims after a moment. "Do you work at The Mad Batter in Buckhead?"

Julia laughs, nodding. "I'll do you one better. I own it."

"I love your peanut butter and jelly cookies," Londyn says

excitedly.

She snorts. "You can thank Imogene for that creation. One day, she asked what good a peanut butter cookie is without jelly."

"Next time I see her, I'll be sure to do that. Until then…" She nods at Julia before lifting her gaze to meet mine once more.

Then she turns, making her way out of the house and into her SUV, leaving me reeling at the prospect of seeing her again.

# CHAPTER SIX

WESTON

"Okay. Spill," Julia orders the second Londyn's car disappears from view.

"Spill what?" I turn from her, retreating down the hallway and into the kitchen. Opening the cooler, I grab a couple of beers, pop the top off each, then hand one to Julia.

"You know what." She follows me onto the covered back porch, sitting beside me on the top step. "Londyn. There's obviously some sort of attraction between you."

"Nah." I brush her off, peering out over the expansive property, almost able to see the ghosts of my childhood dancing before my eyes. Except now it's just Imogene playing with Zeus.

Buying back this house was a rash move, especially once I saw all the work that needed to be done. But now I look forward to spending time here again, doing this exact thing with my sister as we watch Imogene run through the fields and jump into the lake, like we did years ago.

"Don't even try to dismiss it. I saw that shit with my own eyes. Hell, I *felt* it. The electricity…" She shivers dramatically. "It was strong enough to power all of Atlanta for the next century, Wes."

"It's not like that."

"Why?"

"It's just not."

"How did you meet?"

"She fell in a crosswalk during a torrential downpour and was about to get hit by some asshole in a pickup truck. I was in the coffee shop around the corner from the office getting Omar his coffee and saw it all happen. It was stupid, considering I could have been killed, but no one else seemed to care. Hell, some people were even recording it."

"What the hell is wrong with people?"

"I ask myself that on a daily basis," I sigh as I bring the bottle to my lips and take a swig, the drink refreshing in the muggy air. "So I ran out, pulled her out of the way, and carried her into the coffee shop. We talked for a few minutes. Then she left."

"But she gave you her business card. Obviously, there's more to the story if she did that."

"I asked for her number." I chuckle, smiling at the memory. "Shouted it so everyone could hear."

"Really?" She tilts her head, lips pinched together. "That doesn't sound like the Wes *I* know. The Wes who is the antithesis of spontaneous. The Wes who certainly wouldn't draw attention to himself like that."

"I don't understand it, either, Jules. It's like some other power took control and forced me to blurt out those words. So she gave me her business card."

"And?" Her eyes light up in anticipation of the story I've kept from her this past week. A story I thought I'd keep to myself the rest of my life. I assumed Londyn would eventually fade into the recesses of my brain, apart from a memory I'd smile at every time I passed that crosswalk and remembered the day I pulled a woman to safety. But now our paths have more than just crossed. They've collided.

"I texted her to make sure she got home safely."

"That's it?"

"Afraid so. End of story. Until today." Avoiding her curious stare, I peer ahead, unusually preoccupied with Zeus as he marks his territory on a nearby tree.

"You've got a thing for her," Julia states after a pause.

I roll my eyes, but don't look directly at her. She knows me better than anyone. She'd be able to tell in a heartbeat I'm not being completely forthcoming. Hell, she probably already knows that.

"I've told you repeatedly. I don't have time for a relationship. Not with taking over the firm."

"You have time to oversee this." She waves her hand around the massive property I now hold the deed to.

"*Oversee*," I emphasize. "Nash and Londyn will be doing most of the work." I take another long pull from my beer, exhaling on the finish.

"But you'll be checking in. Occasionally helping out. Working closely with Londyn."

I shake my head, knowing all too well what she's getting at. "All the more reason why I shouldn't get involved with her. If it doesn't work out, and I guarantee it won't, it would be awkward."

"Ah-ha!" Julia slams her beer onto the step. The liquid fizzes over the bottle neck, but it doesn't faze her. "I knew it!"

"Knew what?"

"You just admitted it!" She nudges me, her laughter filling the air.

"I didn't admit anything."

"You said it yourself. You don't want to get involved with her because I hired her for the design job here."

"I was speaking hypothetically, Jules. You're only hearing what you want to. But for argument's sake, let's say you're right. You're not, but let's say you are. It would still never work out."

"Why do you say that?"

I narrow my gaze on her. "You know why."

Julia edges toward me. "Because she's black?" she asks quietly.

I pinch my lips together, shrugging.

"I didn't take you for someone who cared about that kind of thing," she remarks somewhat harshly. "Hell, you almost married Brooklyn, despite the fact she's not some trust fund debutante. I thought that's what you wanted. Someone real."

"And I do. Thanks to you."

She blinks, leaning back a little. "*Me?*"

"Yeah." I shrug. "Before you dated Nick, you were desperate for Mom to accept you. Participated in those pageants you hated. Did the debutante thing. Went to Wesleyan because it's where she wanted you to go, even though you would have much rather gone to culinary school. If you hadn't gotten together with Nick, I doubt you would have felt like you were enough. Doubt you would have spread your wings, grown the backbone you have now, and pretty much told Mom to suck it. So when I saw you finally stand up for what you wanted... I don't know. It gave me hope, too, Jules. Hope that I could be happy. That I could have something real, like you have with Nick."

She squeezes her eyes shut, a pensive expression on her face as a gentle breeze blows around us, picking up the familiar aroma of wildflowers and raw earth.

"What is it?" I press.

She lifts her gaze to mine, lips parted, a response on the tip of her tongue. Then she clamps her mouth shut, looking forward. "It's nothing."

A silence passes over us. I can't shake the feeling she's hiding something from me, which is unlike her. She usually tells me everything. We may not have always gotten along when we were teenagers, but in the past several years, especially once I moved back to Atlanta, we've become close.

"Jules, you know——"

"So if you say you want something real," she interrupts before I can push the issue, "why don't you go after it? I know what I saw, Wes. Know what I *felt*. There's something real between Londyn and you."

"I know how it will end, Jules. I've already been there."

"With Brooklyn?" she asks hesitantly.

I nod. "You know how hurt I was after she broke things off."

"You moved your entire world to be near her."

My chest squeezes at the memory of everything I did for it all to come crashing down at the eleventh hour. I'm not bitter, though. Not anymore. Like I told myself in the months to follow, like I still remind myself on occasion, it was better I learned she didn't love me like she needed before we made that lifelong commitment to each other. I thought if I loved her with everything I had, it would be enough. But I've learned you can't force someone to love you if their heart isn't in it. And Brooklyn's heart wasn't in it. Not all of it anyway.

"She broke my damn heart, Jules. And think about it.

Brooklyn… Londyn…" I give her a knowing look. "A bit of a coincidence that they're both named after cities, don't you think? If that's not an omen this is history repeating itself, I don't know what is." My jaw twitches as I shake my head. "No. I'd rather not go through that again. Especially when it will never work."

"Why? Because your mother won't approve?" she sneers.

It doesn't escape my notice she doesn't refer to her as *our* mother. She hasn't in years. Instead, she calls her Lydia, her subtle reminder that the woman never acted as a mother to her, that she only adopted her to appear charitable to her friends. But the second we were no longer in public, she treated her like a nuisance.

"That woman will only approve of someone for her darling Weston if she comes with the right pedigree."

"I don't care about her approval. Not anymore. If I did, I wouldn't have dated Brooklyn. And *because* of Brooklyn, I'm painfully aware that there's only so much a person is willing to put up with when it comes to that woman. And if you thought she was horrible to Brooklyn, imagine how she'd treat Londyn. At least Brooklyn was white."

Julia is more than aware how our parents would react to the idea of me dating anyone who isn't rich, white, and possesses the proper last name. If we didn't have Gampy's and Meemaw's influence, we probably would have thought it normal to judge someone because of their skin color, ethnicity, or socioeconomic status, as everyone else in our lives did back then. Hell, as nearly everyone in my life still does.

"I guarantee there's only so much Londyn would be willing to put up with once she got a taste of the life we've always known."

"That *you've* always known." She pauses before asking her next question, one I'm sure she's wanted to ask for years. "But is this *really* the life you want? Schmoozing clients? Playing their game? Not following your heart because you're worried about what people will say?"

I peer into the distance, unsure how to explain the love-hate relationship I have with my current position as the head of the firm. I've always been passionate about how things were made. Ever since I was a little boy and helped Gampy build the stables on this property, I knew I wanted to follow in my father's footsteps and design buildings.

But I wasn't prepared for the political side of running the business. If it weren't for the charities I founded in order to give back to those who can't afford adequate housing, I'm not sure it *would* be worth it. Truthfully, that's the only thing that's kept me going. Every time I sign a huge contract to build another monstrous highrise in Dubai or a new casino in Vegas, I don't see the bonuses the executive board will receive. I see all the modest houses I can build for those living in shelters after losing their homes in a hurricane or tornado.

"I thought it was when I lived in Boston," I admit finally. "When I was so far away from everything and in my own little bubble."

"But now that you're back with all these people, it's not what you thought it would be."

"It's not what I remember it to be."

Nodding, Julia shifts her eyes forward, a smile tugging on her lips as she watches Imogene swing on an old tire hanging from a large branch, Zeus lying in the shade beneath the tree, acting the part of her dutiful protector.

"Do you remember what Meemaw used to say?"

"Meemaw used to say a lot of things," I joke.

She narrows her gaze on me. With that one look, I know what she's talking about. The one piece of advice I'll always carry with me. That we'll *both* carry with us.

"Sometimes the right path isn't the easiest."

"Exactly," Julia replies, resting her head on my shoulder. "Maybe you're right. Maybe it won't work out. But maybe Londyn is *your* right path. Your key to finally being happy again. You'll never know if you talk yourself out of that first step before you have a chance to take it."

# CHAPTER SEVEN

LONDYN

"How was it?" Hazel asks as she bursts through the door of my condo without knocking.

At this point, I'm used to it. I may rent the second unit of the multi-family house Hazel owns with her husband, Diego, but after I took the self-defense class she teaches and we bonded over our tragic pasts, Hazel's become more like family to me. She's the only person in the world I trust. And that says a lot, considering I didn't think I'd ever trust again.

I look up from my laptop, having spent all afternoon going down the proverbial Pinterest rabbit hole, finding idea after idea for the country house, as I've begun calling Gampy and Meemaw's house.

Meeting her brown eyes as she makes herself comfortable beside me on the couch, I beam. "Incredible. It's just…" I exhale, struggling to find my words. "Everything about it was amazing. It's in the middle of nowhere. I'm not even sure where the downtown area is, since I didn't see anything remotely resembling civilization. Although I did pass about a dozen churches." I snort a laugh. "Pretty sure there are more churches than schools in that part of the state."

Hazel rolls her eyes. "Haven't you learned by now, especially considering you grew up as the daughter of a pastor and were also married to one at one point?" Her voice oozes sarcasm as she continues. "Religion is much more important than education. Just pray and everything will be A-okay."

I give her a half-hearted smile. I don't share the same animosity toward organized religion as Hazel does, although I do struggle with it. Have since my mother died when a disturbed gunman shot up a church. Where was God when that happened? How could that have been part of His plan?

Shrugging off the past, I bring up the album containing the

photos I'd captured and shift my laptop toward her. "Check out some of these pictures."

She inhales deeply, staring in awe at the exterior of the house that looks like it's straight out of a history book.

"Pretty incredible, right?"

"Most people would say it looks like a shithole, but I know you better than that." She laughs.

"It just needs a little TLC. They don't make homes like this anymore. Nowadays, most houses are cookie-cutter replicas of each other. There's no character. No story. But here…" I run my finger along the screen at the closeup shot of the stained-glass window over the front door. "There's history in those walls. I could feel it." I lower my hand, looking at Hazel. "And I know it sounds crazy, but the second I stepped inside that house, I sensed I was about to be part of something greater than merely designing a home. And I didn't even tell you the best part."

Hazel smirks, inwardly laughing at how excited I am over a house. But to me, it's not just a house. "What's that?"

"Look." I scroll through the photos until I find the one I'm looking for. "Pocket doors!"

Hazel bursts out laughing, the sound echoing through the open living space. "Only you would get all hot and bothered by a *door*."

"You don't see stuff like that anymore. There's even a butler's pantry. And a few hidden closets behind bookcases. I'm going to turn one of them into a laundry room, since there isn't one."

Her eyes widen. "No laundry room?"

"The place was built in the 1850s. Apart from a few updates here and there, not much has been done to bring it into the twentieth century, let alone the twenty-first. So that's what I plan on doing, while keeping with the original character."

"So you're taking the job."

"I am," I say, unable to mask the hint of reluctance in my tone.

"What is it?" She pushes a few strands of her chestnut hair behind her ears.

"Nothing," I answer quickly. "It's nothing."

"No. There's something. A minute ago, you were practically coming in your pants over pocket doors and hidden closets. Now, you don't seem so...certain."

I chew on the inside of my cheek, unsure what to tell her about Weston. Wes. All week, I'd convinced myself the spark I felt when we first met was because of my near-death experience. But that same electricity was there today. It was even more powerful, if that's at all possible.

"Come on, Lo." She rests her hand over mine, her gesture comforting. "You can tell me anything."

"I know. I just..." I tilt back my head and stare at the ceiling, wracking my brain for the words I need to explain Wes. "Julia, the woman who hired me, well... She has a brother."

Amusement dances in Hazel's eyes as a grin lights up her face. "Go on."

"And I know him."

"Who is it?" She straightens, brows knitted together. "One of your previous clients? Please tell me it's not the same prick who came home drunk and thought it was a good idea to try to get you into bed, because I'm still pissed—"

I hold up my hand to cut her off. "No. Not a former client. Nothing like that."

"Then who?"

"Remember that guy I told you about? The one who saw me slip in the crosswalk and came to my rescue?"

"Weston, right?"

"Yes." I push out a long breath, running my sweaty palms along my yoga pants. "He's Julia's brother. And an architect, so he'll be quite involved in the renovation and remodel."

She studies me for several protracted moments, analyzing me in a way I'm sure gives away all my secrets. I hadn't told her much about Wes. About the way my body lit up, making me want to lower my defenses for the first time in over five years. I'd simply told her what happened, then of the Good Samaritan who came to my aid. Nothing more. I didn't think I'd ever see him again. I guess I was wrong.

"Why do I get the sense there's more here than him simply being the guy who helped you?" she comments just as my ringing cell phone pierces the room.

I dart my gaze to it. My heart ricochets into my throat, my eyes widening when I see Wes' name pop up on the screen.

Worse, Hazel sees it, too.

"I think that just answered my question," she taunts.

I feign irritation and stand, swiping my phone off the coffee table and heading into the kitchen area. On a deep inhale, I straighten my spine, trying to subdue the butterflies taking flight in my stomach.

"This is Londyn," I answer with all the professionalism I can muster.

"Hey, Londyn. It's Wes."

"Hi. Is everything okay? Or are you calling to tell me your sister changed her mind and decided to go with another designer?"

"*What*? No. No way am I letting you slip through my fingers." He inhales sharply. "I mean, *her* fingers."

I fight back my grin as a warmth spreads over my cheeks. I could listen to him speak for hours and not tire of his deep voice and refined Southern drawl.

"Well, good, because I already have so many ideas for the house. I can't wait to get started."

"And that's the perfect segue to the reason for this phone call."

"What's that?"

"Are you available Friday evening for dinner?"

"Dinner?" I repeat, his invitation catching me off guard.

"To go over a few ideas," he explains. "That's all." He pushes out a nervous laugh. I picture him combing his long fingers through his dark hair, as he did a few times during our brief interactions. "It's not a date or anything."

"Of course." I force a smile, ignoring the unexpected pang of disappointment.

"Not that I wouldn't want to date," he continues. "I just—"

"No need to explain, Wes," I interject, not wanting this conversation to become any more awkward than it already is.

"What time? And where?"

"I was hoping we could get together at my place in Brookhaven. Julia and Imogene will be there, too. They stay with me when Julia's in town checking in on her bakery. It will be low-key and casual. Just a typical family dinner."

"That actually sounds nice."

"Great." Wes' voice is a mixture of relieved and excited. And perhaps a little nervous. "I'll text you the address. Seven o'clock work?"

"That's perfect. I'll see you then."

As I'm about to end the call, Wes stops me.

"Hey, Londyn?"

"Yes?"

He hesitates, then lowers his voice, that sensual tone returning. "It was really good to see you again today."

I close my eyes, sucking in my bottom lip, wanting to tell him how great it was to see him again, too. Instead, I say, "I'll see you Friday." I wince, immediately feeling like a bitch. But if Wes thinks any less of me, he doesn't let on.

"Looking forward to it," he responds.

When the line goes silent, I end the call, heaving out a long sigh. "Me, too."

"You like him, don't you?"

I whirl around, momentarily surprised. I'd all but forgotten Hazel was here. As seems to happen whenever I'm in Wes' presence, the mere act of speaking to him made me oblivious to the outside world. In those few minutes, it was just me and him. No one else.

"Excuse me?" I hold my head high, fixing my expression to one of disinterest as I make my way back to the couch and lower myself beside her.

"Wes." She crosses her arms in front of her chest, a look of superiority about her. "You like him."

"It doesn't matter if I like him. He's a client."

"So?"

"If I want to make a go of having my own interior design business, I need to focus on that. Not spread my legs for my very first client. And even if Wes weren't a client, I'm not

45

interested. Not like that. Unless you've forgotten, I don't date."

"Oh, I haven't forgotten. I just thought maybe after meeting someone who actually makes you feel for a change, you might revisit your stance on your 'no dating' rule," she mocks, using air quotes.

I narrow my gaze. "You know why I don't date. Plus..." I brighten my tone. "I'm happy."

"And I'm the Tooth Fairy."

"I may not go around singing *Kumbaya* and doing Sun Salutations, like you do, but I like my life. I have everything I've always wanted. My up-cycling business has taken off to the point where I struggle to keep items in stock. I have my first real interior design job. On a historic home, no less. And I have you and Diego. What more could I need?"

"Love."

"I have love. You love me. So does Diego."

"That's different. While having a solid support group is important, it will never make up for that butterfly-inducing love we all crave. Trust me." She squeezes my hand. "I understand your reluctance to get involved with someone. It's impossible to know who to trust these days, as you learned yourself. But sometimes you have to say enough is enough and take a risk, come what may. Otherwise, I'm worried you'll only live this half-life."

I'm on the brink of arguing to the contrary, that I'm living the life I've always wanted, but she knows me better than that. She's the only person who has no problem calling me out, pushing me to my limits so I don't retreat into the shell of the woman I was when we first met during her self-defense class.

Throughout the duration of her training, I looked up to her. She became a role model. I admired how strong and resilient she seemed, especially when she shared her story with the class, telling us why she felt compelled to teach self-defense to any woman who needed it.

Like myself, she married young, feeling forced into it. But unlike me marrying my ex so he could be hired as pastor of a rather influential church, she'd gotten married because she was pregnant. Her husband started drinking, grew abusive. After he struck their son, she knew it was time to leave. Unfortunately, he discovered her plan. Out of his mind with rage and too much alcohol flowing through his bloodstream, he confronted Hazel, shot her and their two young sons, aged five and eighteen months, before turning the gun on himself.

Only Hazel survived, albeit barely.

Which is why I still struggle to understand how she was able to put herself out there again after what she went through.

"Weren't you scared?" I ask in a timid voice, feeling unusually vulnerable. "When you started dating Diego? Especially after what you went through, what you lost? How were you able to take a risk again? Trust again?"

"Because if I didn't, he'd win. I survived. I needed to live for Evan and Benjamin." She offers a sad smile at the mention of her sons. "And for me.

"I'm not saying that putting myself out there, putting my *heart* out there, wasn't scary. It was. It was the most terrifying thing I'd ever done after everything I lost. There were times I felt like you do. That I should lock my heart behind an iron fortress so I don't have to experience that excruciating pain again. But if I did that, I never would have met Diego. Never would have experienced his love. And let me tell you, Lo. His love is everything to me."

Peace washes over her as she stares into the distance. "My mama used to always say that life is like a game of chess. Sometimes you're the queen. Sometimes the rook. Sometimes a pawn. But regardless of who you are, the strategy is the same. It's about taking risks and hoping to reap a huge reward. If you don't take a risk, you may miss out on finding that happiness people search for their entire lives. The happiness that might be right in front of you. The happiness you deserve. Just..." She trails off, collecting her thoughts.

Then she returns her blazing eyes back to mine, her expression brightening. "Just keep your heart open to the possibility instead of dictating what will never be because of some misplaced fear about what the future holds. No one can know what lies ahead of us. The only thing we can do is make the most of today. Live the best life we can."

I stare ahead, studying the vintage artwork I found at a flea market that hangs on the wall over the television. Can I really do what Hazel suggests? Can I really keep my heart open after everything?

"You have a decision to make, Lo," she continues when I don't immediately say anything. "Do you keep letting your past control you? Do you keep letting *him* win?"

I tear my eyes back to hers, about to argue I'm not letting *him* win, but she cuts me off.

"Or do you finally take back this last part of your life?" She pinches her lips together, a knowing look crossing her expression. "If you ask me, the answer's pretty obvious."

# CHAPTER EIGHT

WESTON

"You're late," Julia sings as I fly through the door and up the stairs, not even stopping by the kitchen to see her or Imogene. I can't. Not when Londyn's mere minutes away from walking through that same door herself.

Thanks to a few meetings that ran over, I got stuck in the office later than usual. Couple that with the already heavy Atlanta traffic that was even worse tonight, as if karma knew I was desperate to get home, and it's a wonder I made it here before Londyn at all.

"I know," I call back. "I'll be down in ten minutes."

"I've never known you to be ready in less than twenty."

I roll my eyes, ignoring Julia's jab as I step onto the second-floor landing and make my way down the photo-lined corridor and into the master bedroom. I leave a trail of clothes from the king-sized bed and into the bathroom, then take what's probably the world's quickest shower.

Once I wash the sticky Atlanta humidity from my body, I step out and towel off. Wiping the condensation from the expansive mirror above the dual vanity, I tilt my head back, surveying the scruff growing along my face and chin. I consider shaving, something I once did every day. Since Brooklyn left me and I haven't exactly had a woman for whom to shave, I've stopped putting in the effort.

As I peer at my reflection, I wonder what Londyn prefers. Does she like her men clean-shaven? Or would she rather a bit of scruff?

I don't have time to dwell on that, though, as the sound of the doorbell echoes, followed by Zeus' rambunctious barking. After running some product through my hair, I dash into my closet and grab the first thing I find — a white linen shirt and pair of jeans.

Once I'm dressed, I take one last look in the mirror before walking out of my room, my steps quick as I head down the stairs. The instant I round the corner into what I consider the heart of my home — the kitchen, living, and dining area — I'm assaulted with a powdery fresh perfume.

From the moment I laid eyes on Londyn, I thought she was beautiful. But there's something about having her in my house, dressed in a loose black blouse, a pair of skinny jeans, and those same heels I remember from that day in the rain, that makes her even more breathtaking. Her hair frames her face in tight ringlets, complexion smooth, lips shining with gloss. My gaze is drawn to them like a man seeing the majesty of the Grand Canyon for the first time, mesmerized by the beauty, staring in wonder at how nature could make something so magnificent.

"Hi," I say, the slight waver in my voice evidence of the edginess I experience whenever I'm in her presence.

"Hey." She briefly averts her eyes, an adorable nervousness about her that matches my own.

"Hey to you, too," Julia cuts through, reminding me we're not alone.

"Sorry." I head toward my sister, kissing her cheek. "Hey, Jules."

"Impressive." She glances at the clock on the stove. "I was skeptical, but you pulled it off. Ten minutes exactly."

"Told you I could do it."

"I'm calling it a fluke. Or maybe the result of...adequate motivation."

"Did I miss something?" Londyn looks between us, her confusion apparent. "I'm completely lost."

"She always complains I'm worse than a woman when it comes to getting ready."

"I'm a mom," Julia explains with a shrug. "I'm used to needing to be out of the house before the wind changes and my daughter decides she wants to throw a fit."

"I don't throw fits," Imogene protests from the couch in the living room, a coloring book open in her lap.

"Sure you don't." My sister's voice oozes with sarcasm as

she playfully rolls her eyes. Then she redirects her attention to Londyn. "Can I get you something to drink? Do you like wine?"

"I do."

"Red okay? I made lasagna."

My stomach rumbles, the aroma of meat and garlic filtering into my senses. While I'm more than capable of cooking, my culinary skills are no match for Julia's, who's made a career out of it, although her expertise lies in pastries and desserts. Still, she has a gift when it comes to food, much like Meemaw did.

"That sounds wonderful," Londyn offers with a smile. "Do you need help with anything?"

"You're our guest, so just relax." Julia shoots me a look, silently telling me I'm on wine duty, then refocuses on the tomato sitting on the cutting board, bringing a knife up to it.

"Did you find the place okay?" I ask to fill the silence as I stride toward the built-in wine cabinet just off the kitchen.

"I did." She looks around. "You have a lovely home. All the houses out here in Brookhaven are gorgeous, though."

"Where do you live?" Perusing my options, I select a Chianti I purchased last time I was in Italy and bring it back to the island, grabbing a few wine glasses on the way.

"O4W," she replies, using the local nickname for Old Fourth Ward.

"That's a great part of the city." I extend the cutter out of the corkscrew, slicing into the foil around the neck of the bottle, then make quick work of the cork, a pop echoing as I pull it out. "Really on the up and up." I pour some wine into a glass and slide it across the counter toward her.

"I sometimes forget I'm in the city. It's got a nice community feel. People look out for each other there."

"Apartment? Townhouse?" I ask, wanting to learn all the pieces that make up who she is, desperate for even the tiniest bit of information.

"A condo, I guess."

"You guess?"

"One of the instructors at my se——" She stops short, panic

washing over her face just long enough for me to notice before she corrects herself. "My gym," she continues, pushing out a breath. "She and her husband bought a multi-family house several years back. They needed a tenant, and I needed a place to live. Now that I've been there a few years, I forget it's two separate units, since we all come and go from each other's places like we share them."

"Sounds nice. It's good to have people looking out for you." Once I've poured a glass for myself and Julia, I skirt around to the other side of the island, shooing Zeus away, and pull out one of the barstools. "Have a seat."

"Thank you." She drapes her commuter bag over the back of the chair, then hoists herself onto it.

I do my best to ignore Julia's satisfied smirk as I sit beside her. When I unexpectedly brush my leg against Londyn's, I practically jump out of my skin. "Sorry."

She chews on her lower lip. "It's okay."

"How about a toast," Julia suggests through the nervous tension sizzling in the room. I can't remember being this on edge the first time I took Brooklyn out. And this isn't even a date.

"Right." I rip my gaze to hers. "A toast."

"Hope it's a good one," Julia mutters.

"A good one?" Londyn inquires.

"It's this thing we usually reserve just for the holidays or when we have guests over," I explain. "Something we picked up from Gampy. A little sibling rivalry to see who can come up with the better toast."

"Hope you've brought your A-game." Julia waggles her brows.

"Okay." I fully face her. "Let's see what you've got." I steal a glance at Londyn, winking before returning my attention to Julia.

She stands proudly, wine glass raised. "May we never go to hell." She pauses. "But may we always be on our way."

"That'll be a dollar!" Imogene calls out, arm outstretched, palm open, her focus still on her coloring book.

"A dollar?" Londyn asks.

I chuckle. "Julia tends to swear a bit."

"And my darling daughter has brought home her job at school as the polite police. So every time I say a word that's not polite, or swear, I have to pay her a dollar."

"How much have you given her so far?"

"Let's just say her paying for college won't be a problem." She places her glass on the island and reaches into her back pocket, retrieving a small bunch of one-dollar bills. Unfolding one, she walks toward Imogene and slaps one into her palm before returning to us, feigning irritation. "Your turn."

Licking my lips, I clear my throat. "Here's to a long life, and a happy one. A quick death, and an easy one. A good woman, and an honest one. A good wine... And another one."

"Not sure it's as good as mine, but I suppose I'll let you win this round."

"That's what I thought." I smile, bringing my glass toward Julia's, about to clink.

"How about me?" Londyn interjects.

Stopping, I shoot my eyes toward her. "What's that?"

"Can I do a toast?"

"Absolutely!" Julia replies.

"Sorry," I say in a low voice. "I should have asked. I didn't want to put you on the spot."

"It's okay. I mean, I didn't put much thought into it, but it's something my neighbors and I always say before we do tequila shots."

I nod, my lips curving up in the corners, excited for yet another glimpse into who Londyn is. "Go on then."

She raises her glass, smiling as her eyes meet mine. "May the best of the past be the worst of the future."

"I'll drink to that," Julia says, clinking Londyn's glass before mine. Then we all take a sip.

As I savor the robust flavor, my eyes wander back to Londyn, watching as she swallows the liquid, then licks her lips free of the wine residue. A little remains on the corner of her mouth, and I have to stop myself from reaching out and swiping it away with my thumb.

"Would you like to see what I've been working on this

week?" Londyn sets her glass down and reaches into her bag for her tablet.

"Sure. I—"

"Don't worry about any of that." Julia waves her off, interrupting me. I dart my eyes toward her, brows furrowed.

"But I thought you wanted to get together to go over my ideas." Londyn looks from me to Julia, sliding her tablet back into her bag.

"I trust you. I wouldn't have hired you if I didn't," my sister says dismissively. "Plus, you already told me your ideas." She spins around just as the timer on the oven buzzes.

I pinch the bridge of my nose as the realization hits me. Julia never had any intention of discussing the remodel tonight. She planned this to get Londyn and me together. How did I not figure this out sooner, especially after our discussion last weekend?

"I'm sorry about this," I offer, shooting daggers at my sister before looking back at Londyn. "If I had known, I wouldn't have intruded on your Friday night plans. I understand how valuable your time must be." The last thing I want is for her to leave. I'd witnessed her go from hot to cold in the span of a heartbeat on more than one occasion. I fear Julia's hairbrained scheme will have her running as far away as she can.

Instead, Londyn treats me to her gorgeous smile. "Don't worry." Ever so slowly, she gradually leans toward me, her scent wafting around me.

I should look somewhere other than her lips, but I can't help myself. God, they're so full. So mesmerizing. I wonder if they taste as sweet as they look.

As if able to read my thoughts, she licks them, making me harden, my grip on my glass tightening.

"Good food," she begins in a sultry voice, "great wine, and even better company are *never* an intrusion in my book." With a wink, she pulls back.

I watch as she grabs her glass and slowly brings it to her mouth, sipping the wine.

I've never wished I was a wine glass more than I do right now.

# CHAPTER NINE

"You actually made him run naked through the property?" I can barely see through the tears filling my eyes as I sit in the living room of Wes' home, my stomach aching from laughter at the image of a young Wes streaking through his grandparents' massive property after his swim trunks snagged on a branch, tearing them off.

All day today, I'd considered canceling, thinking any discussions regarding the design should be done in a more appropriate setting, not during a family dinner on Friday night. Normally, I wouldn't think twice about having dinner with a client. But Wes is...different. What I feel for him is different. Which is why I should run as far away as I can. But as Hazel reminded me, I need to stop letting *him* control my decisions.

"And that's not even the worst of it," Wes counters, stroking Imogene's hair as she sleeps curled up next to him on the couch. She fell asleep about an hour ago, no longer interested in listening to her mom and uncle share story after story about the summers they spent at their grandparents' country house.

There's something sweet about him as he snuggles with her. When I first met him, I wasn't sure what to think. He seemed so confident, so assured. A man who was always in control of every part of his life. But observing him with this little girl allows me to see his softer, more vulnerable side. I suppose children have that effect on you.

"It gets worse?" I ask, sipping on my water.

Julia grins deviously. "I'd invited a few of my friends from town to come over. Including Evangeline Allen."

"Who's Evangeline Allen?"

"The older sister of one of my good friends. And Wes' first crush. After that incident, I'm pretty sure she was scarred for life."

Wes glances at me with a devious glint. "I'd like to think she saw more than she could handle."

"Sure she did." Julia playfully rolls her eyes, and we all erupt in laughter.

"It sounds like you have some incredible memories at the house." I look between them, unable to see the resemblance one would normally find with siblings.

Wes is broad, tall, with dark hair and penetrating blue eyes. Julia's on the shorter side, although still slender, with golden blonde hair and the greenest eyes I've ever seen. Even their personalities seem to be on opposite ends. Wes appears more soft-spoken and reserved, but when he does speak, it's of importance, not just words to fill the silence. Julia is more outgoing, constantly chatting about whatever comes to mind.

"We do." Julia shares a look with her brother, the affection they hold for each other evident. "Some of my best memories happened there."

"What were your grandparents like?" I ask.

"Amazing," she answers without a moment's hesitation. "They're the reason Wes and I turned out as…normal as we did."

"Normal?"

"We grew up in a world where lunch boxes were Louis Vuitton and sneakers were Jimmy Choo. Or at least they would be if those things existed."

"So your parents had money."

"They did," Wes answers. "They do. Gampy and Meemaw weren't poor, either. They did well for themselves. But unlike our father and his family, they always gave back. Always. Couldn't stomach the idea of having so much when some people had nothing. Gampy would always quote Ronald Reagan and say, 'We can't help everyone, but we can help someone.' So he spent most of his life helping someone, one person at a time. As did Meemaw."

"Unfortunately, that gene never got passed on to Lydia," Julia says.

"Who's Lydia?"

"Our mother," Wes explains quickly.

I wonder why Julia calls her by her first name, but I don't have a chance to ask before he continues.

"Meemaw and Gampy were her parents."

"What did they do for work?" I inquire, then clarify, "Your grandparents."

"Meemaw volunteered at area hospitals as a cuddler," Julia answers.

I wrinkle my brow. "A cuddler?"

"It's exactly how it sounds." Her eyes shine with nostalgia, a heartwarming smile pulling on her full, wine-stained lips. "Some parents can't be at the hospital with their newborns, especially when they're born with medical issues. As much as you want to be there twenty-four/seven, it's not always possible, so cuddlers soothe and snuggle those babies. Sometimes feed them. That's what Meemaw did."

"Wow." I'd never met the woman but can tell I would have liked her. "And your grandfather?"

"He was a lawyer," Wes states.

"District attorney," Julia clarifies. "Then a judge."

"When he retired, he did some advocacy work for the Innocence Foundation, helping people believed to be wrongfully convicted. He even took on some pro bono defense work."

"That's actually what caused the rift between our grandparents and Lydia," Julia adds.

"What? His advocacy work?" I shake my head, confused how anyone would find fault in that. Then again, based on the few things I've picked up, their mother isn't the most sympathetic person.

"That was probably about twenty years ago now," Wes jumps in. "You have to understand. Where we grew up in the Atlanta suburbs is a very affluent community."

"Very...white," Julia emphasizes. "I mean, it wasn't *completely* white, but let's just say, in our school, if you weren't white and wealthy, you weren't exactly welcome."

"What happened?" I press.

"It's been quite a while, so my memory's a little foggy, but a girl a few years older than me ended up pregnant. At fourteen." She gives me a pointed stare. "To make matters worse, her father was the headmaster of our uppity prep school, so you can imagine what a scandal this would be for her family, who were supposed to be nice, Christian people." She rolls her eyes, her disdain obvious.

I swallow hard, knowing all too well what this poor girl must have gone through. After all, I faced this myself. Maybe not at fourteen, but I can sympathize.

"She was a junior debutante, so there was no way for her to participate in all the Southern society bullshit events in her 'condition'." She uses air quotes, her tone oozing with sarcasm.

"Next thing we hear, they arrested a seventeen-year-old from school," Wes explains. "Elijah. Claimed he raped her. According to Gampy, the whole thing was suspicious. He was on the Ethics Board at the school."

"Who?" I ask. "Gampy?"

He nods. "Yes. He'd attended when he was a boy. As did his father. And so on, and so on. Well, when the athletics department wanted to award a football scholarship to Elijah, the headmaster had a few things to say about him, which Gampy overheard, unbeknownst to him. Gampy figured the man saw an opportunity to…cleanse the school and took it."

"Cleanse?"

"Eli was black."

My heart instantly goes out to this poor boy. I never went to private school, but I've experienced my fair share of racism. It doesn't matter where you live, how accepting your neighbors claim to be of people from different backgrounds and cultures. At some point, you'll experience some sort of discrimination based on the color of your skin. It's inevitable. Doesn't make it right, but as my mama taught me, you need to rise above, not stoop to their level, although it's sometimes difficult.

"Eli was a year ahead of me," Wes continues. "I didn't know him well, but I had a few classes with him. He was a good kid. Quiet. Wouldn't hurt a fly, unless they were on the football field." He chuckles to himself, remembering the past. "Like I said, the arrest didn't sit right with Gampy, so he offered to defend Eli."

"Which pissed off Lydia." Julia takes a long sip of her wine before continuing. "After all, she was BFFs with the headmaster's wife. In their eyes, Gampy offering to help Eli was like saying he didn't believe the victim." The more she speaks, the more her annoyance at the situation shows.

"What happened?" I ask.

"The case made headlines, and there were a lot of strong opinions on both sides," Wes states. "Gampy fought to get him a fair trial, which wasn't easy. In the end, no matter what he did, no matter the holes he poked in the supposed narrative or the lack of any physical evidence, it wasn't enough. The jury made their decision before they even walked into that room and listened to opening statements. But Gampy refused to give up the fight. He appealed. Threw everything he had into it."

"Lost everything because of it, too," Julia adds sadly.

"Lost everything?"

"Eli's parents lost their jobs," she explains. "Their employers claimed it had nothing to do with the charges filed against their son, but it's obvious it did. Since this case was big news, they struggled to find other jobs. They could have moved, but they wanted Eli to have a home to return to once charges were dropped and he was released from custody. So Gampy paid all their bills, their mortgage. They already had two kids in college, and he also paid for their tuition so they didn't have to worry about it. That's how strongly he believed in Eli's innocence, especially when the baby was born and... Surprise! It was white. When Gampy brought that up to the girl's father, he argued the baby was light for a black baby. But let me tell you. That baby wasn't just light. Her skin was extremely fair. Even pastier than my Irish skin."

"That must have raised some eyebrows, didn't it?"

"Of course." Julia nods. "Gampy asked to have a paternity test done, which her father refused. But his big mistake was asking for a civil order of support. Which was just vindictive at this point, considering Eli had been sentenced to serve fifteen years in prison and he couldn't remotely afford it. However, the second he demanded child support, Eli had the right to verify his paternity. I'll let you guess how that worked out."

"He wasn't the father," I breathe.

"No, he wasn't." Julia gives me a tight-lipped smile.

"So was his conviction overturned?"

"Gampy tried, based on new exculpatory evidence. Unfortunately, the appeals court claimed that the pregnancy wasn't the sole piece of evidence tying him to the rape. It didn't matter that there was *no* evidence tying him to the rape. Period."

"That's so fucked up," I say, unable to stop myself, although I'm not surprised. The criminal justice system isn't too kind to black and brown people. Once you're arrested, they'll do everything to keep you in the system.

"Gampy fought to free him until his dying day," Wes states. "And Meemaw fully supported his fight. He went to the media. Told the story. It made headlines for a while, and some people put pressure on the legislature to reform the criminal justice system. But then September 11th happened, and the world had a new fight, something more important than one innocent black man sitting in prison."

"Even though we all know there's more than just one innocent black man sitting in prison," Julia adds.

"Did he ever get out?" My heart aches over the idea of this boy sitting in a prison for any length of time for a crime he didn't commit. I don't even question his innocence. I can feel it in my soul, like Gampy probably could.

Wes' expression falls and he solemnly shakes his head. "He hung himself in his cell."

My hands fly to my throat, an ache within. How desperate he must have been to end his life in such a cruel and painful manner. All because one man saw his daughter's promiscuity as a way to eliminate a black man from his precious school. I wish I could say I'm surprised.

I'm not.

I wish I could say Elijah's case is unique.

It's not.

"How did Gampy react?"

"He never found out," Wes says somberly. "He'd passed away a month prior. I think that's why Eli did it. With Gampy gone, he lost hope of anyone else fighting for him."

I swallow through the lump in my throat as we all sit in silence. It's such a tragic story, one that never should have happened. The world needs more people like Gampy. People who are willing to see an injustice and fight it instead of sitting back and allowing it to happen.

"Well..." Julia's bright voice cuts through as she stands from her chair. "Sorry to end the night on such a downer, but I should get that one to her bed before she asks to sleep down here every night."

Wes carefully extracts himself from Imogene, getting to his feet and scooping her into his arms.

"I'll bring her up," he offers.

"I can do it," Julia insists.

"I know, but I've already got her." He glances at me as I stand. "I'll be right back. Make yourself at home."

Julia heads toward me and wraps her arms around me. "Thanks for coming tonight. And for agreeing to work on what will be a challenging remodel."

"Maybe," I say once she pulls away. "But I've never backed down from a challenge."

"Which is why I hired you. Enjoy the rest of your evening, Londyn." She grins, then follows Wes from the living room, their feet quiet as they head up to the second floor.

Now that I'm alone for the first time all night, I blow out a long breath. Tonight went better than I expected. In truth, I wasn't sure *what* I expected. But learning about Meemaw and Gampy, as well as Wes and Julia, was exactly what I needed.

Since I made Atlanta my home, I haven't really made any friends, apart from Hazel and Diego. I've kept to myself. Worked every waking hour of my life. Avoided all serious relationships, not wanting to surrender the control I fought hard to regain. But maybe Hazel's right. Maybe it's time to stop keeping people out. Maybe it's time to start trusting again.

"Sorry about that."

Wes' low voice enters my subconscious as I admire the display of Imogene's baby photos covering the console table behind the sofa.

I notice there aren't any of Wes' parents, as if the family skipped a generation from his grandparents to him and Julia. My heart squeezes at the thought.

"No worries." I flash him a smile before returning my attention to the pictures. "I was just admiring Imogene as a baby. She was beautiful."

"I wasn't around much when she was born since I lived up in Boston at the time. But now I'm able to make up for everything I missed."

His mouth curves up into a smile, his white teeth dazzling against his skin that seems to have seen some sun since I saw him last weekend.

"Do you want another glass of wine? Something else?"

"Thanks for the offer, but I do need to drive." I steal a glance at the clock in the kitchen, surprised to see it's nearly eleven o'clock. "Speaking of which, I should get going. I didn't mean to stay this late. I was having too much fun."

"I had a great time, too. Which is why I'm still wide awake, even though I need to get up at the crack of dawn to get to the house. We're starting on the insulation and drywall tomorrow."

"Did you already get all the wiring done?"

He beams. "Sure did."

"Wow. That was, well...fast."

"Not really." He shrugs. "I knew what needed to be done and didn't wait to take action."

"Most people I know tend to waffle before pulling the trigger on such a huge undertaking."

He closes the distance between us, blue eyes piercing mine as he peers down at me. "One thing you'll learn about me, Londyn, is that when I set my mind to something, I take action. I don't waffle. I do whatever it takes to get what I want."

A shiver trickles down my spine, and I part my lips, on the brink of asking him what it is he wants. But I fear I already know the answer. That he's not just talking about the wiring. If he were, his gaze wouldn't be dark with desire. His breathing wouldn't be uneven. His jaw wouldn't be tense.

"Well then...," I say brightly, increasing the distance before I lose the little self-control I have left. "I'll let you get to sleep."

I head toward the stool in the kitchen, sling my bag onto my shoulder, then continue toward the front door, doing my best to ignore Wes' presence looming behind me, but it's impossible. From the moment we met, everything about him has consumed me. When he's near, his aura envelopes me, making me only think about him, forgetting everything else.

What is it about him that has me all out of sorts when no other man has come remotely close to penetrating my tough exterior? But with one look, one smile, one wink, I want to break all the rules I've lived by for years.

And I can't have that. Not now. Not ever.

I'm about to turn the doorknob when Wes leans past me, his body skimming mine as he covers my hand with his. "Allow me."

My pulse skyrockets as his earthy scent envelopes me. It hypnotizes me, inducing me into a dreamlike stupor. I have no idea how long we stand there, him behind me, his hand covering mine, neither one of us making a move to turn the knob. It's an innocent touch, but this moment is one of the most erotic experiences I've had in recent history. His skin on mine is enthralling, addictive...electrifying.

"I should go," I finally manage to squeak out.

"Yes." His voice comes out a mix between a plea and a growl. "You should."

"Then we need to open the door."

"Yes. We do."

It's silent for a beat before a low chuckle vibrates from his chest, filling the high-ceilinged foyer.

"What the hell are you doing to me?"

I push out a breath, grateful for the break in tension. "The same thing you're doing to me. Which is all the more reason

I need to leave."

"I suppose it is." On a long exhale, my hand still under his, he twists the knob.

My heart deflates slightly when he opens the door and the summer night air makes its way into the foyer, wiping clean whatever just transpired between us. It doesn't seem real. Like we were in a dream and now have been cruelly forced back to earth.

No longer sensing his presence right behind me, I slowly turn around. "Well…" I smile awkwardly, pushing a few curls out of my face, a nervous habit of mine. "Thanks again."

I spin from him, hurrying down the front steps and toward my economical SUV, clicking my key fob. I'm about to open the door when I hear Wes' voice.

"Londyn," he whisper-shouts.

I whirl around, inhaling sharply when I see him advancing toward me, his greedy eyes raking over me. My pulse skyrockets, my core tightening as desire floods my veins. Chest heaving, I back up against my SUV, my body aching for Wes to reach out and yank me against him, despite my brain reminding me it's a bad idea.

But instead of closing the remaining distance between us and crushing his lips to mine in a mind-numbing kiss, he stops a foot away. He scrapes his fingers through his hair, pulling his lips between his teeth, seemingly torn. Then he lifts his gaze to mine.

"Are you busy tomorrow?"

I give him a sideways look. "I thought you were working on the house."

"I am. I… I was thinking maybe you'd want to come help."

"With the drywall?" I arch a brow.

"You don't have to," he adds quickly. "It's not part of your job. I just… I really enjoyed spending time with you tonight. And I'd like more of that."

A few minutes ago, I probably would have agreed, too cast under his spell to think clearly. But now I can And I don't know if spending more time with him is wise. After one night, I find my resolve breaking. What will happen after spending even more time together?

"Wes, I—"

"It's okay," he interrupts before I can voice my concerns. "Don't worry about it. I have more than enough guys who can help." He turns, heading back toward the house.

Worrying my lower lip, I watch him retreat. Of course, Hazel's voice chooses this moment to sound in my subconscious, reminding me to start taking risks again. To stop letting *him* control me. To leave myself open to what could be instead of dictating what will never be because it doesn't comport with my firmly established rules.

Sometimes I really hate that she's such a persuasive voice of reason.

"What time?" I call out as he's about to disappear inside.

He stops abruptly, glancing over his shoulder. "Excuse me?"

"Tomorrow. What time should I be there?"

His eyes light up with the excitement of a kid seeing Disneyland for the first time. "Eight o'clock?"

I nod. "I'll be there."

"I look forward to it."

I fight back my urge to tell him I am, as well.

"Sweet dreams, Londyn," he says smoothly, then closes the door.

Once I slide into my car, I rest my forehead on the steering wheel, heaving out a long sigh. One thing is certain.

This is either a really good idea or a really bad idea.

Either way, I'll find out tomorrow.

# CHAPTER TEN

LONDYN

As I pull up to Gampy and Meemaw's house a few minutes before eight on Saturday morning, it feels like a different place than the last time I was here. When I'd driven down this long, winding path that first time, I'd wondered if I was in the right place, everything desolate and quiet. That's no longer the case.

Several vans and utility trucks line the dirt path. Pallets of drywall sit in front of the porch, dozens of rolls of insulation stacked beside it. From the noise already coming from within, it appears Wes' crew is already hard at it.

I fight the urge to grab my compact out of my purse to check my face, reminding myself I'm at a construction site. As it is, I'll probably be the only woman. No need to make matters worse by one of them catching me applying makeup. Based on the humidity in the air, it'll only take a matter of minutes for it to melt off anyway.

Stepping out of the car, I sling my duffel bag over my shoulder and head toward the house, already getting a few side glances from the crew busy at work. I search for Wes amongst them, spotting him as he walks onto the porch.

Each time I've seen him before today, he's sported three vastly different looks. From commanding businessman. To doting uncle. To the at home dinner with guests.

But this look… Well, this one may be my favorite, if for no other reason than a reminder that this man can go from wearing a tailor-made suit one day to a white t-shirt, ratty jeans, and dingy work boots, his clothes covered with dust and grime, the next. He's like a chameleon. Just when I think I have him figured out, he changes his appearance, making me start my analysis of who he is all over again.

I continue up the gravel path, my sneakers crunching with

each step. There's something so easy and casual about Wes as he gives direction to one of the workmen. I can't help but admire him. The concentration in his gaze. The pull of his biceps against the sleeves of his shirt. The way his jeans fall loosely from his hips, but still allow me to make out the definition of his body.

"Enjoying the view?"

His deep voice pulls me out of my fantasies about what he looks like without a shirt, about how his body would feel against mine.

I tear my gaze toward his, a flush heating my face when I observe the cocky smirk crawling across his full lips framed with scruff. He really gives off a hot, construction worker vibe, something I didn't think possible based on how incredible he looks in a suit. When he crosses his arms in front of his chest, it takes every ounce of resolve I possess to not gawk at his biceps, his defined muscles stretching the fabric of his shirt.

"Londyn?" he says when I don't immediately respond.

"Sorry. Yes." I grit a smile, avoiding his stare as I pretend to push a ringlet behind my ear, despite the fact I'd tamed my curls into a short ponytail earlier. "The house looks like it's coming along quite nicely."

He stalks toward me, intense blue eyes spearing me as he leans toward me. "I think we both know that's not what I'm talking about."

I swallow hard, my heart rate picking up the longer he remains a mere breath away. Then he pulls back, smiling as he touches a hand to my back and leads me toward the house. A man I estimate to be roughly the same age as Wes assesses us as we walk, obviously curious about our somewhat intimate interaction.

"Nash, this is Londyn. She's the interior designer we've hired." He smiles down at me, a hint of pride in his expression as he introduces me. "Londyn, this is Nash, the foreman on this project. He's the only one I trust to oversee all the construction and installation."

"When he's not trying to take control himself." Nash laughs, removing his work gloves and extending his hand.

67

He's on the shorter side, perhaps only an inch or two taller than me. But he still appears to be in decent shape, probably from all the hours of manual labor he must put in every week. "Nice to meet you, Londyn."

"Likewise," I say as we shake.

"If you need anything and can't find me, Nash is the next best thing," Wes explains.

"Good to know. Now, where do you want me to start?"

Nash quirks a brow. "You're here to help?" It's not clear if he's aggravated or impressed by the idea of a woman infiltrating his crew.

"I know how to lay insulation, install drywall. I learned from my father."

"Londyn has her own furniture design company," Wes states. "She up-cycles. There's no doubt in my mind she can handle a utility knife and a staple gun. Anyway, she'll be helping me up in the bedroom, so you won't have another body to keep an eye on." He shifts his gaze to me. "Let's go inside."

The authority in his voice causes a tremor to trickle through me. I don't know why I like it so much, but it makes me momentarily lightheaded.

"I bet she'll be helping you in the bedroom," Nash jokes under his breath as I follow Wes up the front steps and onto the porch.

"I heard that!" Wes shouts without looking back, giving me a sly grin as he steps aside, allowing me to enter the house first.

"Wow," I exhale upon seeing how much he's accomplished over the past week. The drywall in every room has been torn down, fresh wiring, pipes, and air ducts now working their way through the bones of the house. The only things that remain are the fireplaces, and I'm thankful for that. They're too special and unique to destroy.

"I'd hoped they'd be able to extend the gas lines to the fireplaces," Wes says, as if able to read my mind. "But to do so, we would have had to cut into some of the brick and porcelain surrounding them."

"It's not worth it," I reply without hesitation.

He chuckles, touching my elbow and steering me up the creaky stairs that I plan to replace with something much safer, considering Imogene will be spending some time here.

"I had a feeling that would be your response."

"The history of this house is too important to destroy for the convenience of a gas fireplace."

"Agreed."

"What happened to all the doors? Molding? Cabinets?"

"Out in the detached garage. I figured you'd want to repurpose as much of the original materials as you could."

"You figured correctly."

We make our way through the cacophony of hammers and staple guns before coming to a stop in the master suite, natural light streaming in through the windows, aided by a couple of work lights set up in the room.

"Here you go." He hands me a pair of work gloves.

"No need." I set my duffle bag on the floor, which has been covered in plastic to preserve the original hardwood. Unzipping it, I find my gloves and slide them on, waving my hands in front of me. "I've got my own."

"Was that a tool belt I saw?"

With a coy smile, I nod, taking my tool belt out of the bag, as well. I wasn't sure what I'd be doing today, so figured it best to come prepared. Plus, I didn't want the rest of the crew to think I don't know what I'm doing when I've probably been around tools and construction longer than some of them.

"You aren't like any other woman I've met."

"Why? Because I'm not some debutante, like you're accustomed to?" I playfully bat my lashes.

"No." He pulls his lips together. "Well, yes. But most women I've met wouldn't know the first thing about insulation or putting up drywall. They certainly wouldn't own a pair of work gloves or a tool belt. Or if they did, it would be because they saw a pink one in the hardware store and thought it would be cute."

"I've always been fascinated with how things are made. Like my father." I turn from him and walk toward a roll of insulation, carefully unrolling it.

"Does he work in construction?" He takes the top of the insulation from me and starts up the ladder, sliding it between the wooden frame on the top half of the wall while I work it into the stud bays of the lower half.

"It was more of a hobby."

"Then what does he do?"

"You're going to laugh." Spying the blade on the floor by the ladder, I grab it and slice along the insulation, inserting the last bit into the wall.

"Try me."

I raise myself to my full height. "He's a pastor."

"Of a church?"

I snort a laugh. "Unless you know of a different kind of pastor…"

"Huh." He shifts his gaze from me, studying the wall.

"What?"

"Nothing." He shrugs it off. "Just another piece of the Londyn puzzle snapping into place."

He extends his hand toward me, wordlessly telling me to hand him the insulation so we can start on the next section. I do, returning my attention to my reason for being here, fitting the insulation into the next stud bay. When I steal a glimpse at Wes just as he does the same, his arms extended over his head causing his shirt to ride up and expose the hard planes of his stomach, my mouth grows dry. I do everything to stop my libido from fantasizing about what lies at the end of that trail of hair, but she's got a mind of her own, especially around Wes.

"You really are shameless," he comments.

"Just making sure you're doing it correctly." I focus straight ahead, my cheeks heating from getting caught ogling him yet again. "Lord knows how much insulation you can lay while wearing those expensive suits of yours."

"And here I thought you liked how I looked in my expensive suits. At least, that was the impression I got when we first met."

"I do." I quickly snap my mouth shut, gathering my convoluted thoughts. "I mean…" I shake my head. "You just didn't strike me as the type of person who would get your hands dirty, for lack of a better word."

He steps down from the ladder, moving it around me and sliding it farther along. "That reminds me of something Meemaw would say."

"Why do I get the feeling your grandparents had words of wisdom for every scenario facing you?" I finish fitting the insulation, then stand, stretching my legs.

"Because they probably did." He laughs under his breath, a nostalgic gleam in his eyes. "Anyway, one thing Meemaw always said was, 'Before you assume, learn. Before you judge, understand. Before you speak, think.'"

"And now I feel like a total asshole for thinking you were just another hot guy in a nice suit."

"Oh, I am absolutely more than happy for you to think I'm a hot guy in a nice suit, Londyn. That's for damn sure." His eyes flame as a smirk pulls on his lips. "But hopefully as we work together over the next few months, you'll learn something *else* about me."

"What's that?"

He curves toward me, his breath hot on my neck. "I'm not like anyone you've ever met." He lingers for a moment, then turns from me, stepping up the ladder.

"So tell me…," he begins, as if his proximity didn't turn my insides into jelly, "what was it like growing up as a pastor's daughter?"

I squat, hoping to distract myself from Wes' proximity by intently focusing on the insulation.

"For most of my childhood, I didn't realize what my dad did. I mean, I *knew* what he did. But I didn't have any of this ridiculous pressure on me to live a certain way because of who my father was. Not until…" I trail off.

"Not until what?"

I pause as I attempt to formulate a response. What can I possibly tell him without giving him all the sordid details of what led me to walk away from the only family I've ever known? Did I really *walk* away? The phrase suggests I had a choice. I don't feel like I had much choice in the matter. If I did, it was a fool's choice. Damned if I do. Damned if I don't.

"If you don't want to talk about this, we don't have to."

"It's okay." I slide the blade against the insulation, cutting it to fit into the partition, then stand, handing him the fiberglass. "My mama died when I was seven."

He steps down from the ladder, his eyes awash with sympathy. "Londyn, I'm sorry. I—"

"My dad did the best he could trying to raise me, but somewhere along the way... I don't know..." I exhale deeply, recalling my teenage years. "I'd listen to him preach about God's hand being in everything, but I couldn't understand how a God who was supposed to be this all-loving being would take my mother from me. I guess I stopped believing. At least believing like I needed to in order to preserve our relationship."

"So because you questioned your faith, he stopped talking to you?" He tilts his head.

"It wasn't just that. But I think that was the beginning of the end, so to speak. Over the years, our relationship was riddled with other incidents, each causing the rope to fray a little more. After I finished my undergrad and..." I search for the words to explain this without going into any detail. "Well, he didn't support a decision I made that I felt was essential to my wellbeing. And I'm not saying that to sound dramatic. It's true. If I'd followed the path he wanted, I probably wouldn't be alive today. So, for my own preservation, I needed to go in a different direction."

I crouch down, refocusing my attention on the wall. It normally takes months for me to share anything remotely having to do with my past. But with Wes, it just feels right.

It felt right with *him*, too, though.

"So I packed up my things, came to Atlanta, decided to get my master's in interior design, and haven't looked back since." I push out a nervous laugh, averting my eyes, embarrassed by how much I shared with him, albeit in vague terms. But after last night, after hearing all about Gampy, I get the feeling Wes can understand. That he doesn't judge me. That he doesn't *blame* me.

"I'm sorry you were in a position where you felt like you

had to choose. It takes a strong person to stand up for what they believe in, especially to their own family. And for the record…"

When he trails off, I stand and arch a brow. "Yes?"

"I, for one, am grateful you chose the path you did."

"You are?"

"I am. It's like…the butterfly effect. You're familiar with that, correct?"

I nod. "The theory that one small disturbance can set into motion a chain reaction leading to a large shift in the state of things."

"Precisely. Had you not had a disagreement with your father, you never would have come to Atlanta and studied interior design. You never would have gotten a job working for Margo St. James. She never would have fired you. You never would have attempted to cross a busy intersection in a torrential downpour." His voice becomes lower, more sensual, the space between us decreasing with every thumping beat of my heart. "And our paths never would have crossed." He stops a mere whisper from me, my insides coiling from his proximity. "If you ask me, that would have been a damn tragedy."

Heat builds on my cheeks, my stomach in knots. It's been years since a man has spoken to me with such conviction, such honesty. And just like with *him*, it makes me want to tell Wes everything, share my deepest, darkest secrets.

But I'm not the naïve young girl I was all those years ago. I've been hurt in ways I never imagined possible. And I still carry that pain as a reminder to not trust so easily.

I'm riding that seesaw. One second, I want to take a risk with Wes, like Hazel encouraged me. But all it takes is one reminder of how badly I was hurt to make me retreat back into my protective shell.

Clearing my throat, I spin from him. "You're only saying that because you were in desperate need of a designer who wouldn't destroy the memories you have of this house," I joke.

When he doesn't immediately respond, I glance at him. His eyes are narrowed on me in an analytical stare. I can only imagine how my emotional whiplash must be confusing Wes. It confuses me, too.

On a long exhale, he climbs back up the ladder. "That's true." He takes the final bit of insulation from me and fits it into the last stud bay. "But I'm really glad that designer is you."

I keep my gaze trained forward as I work the fiberglass into the walls, torn between telling him I'm glad, too, and protecting myself. After everything I've been through, it's all I know. Nearly every other person in my life has disappointed me.

All reason tells me Wes is no different.

# CHAPTER ELEVEN

WESTON

A rare stillness surrounds me as I step into the foyer after helping Nash load the unused materials into the van, the house now a blank canvas, ready for Londyn to work her magic. I worried this place would lose its character when we gutted it in order to install new electrical, plumbing, and HVAC, but it's still here. It's in its bones, and I can't wait to see what Londyn does with it.

Making my way into the kitchen, I open the cooler and grab a couple of beers before heading toward the back porch. I pause in the doorway, taking a moment to admire Londyn as she sits on the top step, eyes closed, a peaceful look on her face that's shiny with perspiration.

I have to hand it to her. She held her own today. At times, she even made my crew look bad, refusing to take a break when everyone else did. She definitely made *me* look bad, but I don't mind. I'd gladly suffer through nicking my finger with the staple gun because I was checking out her ass again if it meant I could have more of these moments with her.

Sensing my presence, she opens her eyes and glances over her shoulder. As she's about to stand, I shake my head. "Stay." I lift the two beers. "Figured you could use one after today." I lower myself beside her and hand her the beer.

"Thanks." She brings her bottle toward mine, clinking them.

"You bet."

I swallow a sip of my beer, the cold liquid refreshing after spending nearly ten hours working in the humidity. It's certainly not what I'm accustomed to. I'm used to sitting in an air-conditioned boardroom while dressed in a suit. I forgot how much I liked this part of the job. It's what sparked my passion to design buildings in the first place. It makes me want more of this.

"It's so peaceful here," Londyn remarks after several quiet moments, the only sounds the ambient music of nature. "Like you can forget everything else and just enjoy the moment." She takes a long pull from the bottle, finishing on a satisfied exhale. "I can see why you and Julia loved coming here as kids. It's so different from Atlanta."

I nod, peering into the distance, feeling like no time has passed since those summer days I'd sit in this very spot, Gampy at my side, sipping on a sweet tea or lemonade, the sound of Meemaw cooking in the kitchen cutting through the chirping birds and buzzing mosquitos. The birds still chirp. Mosquitos still buzz. But I'll never again sit beside Gampy as he tries to impart words of wisdom, or listen to Meemaw teach Julia how to make whatever comfort foods she would fill our bellies with that evening for supper.

"It really made my childhood memorable. If it weren't for Gampy and Meemaw..." I shake my head, struggling to find the words. "You probably picked up on it last night, but my parents haven't always been the best role models."

"It wasn't too difficult to figure out."

"I don't have as antagonistic a relationship with them as Julia does." I laugh to myself. "Kind of hard to work with your father if you don't get along."

She whips her eyes to mine. "You work together?"

"More or less." I shrug. "I come from a very long line of architects on my father's side of the family. My father's an architect. *His* father was an architect. His grandfather was an architect, and so on."

"So you had no choice but to become an architect, too," she states, assuming she has me figured out.

"Actually, I *wanted* to be an architect, but not because of my father. What he did never intrigued me. Whenever I saw him working, he was sitting at a drafting desk, drawing up plans. Granted, I actually enjoy that part of it now, but when you're a ten-year-old boy, there's nothing exciting about that. There's a reason no young child says they want to be an accountant when they grow up."

"True."

"I wanted to do something with my hands. So, in reality, it was Gampy who inspired me. From the moment I could lift a hammer, he taught me how to build, taught me the science and physics behind it all before I even took a single architecture class in college."

"What kinds of things did you make?"

I nod at the long, wooden building beside the overgrown horse paddock in the distance. "I helped him build those stables. I was probably only nine or ten at the time. After that, I knew that's what I wanted to do." I heave a sigh. "And for a while, that's kind of what I did for the firm, at least when I was fresh out of college. I designed buildings, then supervised the implementation of my design. But as I gained more experience, I moved up in the hierarchy of the firm, spent less time on job sites and more time in the office to the point where I barely remember what it's like to do the actual building anymore. I always knew I'd eventually take over the firm. It's been run by a Bradford since my great-great-great-great-grandfather started the business as a one-man operation during Reconstruction. But…" I shrug.

"It's not what you thought it would be," Londyn says. It's not a question. More an observation.

"I know what it must sound like. That I'm complaining about having security in a job that pays well enough for me to live comfortably for the rest of my life. Believe me. I have absolutely nothing to complain about there."

"But you're not happy."

I pinch my lips together, staring out over the meadows, wishing things were as simple as they were when I was a kid running through those fields.

"I don't think I've been happy in years." I lick my lips. "Actually, that's not entirely true." My gaze shifts to hers, skating over her clear skin, the smattering of freckles across her nose, her lips shining from the remnants of the beer. "Today made me happy." I allow my statement to linger in the air for a moment before turning to look out over the property once more. "I'm not sure if it's because of the house,

77

or the memories, or getting to know you better, but I loved every second of today."

"Even when you were just a few millimeters away from stapling your hand to the drywall and needing me to rush you to the nearest hospital?" She arches a thin brow.

"Yes." I chuckle. "Even when I nearly stapled my hand to the drywall." I hold up my now-bandaged pinky finger. "Even if I *had*, I wouldn't trade today for anything. I felt...useful."

"And you don't feel useful at your job?"

"More like a puppet." The words leave me before I have a chance to consider them. "I got into this field because I loved seeing a project go from a concept, onto paper, then become an actual building, whether it be a stadium, or skyscraper, or someone's home. Now my days are spent schmoozing clients so they'll keep using our firm instead of taking their business to a younger one that promises to do the job quicker and cheaper. Sometimes I feel like I'm just a glorified salesman who knows a thing or two about designing buildings. Not someone who spent years studying what materials can be used in a highrise in San Francisco to prevent it from tumbling down during the next big earthquake."

She seems to consider my words for a moment. I have no idea what came over me, why I felt the need to be so forthcoming. But I can complain all I want. I'll never walk away from the firm, regardless of how unhappy I am. I can't, not when hundreds of employees count on me so they can provide for their families.

"Do you want to know what prompted me to start my up-cycling business?" she asks.

"What's that?"

"After moving to Atlanta, I was in a pretty dark place, wondering if I'd made a mistake in leaving the only family I had. I was depressed, struggling to make ends meet. I had debilitating anxiety that sometimes made it hard to leave my apartment to work my minimum wage job. So my roommate suggested I go to a support group at a local church for people who..." She pauses, giving her next words careful consideration. "Well, for people who were going through what

I was.

"It was difficult at first. I was raised to believe the only help and guidance I needed should come from the church and God. But after a while, I realized sometimes help can be found in other places. Can be found in other people who empathize. And it was at one of these meetings that another woman mentioned finding one thing in life that gave you joy and spending a few minutes of your day doing that. Didn't matter if it was underwater basketweaving. It was important to have one bright spot in your day so you didn't feel weighed down.

"On my way home from work that night, I noticed a beat-up old trunk on the side of the road with a sign that said free. So I loaded it into the back of my car and brought it to my apartment. I wasn't sure what I was going to do with it, but the next day, instead of buying groceries with my last twenty dollars, I went to the hardware store and got some supplies. During the next support group meeting, I spoke about finally finding something that gave me joy and how it changed my outlook. Even showed a photo of my project to the group. Another member fell in love and offered me a hundred bucks on the spot for the old trunk that was now a funky little coffee table."

"That's incredible." I smile down at her. I don't know her whole story quite yet, but with just the bits and pieces she's given me, I know Londyn is a strong, tenacious woman.

"I guess what I'm trying to tell you is that maybe you should find something *you* love. Something that gives you joy. Then your job may not feel so lacking. It worked for me."

I consider her words, wondering what brings me joy. Sure, there's Julia and Imogene. Whenever I spend time with that little girl, my heart brims with love. But I'm not sure that's what Londyn's talking about. Just like she found joy when she returned to her passion of up-cycling furniture, maybe that's what I need to do, too.

I rest my forearms on my knees and steal a glance at Londyn, my mind spinning, excitement bubbling inside me at the idea taking shape. I hadn't even considered it when I won this place in auction, but it feels right.

"What do you think about helping out a little more?"

She tilts her head, brow creased. "What do you mean?"

"This house. I don't know about you, but I really enjoyed today."

"I did, too." She gives me a small smile.

"Maybe this is what I need in my life. Get back to what I love. Get my hands dirty, my body sweaty, and my fingers bloody."

"You're going to do all these renovations yourself?" Her tone is heavy with disbelief.

"Not all by myself." I gently nudge her with my shoulder. "I'm hoping you'll help. I'll pay you more, of course. Don't want you to think I won't. But maybe when I'm at the office during the week, you can look for window treatments, lighting, and cabinets… Whatever designers need to make a space beautiful. Then on the weekends, we can work on the house. Together."

"Just us?"

"I'll call in Nash and his crew on some of the bigger installations. My ancestors built this house. My happiest memories occurred here. I almost feel like I owe it to their legacy to make my own mark, not just pay a crew to do the work while I sit in the comfort of my house or office. So what do you say?"

Blinking, she looks forward, seeming to carefully weigh the pros and cons of my rash proposal for what feels like an eternity. I don't think I've ever been so anxious for someone to say yes. Not even when I proposed to Brooklyn in an upscale Boston restaurant, dozens of eyes on us.

"Okay," Londyn finally says, returning her gaze to mine.

"Okay?"

"Yes. Okay. I'll help you."

Before I can think about what I'm doing, I fling my arms around her, pulling her to me, her powdery aroma now mixed with a hint of sweat. But it still has me craving her in a way I shouldn't. She stiffens, inhaling a sharp breath, and I quickly drop my hold.

"Sorry. I just… I guess I got a little excited." I lower my

eyes, running my fingers through my hair.

"It's okay. Just surprised me. That's all." She smiles. "I just have one condition."

"What's that?" I expect her to tell me no more displays of affection or flirting, as we've done a time or two today. I can't help it when I'm around her. I forget who I am. Forget about the responsibilities placed on my shoulders since birth.

"We'll work on this house together, but you can't be here for any of the finishing touches."

"But—"

She shoots up her hand. "This is non-negotiable. You can help with painting, tiling, and installing cabinets. Stuff like that. But that's it. The last week, you don't step foot in this house."

"May I ask why?"

"I don't want to miss out on the reason I went into this field in the first place."

"Which is?"

"That moment y'all see your new home for the first time. I know it sounds insignificant. But for me, that moment…" She shakes her head. "It's—"

"Magic," I finish.

"Yeah." She smiles. "Magic."

"I wouldn't want you to miss out on the magic. You have my word. The last week, I won't step foot in the house." I extend my hand toward her, a single brow arched. "Do we have a deal?"

She eyes my hand warily, but soon places hers in it. "We have a deal."

# CHAPTER TWELVE

WESTON

"What do you think? Looks good, right?" Londyn steps back to admire the walls we've spent the better part of today covering in wallpaper.

I was a bit hesitant when she suggested wallpaper as opposed to paint in the formal living room, worried it would make it appear dated, and not in a historic way. But as she's done every time I questioned her over the past several weekends we've spent renovating this house, she convinced me to trust her, and I'm glad I did. It really complements the charm of the home, especially when coupled with the fireplace. I can only imagine how it will look when fully furnished.

"Once again, I stand corrected." I flash her a smile as I wipe sweat from my brow. "I'm officially never going to question your design choices again, because you're batting a thousand."

"Picture it with some vintage pieces," she adds excitedly, brushing a bit of dust off her white, sweat-dampened t-shirt. "I found a chaise lounge from the early 1900s at an estate sale the other day, and it will look perfect in this room."

She reaches into her back pocket, retrieving her cell, and pulls up a photo, stepping beside me. I do my best to focus on her phone and not her proximity as she scrolls through the images she's taken of the chaise in what I assume to be her workshop.

Several other pieces of furniture in various stages of restoration are stacked against the walls, a workbench in the center of the space. Another glimpse into who Londyn truly is. Yes, it's just a workshop, but to me, it allows me to learn more about this woman who's consumed my thoughts since our first meeting.

"It doesn't look like much right now."

"Not sure what anyone would see other than something that's destined for the junkyard." I nod at the image. The legs are barely attached, the velvet upholstery torn and faded.

"It just needs a little love." She clicks off her screen, shoving her phone into the back pocket of her shorts. "Just like this house. And look what a little love did for it."

She spins around, admiring the work we sweated over all day. It's no wonder people choose to paint instead. Putting up wallpaper and lining up the pattern so it's seamless is damn tedious. But she promised it would be worth it, and it most certainly is.

"I understand this isn't what you signed up for." I wave my hand around. "You probably would've much rather spent your time on the actual design work and supervising my crew to make sure they didn't fuck it up, not get roped into doing the grunt work yourself. So I really appreciate you being here. Doing this with me."

"Honestly, there's no place I'd rather be." She flashes me a sweet smile, a vulnerability about her. "I'm not sure what I'll do with myself when we finish this house." With a shallow sigh, she cranes her head back, admiring the original coffered ceiling she was able to salvage. Then she brings her eyes to mine. "I'll miss this."

"I'll miss this, too," I admit, stepping toward her.

The mood shifts, everything going still. Cicadas no longer buzz in the distance. The breeze blowing through the fields calms down. The birds fall silent. All I can focus on is Londyn. This carefree, mysterious, charming woman who's invaded my every waking thought these past few months.

As much as I've imagined what it would be like to wrap her in my arms, to press my mouth to hers, to taste her lips, I haven't, sensing a hesitation and reluctance on her part. At first, I assumed it was simply because I'm her client. But over the weeks, she's become more than a designer to me. Just like I've become more than a client to her. Still, there's something keeping her closed off. I feel it in my soul.

But today, she doesn't retreat as she's prone to do. Instead,

83

she keeps her gaze focused on me, her lips parting slightly. With slow steps, I advance, silently pleading with her to stay in this moment with me, to allow herself to feel this insane connection that's only grown deeper the more time we spend with each other. She moistens her lips, causing the ache that's taken up permanent residency in my body to grow stronger. I reach for her cheek—

"It's so pretty!"

Londyn and I jump away from each other, tearing our eyes to the doorway as Imogene walks in, oblivious to the tension vibrating between us. Or at least the tension that *was* vibrating between us.

"Much better than the boring white walls from before." She continues into the room, spinning a slow circle.

"Imogene, be careful." Julia rushes in behind her, out of breath, obviously having chased her into the house. Then she stops, taking in all our hard work. "Wow. She's right. This is gorgeous." She glances at Londyn. "You two work well together. First, the amazing work on the two upstairs bathrooms, now this?"

"We have it down to a science by now," Londyn responds, her tone even. I glance at her, wishing I could read her thoughts, see what's going through her mind after our latest "moment". At the very least, I can sense she's torn.

I struggle with this, too, unsure if I want to put myself through the inevitable heartache like I suffered with Brooklyn. But for Londyn, I don't think that's the only thing holding her back. I imagine it's something bigger. Is it related to the story she told me about her father? How he turned his back on her when she needed him the most? To say I've been curious about what exactly their disagreement entailed is an understatement. Still, I haven't pressed.

"I imagine," Julia replies. "I can't wait to see the final product. I know it'll be worth all the effort y'all have put in."

"I hope so."

"So what brings you and Imogene here?" I ask. "I thought you two were going to spend the day doing some fun things in the city, since you'll be heading back to Charleston in a few weeks."

"That *was* the plan. I told her she could decide what we'd do. Anything she wanted. I assumed we'd go to the puppet museum or Legoland. Something like that. Do you want to know what she asked to do?"

"What's that?"

"Come here."

"That's really sweet," Londyn sighs, nudging me. "Wanting to come out here to see you."

"Well, that's only half of it," Julia interrupts. "When we were in the downtown area last weekend, she noticed the signs for the county fair starting today. So that's why she wanted to come. To go to the fair. More specifically, to go on all the carnival rides." She grits a smile. "I'd rather get a Brazilian wax than suffer through that."

"Jesus, Julia," I groan. "Not the mental picture I need right now."

"But it's true. Remember all those kids we used to play with when we came here for the summer?"

"We got along with some of them."

"True. But there were quite a few we didn't get along with, weren't there?" She gives me a knowing look. "Quite a few Gampy and Meemaw didn't get along with, either."

I blink, my shoulders falling. "Oh." I hadn't thought much about what spending time back here would mean. Hadn't really thought twice about running into any of the people from our past.

"Exactly. But it's what Imogene wants."

"What do I want, Mama?" she interrupts, sidling up next to Julia, the resemblance between them uncanny.

"To go to the fair!" Julia switches to mom mode in the blink of an eye, not letting on that it's the last thing she wants to do on a Saturday evening. "So let's get going and leave Uncle Wes and Londyn to finish up."

"Can't they come with us?" Imogene asks, her expression pleading.

"Oh, sweetie. They're busy working on the house right now. But maybe—"

"We can go," Londyn interjects.

Julia and I both fling our eyes to her. I'm not sure who's more surprised. My sister or me.

"If you don't mind, that is," she continues. "We did finish several hours ahead of schedule."

"Thanks to your expertise," I remind her. "If I had to do this on my own, I'd probably still be Googling the proper way to apply wallpaper. Hell, I undoubtedly would have ditched the idea and went with paint instead."

"And you would have chosen the worst color for this room," she retorts with a smile.

"Most definitely," Julia agrees, the two of them having a laugh at my expense. I won't complain, though. Not when I finally see the spark back in Londyn's eyes.

"What do you say, boss?" Londyn asks.

I inwardly cringe at the term. She's referred to me as "boss" a few times, always immediately following a more...personal moment between us, as if it's a reminder of who I'm supposed to be to her.

"Think we can cut off work early tonight and spend some time with your sister and niece?" She lowers her voice. "Julia might like the company."

She doesn't have to say another word for me to understand. I should have been the first to offer to go with Julia. Even if the likelihood of running into anyone who will recognize us is probably low, I wouldn't want her to go and something to happen.

"You know what? I think that's a great idea. We'll all go."

Imogene cheers, jumping up and down, as Julia mouths, *Thank you.*

"Do you mind if I take a few minutes to freshen up?" Londyn asks. "Maybe shower this awful humidity off me?"

"Sure. Take your time." I smile, my gaze following her as she grabs her duffle bag and heads down the hallway.

"She's got a change of clothes?" Julia sidles up next to me. Her voice has a teasing quality to it that's reminiscent of our teenage years when she'd pester me about girls I had a crush on.

"She started bringing a change of clothes a few weeks back."

"Any reason for that?"

"The heat's been brutal, so once the upstairs bathrooms were completed, she's been taking a shower after finishing up for the day."

Julia tilts her head, her eyes alight with mischief. "Why would she need to do that if she's just going home? Doesn't she have a shower there?"

"Of course she does." I pinch my lips together, averting my gaze. But I know my sister. She's like a dog with a bone when it comes to this kind of thing, especially about anything to do with Londyn.

For weeks, she's been nagging me for more information, encouraging me to finally make a move and ask her out. She won't let up until she knows everything. So instead of admitting I've spent the past several weeks fantasizing about kissing Londyn, I throw her a tiny bone.

"We've been having dinner together."

"Is that right?"

I roll my eyes. "Not like you're thinking. It's a long drive back to Atlanta—"

"Not that long," she interjects. "Just a little over an hour, depending on traffic."

"Regardless, the least I can do is feed her before she drives back."

"Feed her *what* exactly?" She waggles her brows.

I push past her, heading up to the master bedroom to get ready. "You're sick."

Her laughter fills the space. "But you still love me."

"Debatable."

# CHAPTER THIRTEEN

LONDYN

The sights and sounds of the county fairs of my childhood surround me as I stroll beside Julia through trampled grass. Wes and Imogene walk several feet in front of us, their hands clasped together, her laughter echoing in the late afternoon air.

Since we arrived here a half-hour ago, I've barely been able to take my eyes off Wes and the way he is with Imogene. Over the past few months, I've witnessed their interactions, but not for prolonged periods of time. Not like this. The affection he has for the little girl is evident. And it's clear she worships the ground he walks on.

"He's the best thing that's ever happened to her," Julia says, reading my thoughts.

I lift my eyes to hers, smiling.

"And to me," she adds, glancing down at her feet. A bit of vulnerability surrounds her, which is unlike the strong-willed woman I've gotten to know.

"You two seem to have a really close relationship."

"We've certainly had our fair share of disagreements. What siblings don't?" She laughs, her expression lightening for a moment before turning serious. "But he's always been there when it mattered." She pauses before continuing. "Did Wes mention I'm not his real sister? Not by blood anyway."

I blink, slowing my steps as I wrap my brain around this revelation. I don't know why it catches me so off guard. Wes and Julia look nothing alike, so it shouldn't come as such a shock. Now I'm even more intrigued to learn about this part of her... And Wes.

"No, he didn't."

"Which is so like him." She shakes her head, smiling fondly. "When we were kids and someone brought up the fact I wasn't born into his family, that I'm not a true Bradford, he'd kindly but firmly remind them I'm his sister, regardless that we don't share the same DNA. But that's just the type of person Wes is. Kind. Loyal. Protective."

"Were you adopted at birth?"

"I was about Imogene's age." She shoves her hands into her pockets. "My birth mom had a drug problem that eventually got the better of her. I think I was taken away from her when I was four or so. I bounced from foster home to foster home for a while. I guess being raised by a drug addict for four years had some psychological effects a lot of families weren't prepared for. But once my mom overdosed, it made me eligible for adoption. To be honest, I didn't think I'd ever be adopted. I'd once overheard my social worker saying that the older kids got, the harder it was to find a family willing to raise them. Not completely impossible, but many potential adoptive parents prefer a baby. Not a maladjusted six-year-old with emotional problems." She smiles sadly.

"How did Wes' parents become interested? Based on the little I've picked up from you and Wes, they don't seem like the type of people who'd do anything that didn't benefit them."

"You're right about that. Apparently, one of Lydia's friends decided to become a foster mom in order to look…charitable. These women suffer from what I like to call *one-up syndrome*. They're constantly looking for a way to out-do one another. So if Lydia wanted to one-up her so-called friend who decided to foster, she needed to adopt. On paper, Lydia and James are the perfect candidates. Wealthy. Great neighborhood. A private school education. Able to afford the therapy I required. But that's all the Bradfords are. Perfect on paper. When you get a peek into the family's private life, you're in for a rude awakening."

"I take it you didn't exactly like life as a Bradford."

"I tried. I really did. I was so worried about messing up. Worried they'd decide they didn't want me. So for years, I did everything to be the perfect daughter I thought Lydia wanted. Just like Wes. All his life, he had unrealistic expectations placed on his shoulders to be the perfect son. The perfect student. The perfect, well…everything. But I eventually broke free. Met someone who…" She hesitates, pulling her lip between her teeth in contemplation. Then she shakes her head. "Well, someone who made me realize I'm enough as I am, more or less."

"And Wes? Has he realized that?" I ask, although I fear I already know the answer.

"I don't think he has," she says with a sigh. "He still tends to carry the weight of the world on his back. Which was why buying back Meemaw and Gampy's place was so important." Her face lights up when Imogene glances back at us, beaming enthusiastically as we approach a few carnival rides I'm convinced she's about to drag Julia on. "Why it was important to us. I hope he's able to feel what we did all those years ago whenever we spent time there."

"And what's that?"

"It's the only place either of us could feel normal, could feel love."

"You didn't have that with your adoptive parents?"

"Not even close." She pauses, then adds, "Neither did Wes."

I stop walking, those three words hitting me harder than they should. I knew he didn't have the best relationship with them as an adult. But to never feel a parent's love, even as a young child? I couldn't imagine. My life may not have turned out like I'd envisioned, but at least I knew my mother's love. *Felt* my mother's love. My heart breaks for the little boy who never experienced that. Whose mother probably only got pregnant because another woman in her social circle was.

"Mama! Mama!" Imogene's excited voice cuts through, and I look to see her tugging on Julia's hand. "Can we go on the Ferris wheel?"

"You know it goes pretty high."

She scoffs. "That's okay. Uncle Wes told me I'm fearless."

"And that you are, my love." Julia tousles her daughter's hair, then looks at me. "Guess I'm going on the Ferris wheel." She feigns enthusiasm. "Joy of joys."

She allows Imogene to pull her along the dusty field, past various carnival games offering large stuffed animals as prizes, and toward the ticket booth. Julia purchases the necessary number of tickets as Wes and I stand off to the side. I crane my head back, the setting sun making it difficult to see the top of the Ferris wheel.

"Aren't you guys coming?"

I tear my eyes forward, praying the voice that sounds alarmingly like Imogene's doesn't actually belong to her. Unfortunately, my prayers go unanswered, as they have most of my life.

"I—" I glance between her and the Ferris wheel, heat covering my cheeks as dread sets in.

"Please?" Imogene clasps her hands together, her eyes imploring me.

It's official. The little girl is some sort of witch, because when she peers at me like that, I am powerless to tell her no, regardless of the sweat forming on my nape over the idea of being suspended in the sky on that thing.

"She's good, isn't she?" Wes whispers into my ear.

"A master at her craft, it seems."

"What do you say? Want to go for a ride?" He extends his hand toward me.

I look from him, to the spinning circle of death, then back, unease visible on my expression.

"Come on. It'll be fun." He grabs my hand and drags me toward the ticket booth, buying two.

"I'm not sure I'd call getting on a ride that's been disassembled and reassembled dozens of times in a year by minimum wage workers fun. Have these even been inspected?"

"Don't tell me you've never gone to a carnival before." He returns his change to his wallet, then places his hand on my back, steering me into line behind Imogene and Julia. "Or is that not something a preacher's daughter does?"

"I've been to carnivals. When I was younger. When I didn't realize how unsafe these things are."

He smirks, acting as if he doesn't have a care in the world.

As if we're not about to get on a treacherous carnival ride and pray we don't plummet dozens of feet to our death.

"True, but if we do die, at least we'll have a good death story."

"I'd rather have an interesting *life* story. Like, here lies Londyn Bennett. She died at the ripe ol' age of 108. She attributed her longevity to a daily dose of bad reality television, an overabundance of carbs, and not riding on rickety-ass carnival rides."

His eyes light up in amusement. Then he leans into the crook of my neck. I go still, barely breathing, his proximity enthralling, exhilarating, and so wanted, yet equally petrifying at the same time.

"Come on, Lo. Live a little."

A shiver trickles down my spine, my limbs weakening. How can I tell him no when my childhood nickname on his tongue sounds so satisfying? So pleasing? So captivating?

"Okay," I whimper.

"That's my girl."

I don't even have to look at him to see the smile crossing his mouth, able to hear it in his voice.

"Let's go." He tugs me forward, and I snap out of the spell his words and proximity had cast over me.

When I see we're at the front of the line, a chill envelopes me, my stomach roiling. I'd hoped to have a few more minutes to mentally prepare myself, but I barely even have a few seconds, my anxiety increasing as Wes hands our tickets to a bearded man working this wheel of doom.

Imogene waves excitedly from their carriage as Wes leads me toward the one directly behind them, the safety bar dangling open. She's only six, yet doesn't seem to be scared. If she can be fearless, so can I. At least that's what I tell myself as I allow the carnival worker to lock Wes and me inside.

I face forward, not looking up or down, and blow out a breath. When we lurch forward, I clutch the bar in a vice-like grip, my knuckles turning white.

"Jesus, Mary, and Joseph," I mutter under my breath as the ground moves beneath us. Thankfully, we come to a hard stop just a few seconds later.

"I never would have pegged you for someone who was scared of heights." Wes chuckles. "Not after seeing you jump up and down ladders like a damn trapeze artist these past few weeks."

"I'm not scared of heights." I loosen my hold to flex the stiff muscles in my fingers. "Just falling from heights because of some completely preventable malfunction."

"You won't fall." He fixes me with a serious look.

"You can't guarantee that."

He shrugs. "You're right. I can't."

"Way to make me feel good about this decision." I laugh nervously, doing my best to focus straight ahead and not down. We're probably only ten feet off the ground, but as far as I'm concerned, it may as well be ten miles.

"I do what I can."

When we begin moving once more, I instinctively grab onto his hand, squeezing.

"Damn, Londyn. You're going to break my fingers if you keep that up."

I shoot him a glare. "You deserve it for dragging me onto this death trap." When we stop a few seconds later, I relax my grip, smiling to myself when he shakes out his hand with a wince. "And you can call me Lo if you want. That's what my mom called me."

He shifts toward me the best he can when trapped in this tiny, open-air bucket. "What was she like?"

I stare into space, imagining her smile as she sang to me. "Beautiful. She had the most amazing voice."

"She was a singer?"

I nod. "Not professionally, but she could have been. She was always smiling. And her laugh..." I sigh, remembering her vivacious laughter that filled our home every day. "We didn't have a huge house, and there were some months I could tell money was tight, but I never doubted her love for me."

I can sense Wes' hesitation before he asks his next question. "What happened to her? You'd mentioned she died when you were young."

93

I don't say anything right away, torn. For years, I've barricaded myself behind a wall, not sharing my past with anyone, unsure whom I could trust. From the beginning, I sensed Wes was…different. Which is probably why I actually want him to know this part of me. Want him to see who I really am. Want him to understand where I come from, why I am the way I am.

"I was seven when she was killed."

"How?"

"Wrong place. Wrong time." I meet his gaze. "Do you remember hearing about a church shooting in Virginia twenty years ago? It was a pretty big deal since it was right after Columbine."

He nods, the motion almost imperceptible.

"That was my father's church."

"Londyn…" His voice is laden with sympathy and something else. Heartache. But how could that be? He didn't know me then. Didn't know my mother. Still, the pain in his expression is real. There's no mistaking it. He's not just acting this way because he thinks it's what I need, as *he* so often did all those years ago. Wes' reaction is honest. Maybe I *can* trust him with more than what I've allowed him to see.

I face forward again, staring into the distance. They say people who have witnessed a traumatic event can often recall the tiniest details, even decades later. Just like I can still remember what I was wearing. Still remember the math problem I was working on. Still remember what song they were rehearsing when gunshots rang out.

"She led the choir and was holding a rehearsal. Sometimes I'd sit in a pew and listen. That night, I decided to sit in my father's office and do homework while he worked on his sermon for the week." I swallow hard. "There were screams. Shouts. Gunshots. I distinctly remember my father jumping to his feet, torn between protecting me and helping his choir. In the end, he grabbed me, rushed me out the back entrance, and hid me in the car, all the while listening to the gunshots taking more and more lives. In the end, twelve people died. Another six were gravely injured but survived. I was young when it

94

happened, but not too young to realize my father might have been able to save some of those people, maybe even my mother, if he hadn't rushed me to safety."

"You can't think that way," Wes urges, his gaze intense. "I'm not a parent, but there's no doubt I'd do the same thing if it were Imogene. No question."

"It's always messed with my head a bit. It's why I always strove to do everything to make my father proud, do whatever he asked, make him think he didn't make a mistake in saving my life instead of someone else's. So when I say I've struggled with guilt these past several years since I left the church, left him, that's what I'm dealing with."

"Why did you leave the church?" he asks. "What happened to make you walk away? It sounds like you were close with your father at one time."

"I was. I..." I chew on my lower lip.

He covers my hand with his. "It's okay. Whatever it is, I won't think any less of you."

He says that now, but he doesn't know the truth. My father saved my life. But me? I took a life.

"Let's talk about something else." I pull my hand from his. "The last thing I want to talk about on this thing is death, considering mine feels pretty fucking eminent," I joke, lightening the tension.

"Do you not like to fly then?" he asks after a beat, not pressing me for more information about my past.

"Actually, I love it. But planes go through rigorous safety checks. This thing..." I wave my hands around, sucking in a breath when I see we're circling in the late afternoon sky, the sun setting on the horizon turning the sky a beautiful pink hue. I swallow hard as we near the top, panic setting in.

Wes reaches over, clutching my hand in his. I rip my eyes toward his as a comforting smile tugs on his full lips.

"Just think about something else, Lo."

"L-like what?" I ask, my stomach seeming to do backflips. I'm not sure if it's from the motion of the Ferris wheel or the feeling of Wes' skin against mine. Perhaps a bit of both.

"Whatever makes you happy."

95

I push out a shaky laugh. "Don't tell me you're about to go all Julie Andrews on me and break into song."

"Julie Andrews?" He scrunches his brow. "I don't follow."

"Yeah. That scene from *The Sound of Music*. When all the kids get freaked out because of a thunderstorm and run into her room, where she serenades them with 'My Favorite Things'."

"It's been quite a few years since I've seen that movie, but don't worry." He flashes me a debonair smile. "I have absolutely no intention of breaking into song. Pretty sure that would have you scrambling to leap off this *death trap*, as you call it, heights be damned."

I throw my head back, laughing harder than I have in quite a long time, despite being on a decrepit carnival ride where my next breath could very well be my last.

"Okay then. Singing's out. Duly noted." I pretend to make a note on an imaginary pad. "How about you tell me what makes *you* happy? Maybe it'll work on me."

"Perhaps." He pinches his chin, deep in thought. When he opens his mouth, I expect some profound answer. Instead, he serenades me with the first verse of "My Favorite Things".

I playfully jab him in the side with my elbow, the sound of our laughter carrying over the dings and alarms from nearby carnival games and rides. Then Wes slings an arm around my shoulders. A few days ago…hell, a few *hours* ago…I probably would have shrugged him off, wanting to keep the lines between us from becoming blurred. But I'm starting to realize we blurred those lines the second he risked his life to save mine all those weeks ago. In that one act, we became bound to each other, an impervious connection growing stronger with each minute we spend together. One we're powerless to fight.

"This," Wes murmurs into my ear, his warm breath on my skin causing goosebumps to break out.

I turn toward him, my mouth growing dry from the sincerity in his deep blue eyes. "What do you mean?" I ask, scared of the answer, yet also hoping it's the one I want.

"This, Lo." He inches toward me as he pushes several of my curls away from my face. "This right here makes me happy. Spending time with you."

"This makes me happy, too," I barely manage to squeak out.

"I was hoping you'd say that."

With agonizingly slow movements, he gradually erases the space between us. But what's only a matter of inches feels like a mile as his breath dances on my lips, my mouth watering at the promise of his kiss.

For weeks, I've imagined how he would kiss. Would it be controlled and dominating, like the man he appeared to be during our first meeting? Or would it be soft and sincere, like the man I learned he could be during the times he listened to me talk about my past? Or would it be desperate and needy, like the way he's currently peering at me, a man at the end of his rope?

My chest heaves, every synapse in my body firing when his lips faintly brush against the corner of my mouth. Before I can push forward or pull back, the Ferris wheel comes to an abrupt stop, jostling me, my forehead bumping his face.

"Shit." I lean back, horrified as I watch Wes rub his nose. "Are you okay?"

"Yeah." He chuckles. "Just...bad timing, I guess. Story of my life. Perpetually a dollar short and a day late, as Gampy would say." He winks, then slides out of the bucket once the carnival worker unlocks the safety bar. "Shall we?" He extends his hand toward me.

"Yes." I place my hand in his and he helps me down from this wheel of death, our fingers remaining locked as we make our way back to the frenzied atmosphere of the fair.

"Did you have fun, Uncle Wes?" Imogene asks, excitement oozing from her voice.

"It certainly looked like you were having fun." Julia waggles her brows, which causes my cheeks to warm in embarrassment.

I'd been so immersed in Wes and our conversation, I'd all but forgotten Imogene and Julia were in the bucket right in front of us and could see everything. From the way he held my hand. To the way he slung his arm around my shoulders. To

97

the way he nearly kissed me.

"And for the record…," Julia continues, grinning deviously, "I wholeheartedly approve."

# CHAPTER FOURTEEN

## WESTON

I can't stop holding her hand. Can't stop brushing my thumb along her knuckles. Can't stop wishing we had a few more seconds on that Ferris wheel so I could get a better idea of how her lips taste. Because I'm certain she wanted me to kiss her. And god, do I want to kiss her.

"Weston? Is that you?"

The familiar voice pulls me out of my daydream. It's probably for the best. If I don't stop thinking about kissing Londyn, I won't be able to hide the need brimming inside me.

I slow my steps, searching for the source. When I spot a booth advertising *Georgia's best peach cobbler*, my mouth salivates over the memory of Miss Clara's peach cobbler.

"Oh, it *is* you!" The stocky woman wipes her hands on a dishtowel, then issues orders to a couple of teenagers working the booth before ducking underneath the counter and making her way toward us.

"Miss Clara," Julia greets warmly as the woman approaches.

Her dark brown hair is now mostly gray, her skin has a few more wrinkles, and she probably carries a bit more weight, but her smile is as infectious and heartwarming as it was all those years ago whenever Gampy and Meemaw took us to her diner after church on Sundays.

She shifts her gaze to Julia's petite frame. "You can't be sweet little Julia, can you?"

"I'm not so sure Julia was ever sweet," I joke, to which my sister jabs me in the stomach, making me nearly double over.

"Glad to see some things haven't changed," Miss Clara comments. "That you two still bicker like you did all those years ago. But you still love each other just the same." Her lips kick up into a nostalgic smile, her eyes glassing over, probably remembering Meemaw and Gampy as she peers at two walking memories of the past. Then her gaze shifts downward. "And who is this beautiful child?"

"This is Imogene," Julia says proudly. "My daughter."

Miss Clara covers her heart with her hand, her chin trembling. "You named her after your meemaw." She shakes her head, struggling to reel in her tears. It doesn't matter how many years have passed since we lost them. It still affects Miss Clara. Just like it does Julia and me. Especially Julia.

"I did."

"It's a beautiful way to honor her memory. Such a tragedy what happened to them, but I know God welcomed them home with open arms." She pulls her lips between her teeth as she glances between Julia and me, soaking in our changed appearance with the affection of a grandmother.

"Well, look at me getting all teary-eyed." Her voice brightening, she swipes her cheeks. "I must be making a right fool out of myself, and in front of your...wife?" Her tone rises in pitch as she looks between Londyn and me.

"No," I say quickly. "Not my wife." I blow out a nervous laugh and run a hand through my hair.

"Oh, well, after hearing about your engagement a few years ago, I'd assumed—"

"No. Not married," I interrupt, sensing Londyn's curious eyes on me.

I turn to her, struggling to come up with an explanation. Should I have told her about Brooklyn? Does it matter?

"Londyn," I begin, so as to not stand with my proverbial foot in my mouth, "this is Miss Clara. She owns the diner in town that Gampy and Meemaw always took us to when we were kids. Miss Clara, this is Londyn, my..." I shake my head, unsure how to explain who Londyn is to me. Designer seems too...impersonal. But I suppose that's what she is. "Interior designer," I finally say.

"I see." Miss Clara grins, a devilish glint in her eyes, obviously discerning there's more between us than designer and client. "Well, it's wonderful to meet you, Londyn." She extends her hand.

"You, too," Londyn says as they shake.

"I won't keep y'all from your fun. I'm sure Miss Imogene here would much rather go on the rides than stand here and talk to some old lady. How long are y'all here? Or did you just drive in for the fair?"

"Actually, Wes bought Meemaw and Gampy's old place," Julia explains, her eyes filled with pride. "Stumbled on it on the auction block and made sure he got it back. Returned it to the rightful owners. We're renovating it, with Londyn's help. Well, more like she's helping Wes. Home improvement and me don't really mix." She laughs.

"Is that right? So you're going to be spending time here in town then?"

"Once the remodel's done, yes," I reply. "Might take a few more months, but we're getting there." I flash Londyn a smile.

"Well, bless my soul." Miss Clara exhales a satisfied sigh. "This is fantastic news. I'll be sure to keep an eye out for y'all at the diner. I'll even seat you at your gampy's favorite booth."

"That sounds fantastic." I lean down to kiss her cheek. "Great seeing you, Miss Clara." When I pull back, she brings her hands to my arms, squeezing my biceps.

"You, too, Weston dear. Really great to see you." She drops her hold on me and pulls Julia in for a hug. "So wonderful to see your beautiful smile again, darling." She holds her for another beat before releasing her, looking down at Imogene. "You behave for your mama and uncle. Okay?"

"Yes, ma'am," Imogene answers politely.

"I'll be seeing you around." Miss Clara waves as she retreats through the crowd, sidestepping children carrying cotton candy and caramel apples. She looks back over her shoulder. "And nice to meet you, Londyn. I hope to see much more of you sometime soon."

"Me, too," Londyn replies as Miss Clara ducks back into her booth.

"Come on, Mama. Let's play some games." Imogene grabs Julia's hand and tugs her toward the booths overflowing with stuffed animals of all sizes. Londyn and I follow.

"She seemed sweet," she comments after a few silent

moments as I toil over which bomb to address first. Do I start with how my grandparents died? Or should I discuss the fact I was once hours away from being married? Neither of them are events I enjoy talking about.

"She's probably the kindest and most generous person in this town."

"You can tell she holds your grandparents in very high esteem."

Her hand brushes against mine, sending a rush of excitement through me. Needing to feel her skin, I link a pinky with hers to test the waters, unsure if she's upset I hadn't told her about my engagement. When she doesn't pull away, I intertwine the rest of my fingers with hers.

"She's one of the good ones. She'd always remain in the diner after it closed at night to prepare meals for some of the area children who didn't get fed at home, especially during summer when school was out of session. I wouldn't be surprised to learn she still does it. It's why she got along so well with my grandparents. She was a giver. Like them."

"Like you, too," Londyn offers.

I part my lips as I contemplate her statement. I've never considered myself a giver. Not like my grandparents, who devoted their entire lives to helping people. I do what I can, but it doesn't come remotely close to what Gampy and Meemaw did during their lifetimes.

"Don't even try to say you're not," she argues. "That day you helped me in the rain, I saw you with Omar. You gave him the coffee and pastry bag you'd had at the coffee shop. Which makes me think either you gave him your own coffee and danish, or you bought them specifically for him. I could be wrong, but I'm leaning toward it being the latter."

"It's not his fault he's homeless. He's a vet. Fought in Vietnam, for crying out loud. He deserves better than what he got."

"Like I said." She smiles up at me and squeezes my hand. "You're a giver."

"Can we play that game?" Imogene asks from up ahead.

I turn my attention forward, watching her dart toward a

booth that's framed by dozens of stuffed animals, many of them close replications of Disney characters. Along the back wall are several stations of milk bottles arranged in a pyramid. I remember this being popular when I was a kid. I'd assumed these games would have advanced with technology. I guess that's the reason baseball is considered America's pastime. It's timeless. Just like this game of requiring someone to knock down the bottles with a baseball.

"Sure, sweetie." Julia hands the man the requisite cash to cover the cost of six balls, then kneels, giving Imogene some tips on how to throw a baseball.

"So it's true."

I hear the voice from behind me, but I don't immediately pay any attention, too immersed in watching Imogene wind up and throw the baseball with more heat than I thought she could at her age. Truth be told, her aim is pretty spot-on, too, only an inch shy of hitting the bottles. More proof that she is most certainly her mother's daughter. Julia was always more interested in sports than makeup and fashion, much to my mother's horror.

When I feel a tap on my shoulder, I drop my hold on Londyn's hand and spin around, coming face-to-face with a ghost from my past. I'm surprised I even recognize Grady Stowe, an asshole whose nose I once broke when I overheard him talking about Julia in a way I didn't think appropriate or respectful. I have a feeling he probably still hasn't learned that lesson. His red hair has prematurely thinned, creating a bald spot on the top of his head. His stomach bears evidence of years of drinking beer, his overall unkempt state giving the impression he's not married. A fact I confirm when I notice his barren ring finger.

Then again, I'm not one to talk. I've never been married, either.

"Can I help you?"

"I said… So it's true."

"What's true?" I ask firmly, widening my stance and crossing my arms.

He licks his lips, stealing a glimpse at Londyn. Instinct kicks in and I step in front of her, blocking her. Not out of shame or embarrassment, but to protect her from whatever Grady wants, why he felt the need to approach me when we haven't spoken in ages.

Even when I spent my summers here, I was never exactly friendly with Grady. He was, as my Gampy called it, bad news. The whole family routinely got into trouble and were frequent visitors to the local jail. It wouldn't come as a shock to learn Grady followed in his father's footsteps and has made a career out of stealing to make a buck instead of earning one the honest way.

"That you turned out like your grandfather." His lip curls as he peers over my shoulder, sneering at Londyn in disgust.

I've never understood how someone could hate another person based on their appearance, something they have no control over. It's why I never understood my parents all that much. Their entire existence revolved around judging people. If you didn't wear the right clothes, didn't get invited to the right events, didn't have the right friends, you were too insignificant for them to waste their time on. I still don't know how two people as loving and generous as my grandparents could raise someone as spiteful and judgmental as my mother. Then again, as Meemaw often told me, some people lose sight of who they are when money's involved.

Grady pushes up his shirt sleeves, revealing what appears to be a rudimentary tattoo in the shape of a swastika on his right arm, which he probably got in prison.

*Great.*

"That you turned into a nigger-lover, too."

Suddenly, everything falls quiet. I no longer hear the dinging from the carnival games. Or the constant chatter of people lining up for food. Or the motors on the nearby rides. It's like I'm in a tunnel. Just me, Grady, and my anger at the derogatory word, one I can't even stomach to repeat.

Oblivious to the crowd growing around us, I reel back, looking forward to the feel of Grady's flesh meeting my fist. But I'm stopped mere inches shy of his chin, a strong pull on my elbow preventing me from making contact.

"Stop," Londyn orders, jumping between us. Her voice is firm, lips pinched into a tight line, eyes pleading with me not to do this.

"But—"

"No. It's what he wants, Wes. I've dealt with people like him all my life." She shoots a spiteful look in Grady's direction. "Small-minded pricks who only stand for something easy, like hate. Don't stoop to his level. You're too good a person to do that."

My gaze floats between Grady and Londyn, then to the assembled crowd. But that's not what causes me to reconsider. It's the expression of fear on little Imogene's face as she peeks out from behind her mother. My heart squeezes that she had to see this. That she had to witness hate, something no child should ever have to experience.

I briefly close my eyes in resignation, lowering my fist. "Okay."

"Pansy," Grady remarks under his breath as I retreat.

Stopping abruptly, I advance toward him, wiping the cocky, self-satisfied smirk off his face in one swift motion. I get nose-to-nose with him, nostrils flaring, jaw tense.

"Make no mistake, Grady," I snarl. "If you come near her or the rest of my family, I won't hesitate to destroy you."

"Are you threatening me?" he guffaws, a few of his friends from back in the day assembling around him. I didn't like them then. And I don't like them now. But I'm no longer the scrawny, awkward teenager he remembers me to be. I'm a man with enough resources at my disposal to make their lives extremely difficult. And enough physical strength to easily overpower them if circumstances require.

"Not a threat." I adjust my posture, holding my head high, an air of authority about me. "A promise. And when I make a promise, I keep it. So if I were you, I'd keep your distance. You may still be the same inconsiderate prick. And maybe that's the one thing we have in common. That our personalities haven't changed much since the last time we saw each other. Because I assure you. I will still do whatever it takes to protect those I love."

105

He opens his mouth, but I cut him off.

"Whatever it takes," I repeat, my voice infinitely more threatening. I level a stare on him, then turn, extending my hand to Londyn.

She looks at it, hesitating, but to my relief, she eventually takes it. I need her skin against mine right now. It's the only thing that seems to calm me, rage still bubbling in my veins.

We silently make our way from the fair and toward the car, no longer in the mood for carnival games and greasy food. Even Imogene remains unusually quiet, a feat for the little girl who tends to talk from the second she wakes up in the morning to the instant she falls asleep.

As we approach Julia's SUV, Imogene breaks the silence. "Mama, what was that word the mean man called Uncle Wes?"

We all stop walking as Julia crouches down to her level so she can look into her eyes. I don't envy my sister right now. How do you teach a six-year-old about hate when their entire existence is based on love?

"That's an awful word, one we never say. You laugh when Mama says shit, ass, and the occasional fuck, but under no circumstances is what that man said allowed to be spoken in our house. Ever," she emphasizes.

Imogene nods, eyes wide, the tone of Julia's voice carrying the importance of what she's saying.

"It's a cruel word," she continues, then softens her voice. "One used only by people whose hearts are filled with hate. And your heart isn't filled with hate, is it?"

Imogene shakes her head, her eyes brimming with innocence. "No. Like you tell me, it's pure and filled with love."

"That's right, baby." Julia brings her hand up to Imogene's smooth cheek, caressing her skin.

"Then why is his heart filled with hate? Do you think maybe he just needs a hug?"

I look from Imogene to Londyn at my side. Releasing her hand, I drape my arm around her shoulders, pulling her toward me. I half expect her to push out of my embrace, the gesture too forward for…whatever we are. But she doesn't. She nuzzles into me, lifting her gaze to mine and smiling sweetly.

"I don't know," Julia replies. "Sometimes that happens. Some people are scared of things that are different. Of people who are different."

Realization washes over Imogene's expression as she looks at Londyn. "He didn't like Miss Londyn because her skin's different than ours?"

"Yeah, baby. He saw something different and got scared. But Miss Londyn doesn't scare you, does she?"

"No. I like having her around." A grin crawls on her lips as she leans close to Julia. "And I think Uncle Wes *really* likes having her around," she attempts to whisper, but she hasn't exactly mastered that skill quite yet.

I peer down at Londyn, her eyes shining, and offer her a slight shrug, silently telling her my niece isn't far off. That I *do* enjoy having her around. Normally, I might be embarrassed, but not right now. Not when Londyn settles even further into my embrace.

"I think so, too," Julia continues. "That's because we all have love in our hearts, even if someone doesn't look like we do. What's on the outside isn't nearly as important as what's on the inside." She moves her hand to cover Imogene's chest. "Isn't nearly as important as what's in here. I don't want you to ever forget that, okay?"

"Okay, Mama." She smiles, then pinches her lips together, her expression serious, as if about to ask a question of the utmost importance. "Can we get ice cream on the way home?"

The tension immediately evaporates, all of us breaking into laughter.

Julia stands, placing her hands on Imogene's shoulders and leading her toward the car. "Of course, baby."

# CHAPTER FIFTEEN

LONDYN

"Want a beer to take the edge off?" Wes turns to me as we stand in front of Gampy and Meemaw's house after watching Julia and Imogene drive off on their way back to the city.

"It's been a long day." I smile, but it's obviously forced.

We've worked much later before, and I've had no qualms about staying for a beer and some burgers before heading home. But things feel…different. I can't quite put my finger on it. I should feel grateful Wes stood up for me like he did. But I hate he had to do that.

"I should head back. Get a good night's sleep."

"You can crash here if you want. You can take the bed in the master. I've got an extra sleeping bag I can use."

Once I learned Wes had been staying here on the weekends, I focused my attention on getting one of the bedrooms into a somewhat useable state. It still needs paint and other details, and the bed is just a simple frame for the time being, but it's better than sleeping on the floor.

"I didn't take you for the roughing-it type," I joke in an effort to cut through the solemn atmosphere that even ice cream couldn't fix.

"There's still a lot about me that I think will surprise you."

"I think so, too," I murmur.

"But I also have an air mattress." He beams.

I laugh, which feels good, especially after tonight. "Of course you do."

"Come on, Lo," he pleads, becoming serious once more. "One beer. At the very least you can hold a beer and sit with me so I don't feel like I'm drinking alone. After tonight, I could *really* use a beer. And a friend."

As much as I'd love to go home, curl up in my bed, and

forget about tonight, I can't ignore the pull I feel toward him, so powerful and all-consuming. He's the one person in recent history I struggle to deny, although all reason tells me I should.

"Okay."

"Okay." Wes places his hand on my lower back, leading me up to the front porch.

After unlocking the door, he allows me to walk in ahead of him. Neither of us says a word as we head to the barren kitchen. He opens the mini fridge he brought here a few weeks ago and grabs two beers, popping the top off both. Handing me one, we walk out to the back porch I plan to transform into an outdoor entertaining space, complete with dining area and built-in grill. Right now, though, it's still a rundown old porch. But that doesn't matter. After a long day of working on the house, this has become one of my favorite things. Sitting on the top step, drinking a beer, Wes at my side.

Assuming our normal spots, we sit in relative silence, apart from the typical sounds of a country evening. Frogs croaking. Insects buzzing. Owls hooting. Despite the symphony of nature surrounding us, it's remarkably peaceful.

"Are you okay?" Wes asks after a while. "With what happened earlier?"

I look away from a few lightning bugs dancing in the distance, my eyes locking with his. "It's not the first time I've been called something like that. And it won't be the last."

His shoulders fall as he shakes his head. "It's so fucked up. The Stowes have always been like that, though."

"What? The town assholes?"

"Yeah. Definitely." He leans his forearms on his thighs, taking a long sip of beer. "Although, technically, his family lives the next town over. At least they did when we were kids. People called their neighborhood Stoweville because half the residents of the trailer park were all Stowes. When they weren't locked up for their latest robbery or car theft, that is."

"That would explain why he didn't sound like he was a big fan of your gampy."

He barks out a laugh. "Understatement of the year. The Stowes always hated Gampy. He'd been the prosecutor, then

109

judge on a few of the cases where they were the defendants."

I nod, not surprised. I'm normally not one to judge someone based on their appearance, having been the victim of that my whole life, but Grady had a rough look about him, one you only get after doing hard time.

"What happened to your grandparents?" I ask softly.

He doesn't immediately respond. Instead, he keeps his gaze focused straight ahead.

"I'm sorry, Wes. I didn't mean to pry. After what Miss Clara said, I—"

"It was almost fifteen years ago now," he interrupts. "I was up in Boston for college, so I wasn't around." He pulls his bottom lip between his teeth, and I can tell the memory is difficult for him.

So just like he offered me comfort when I spoke of my mother, I do the same, covering his hand with mine, squeezing. The instant I do, raw need courses through me from the simple act of my skin touching his.

"As I'm sure you're aware, we're not exactly accustomed to winter weather all that much down in these parts."

"Certainly not," I laugh under my breath.

"Right. Well, as you may recall, Meemaw volunteered as a cuddler at the hospital, which is about twenty minutes from here."

"I remember."

"She was working one of her shifts when what was just supposed to be a rainstorm turned to ice, then snow. She called Gampy to tell him she would stay at the hospital until the roads were better, but he insisted on picking her up since it was a special day." He forces a smile. "Their fiftieth wedding anniversary."

"Oh god." My hand flies to my mouth, my stomach churning over what I fear he's about to tell me.

"You know that bridge you cross on the way into town? The Hammond Bridge?"

I nod.

"Their last name was Hammond."

A lump forms in my throat. I've never met Wes'

110

grandparents, but I feel like I have. Hell, these days, I feel closer to the ghosts of his past than I do my own.

"Gampy lost control of the car on a patch of black ice and they went over the side of the bridge. Cause of death was drowning."

"Oh, Wes…"

Tears brim behind my eyelids. I'm not sure why I'm crying. Because of what happened to them? Or because I never got the chance to meet the two people who had such a profound impact on this man I've become rather fond of over the past few months?

I inch closer to him, wishing there were something I could do or say to make it hurt less. But I know better than anyone that's not the case. It doesn't matter how many years have passed. Some deaths you're not meant to get over. Some are meant to stay with you, remind you of the importance of carrying on.

So, instead of filling the silence with meaningless condolences, I rest my head on Wes' shoulder, making sure he knows he's not alone. That was all I wanted when my mother died. To feel like I wasn't alone.

"I like this," he murmurs, moving his arm and draping it around my shoulders.

"Me, too," I admit, stretching my legs in front of me, melting into him. I close my eyes, inhaling the sweet country air, serenity washing over me, something I didn't think possible after the incident at the fair. But that seems to be the effect Wes has on me. He makes me forget everything for a minute.

"Londyn…," Wes says after several moments of listening to nature rustling around us.

The uneasiness in his tone gives me pause, and I look at him. I'm on the verge of asking what's wrong when I feel something brush over my ankles.

"Don't. Move," he warns, his intense gaze focused on whatever it is.

I slowly turn my head, my lungs desperate for air when I see a snake slithering up the bottom step and across my outstretched legs.

"Is that…," I begin with a quiver, my muscles tightening, a chill enveloping me.

"Shh," Wes hushes me so as to not draw the snake's attention.

But it doesn't work.

The trembles overtaking me alert the snake to the fact that I'm a possible threat and not an inanimate source of warmth. Its body coils, everything about it making me confident it's about to strike.

When it hisses, I jump up with what feels like superhero-like speed. I squeeze my eyes shut, not wanting to watch as it clamps its mouth onto my leg. But that never happens, the sound of metal thumping into wood cutting through the air.

I still, peeking through a slightly open eyelid to find Wes standing over the now decapitated snake, a shovel in his hand.

"Jesus, Mary, and Joseph," I exhale as I hop from foot to foot, shaking my hands, my flesh crawling.

Wes leaps up the steps and toward me, eyes awash with concern. "Are you okay?"

"I hate snakes," I cry out. Without thinking, I wrap my arms around him, desperately trying to get my feet off the ground for fear the headless snake will mutate and grow back multiple heads, like the hydra Hercules battled. "I fucking hate them."

"I don't think they're on most people's list of favorite things."

I pull back, shaking my head. "No. I mean, I am absolutely fucking petrified of those damn things. It's completely irrational, because most of them aren't dangerous—"

"Well, that one was," Wes interrupts, nodding toward the snake carcass to the left of the stairs. "Copperhead. With all the overgrown brush, I guess they made a home out here. We'll need to get a landscaper out here soon so Imogene doesn't have a run-in with one."

"If you're trying to make me feel better, it's not working."

Wes pulls me closer, a hand splayed on my back, kissing the top of my head in a pacifying way I've seen him do to Imogene countless times.

"It's okay," he soothes, running his fingers up and down my spine. "You're okay. I got you."

"I hate them. I hate them. I hate them," I repeat, clutching onto his t-shirt with my fists as I remain in his embrace, doing my best to get my emotions under control.

Wes doesn't react, just continues to hold me, keeping me safe in his arms. And that's the thing. I actually *feel* safe. I do every time I'm with him.

"Better?" Wes asks when I stop trembling, my breaths slowing.

I nod against his chest, inhaling deeply, his familiar woodsy scent wrapping around me. "Better."

"Good." He pulls back slightly, but doesn't drop his hold on me, keeping me in his arms.

My pulse kicks up when he pushes a few curls away from my face, his thumb skating across my skin. A shiver trickles through me, and not from the breeze wrapping around us or my lingering fear. From the way he peers at me. So much heat. So much want. So much hunger. It has my stomach doing backflips.

"Londyn…" His voice is deep, husky, guttural.

"Yes…"

"Londyn…," he repeats, clutching my cheeks in his strong hands.

"Yes." My eyes flutter closed as he pulls my lips toward his.

But he doesn't kiss me. Just stays in this magical place where dreams are made and hope lives. This place where two souls are about to feel each other for the first time. This place that's home to so much anticipation and promise.

When I don't retreat or push him away, he moves a hand to the small of my back, yanking me against him. And then it happens. What I've fantasized about more times than I care to admit. He erases the last bit of space between us, his lips soft and sweet as he tests the waters. Relishing in this first touch, a tingle spreads over me, heating me from the inside out.

Does he understand the magnitude of this moment, too? Is

113

that why he's taking his time, not rushing through this to get to the good stuff? Because in my mind, it's all good stuff with him, even this barely-there meeting of our mouths.

His self-control doesn't last too long, though. Before I have a chance to catch a breath, he deepens the exchange, his kiss bruising and greedy, leaving me thoughtless. Mindless. Defenseless. But in the best way possible.

Digging his fingers into my scalp, his other hand guides me backward, tightening when my back comes into contact with the wall. He circles his hips, the feel of his erection against me causing my craving to ratchet up another level. I hook a leg around his waist, desire pooling between my thighs at the feel of him. God, it's been so long since I've felt like this, so needy and free.

He briefly pulls back, eyes locking with mine. "God, you taste better than I imagined. And I've certainly imagined."

Before I can speak, he dives in for another impassioned kiss, this one even more hungry. I curve into him, succumbing to him. It's been years since I've allowed a man to kiss me like this, hating how vulnerable a kiss could make me. How many lies can be masked in one gesture. But I don't feel any of that with Wes. All I feel is his respect. His admiration. His undeniable passion for me. Passion I've denied for weeks. Passion I don't want to deny any longer. Passion I deserve.

I run my hands down his back, lifting his shirt and digging my nails into his flesh. As I continue my exploration of his body, my touch confirms what I'd imagined the countless times I mentally undressed him. Broad shoulders. Defined chest. Chiseled abs.

He breaks away from my lips, both of us panting. Then he buries his head in the crook of my neck.

When he scrapes his teeth against my flesh, I throw my head back on a moan, my veins on fire from his scintillating touch. My chest heaves. My heart races. My soul sings. All from this unassuming man's touch.

He pushes one of the thin straps of my sundress off my shoulder, kissing the exposed skin. "Is this okay?" He floats his gaze to mine.

"Yes."

"Good."

He smiles slyly before pushing the top of my dress farther down, exposing more of my cleavage. He trails kisses from my shoulder, along my collarbone, and down the crest of my breast. Drawing a line with his tongue, he stops just shy of my bra. Then he flicks his eyes back to mine, a hint of mischief within.

"Is this okay?" he asks again.

"Yes," I reply, this time with more desperation, more urgency.

"Good."

He returns his attention to my breast, his mouth warm on my skin. He dips a finger beneath my bra, lightly grazing my nipple. But it still causes an inferno to erupt in my core, burning everything in sight. I'm no longer Londyn. No longer this man's interior designer. I'm just a bundle of hormones in desperate need of release.

"Is this okay?" he repeats.

"Yes," I answer frantically. I couldn't tell him no even if I wanted to. But right now, I can't remember wanting anything more in my life, the tension that's been building with each moment bubbling over, scorching everything in sight.

"Good."

His deft fingers push down my bra cup, revealing my breast. He lifts his eyes, jaw tight, nostrils flaring.

"You are so fucking beautiful, Londyn." He crushes his lips to mine in a punishing kiss before tearing away, leaving a fire in his wake as he makes his torturous journey back down my frame.

I hold my breath, watching as he stops a mere whisper away from my nipple. He blows on it, the warmth causing it to pebble even more. When he finally takes it into his mouth, I moan, synapses firing inside me, reawakening parts of my body I'd forgotten existed.

I thrust against him, but it's not enough, nothing able to extinguish the flame he lit with his kiss, his touch.

He squeezes my thigh, his hand traveling upward and

pushing the skirt of my dress higher as his tongue circles my nipple with more hunger before pulling back, leaving me bereft and needy.

"Is this okay?" he asks, sliding his hand even higher up my leg, lifting his eyes to meet mine.

"Yes," I answer, not a hint of hesitation in my tone.

Reaching my panty line, he teases it with one finger, ghosting my center. When he feels how much I want him, his eyes widen before darkening.

"Is this okay?" He lifts my panties, but doesn't push them to the side. Not yet.

"Yes." My voice is barely audible, too many sensations rushing through me. If we were anywhere else, I might stop him, not wanting anyone to see. But we're all alone out here, no other house visible for miles. It's just us. And this all-consuming need.

His expression even, he slides my panties aside, the warmth of his finger so close to my center pushing me to the edge of all reason. *Past* the edge of all reason. Because I am out of my mind with lust. In another time. Another place. Where all I care about is letting go.

He brings his thumb to my clit, the contact sending a charge straight to my core.

"Is this okay?" he asks a final time. The restrained want in his chiseled expression, as well as his voice, is evidence it's taking everything he has to keep his wits about him.

"Yes," I respond, thrusting slightly against him, urging him.

His lips descend on mine, his teeth nibbling on my bottom one. "God, I was hoping you'd say that."

When he presses his thumb more firmly against me, I'm helpless to contain the moan that escapes my mouth, utter bliss rushing through my veins. Everything about this moment feels like a dream.

An erotic dream I want to have again and again.

"God, you're so wet, Lo," Wes groans, his motions propelling me higher and higher. "Do I turn you on this much?"

"Yes," I breathe, my grip on him tightening when he pushes

a finger inside me. My core clenches, the fullness of his finger inside and thumb on my clit unraveling me to the point of oblivion.

"Fuck," he hisses, adding another finger, stretching and tormenting me. Our heavy breaths intermingle as we succumb to everything we've fought for weeks. "Do you have any idea how many times I've thought about how you would taste? How you would feel?"

"How many?" I ask, our gazes locking as he continues to torture me.

"Too many, Londyn." He lowers his mouth to my neck, biting and sucking on that sensitive spot just below my earlobe. "So fucking many. So many nights I've jerked off to the fantasy of burying myself inside you."

"Oh god," I whimper, more turned on than I thought possible.

I don't know what I expected Wes to be like in the bedroom, but I hadn't anticipated this. For the gentleman I assumed him to be, he can certainly bring the heat when the occasion calls. And the fire ravaging through me from his words right now is enough to rival when Sherman marched on Atlanta, setting everything in his path ablaze.

"That's right, baby," Wes grunts. His motions become more frenzied, sensing my impending orgasm. "See how good we can be together? How good I can make you feel?"

"God, yes." When he slips another finger inside, I can no longer hold back, my body a slave to him. I come undone, lights flashing behind my eyes as waves of one of the most intense orgasms I've ever had fills me.

Wes isn't the first person I've fooled around with since *him*. But he's the first person I feel myself craving in a way I never thought possible. With his kiss, his touch, his words, I've lowered my defenses, allowing myself to be vulnerable for the first time in years.

And I don't know what to think about that.

"What just happened?" I exhale, my chest heaving.

Wes nuzzles my neck. "Hopefully something amazing."

As I start to come down, the lust that had been my primary

motivation mere seconds ago wanes and is replaced with guilt. Remorse. Shame.

Just like all those years ago.

Clarity overtaking me, I push against him. The sudden force startles him and he stumbles backward, looking just as confused as I feel. Part of me wants to throw caution to the wind and pull Wes back to me, see how far we can take this. But the other part knows this entire situation is a ticking time bomb. Once Wes sees behind the mask, has a taste of the darkness inside me, he'll run. After all, the Londyn he just kissed isn't the real me. I'm not even sure who that is anymore.

I'm not sure I've ever known.

Doing my best to speak through my labored breaths, I fix my stare on Wes. "This…" I shake my head. "This was a mistake," I manage to say.

Then I spin on my heels, hurrying away as quickly as my feet will carry me, praying he doesn't follow.

# CHAPTER SIXTEEN

WESTON

I blink as Londyn puts space between us, leaving me confused about what just transpired. How could she have gone from hot to cold in the span of a heartbeat?

I shouldn't be surprised. Our entire relationship has been a tumultuous seesaw of ups and downs, with not much in between. But I thought I finally had her. Finally burst through the walls she seemed to erect around herself.

Maybe I was wrong.

"Londyn!" I call after her, my heart still hammering from the feel of her. The sound of her. The taste of her. I knew when we kissed it would be electric. I didn't expect it to be so explosive.

And I certainly didn't expect it to implode just as quickly.

Londyn quickly scurries through the house and toward her car, not so much as glancing back at me. I propel myself after her, refusing to let her run away without talking through whatever has her spooked. Because there's no doubt in my mind that something spooked her. But what?

"Londyn," I repeat as she fumbles for her keys, her hands shaking violently. But she still doesn't acknowledge my presence. "Londyn!" I shout once more, grabbing her elbow and forcing her around.

The second I do, I regret it. Her eyes fling wider than I've ever seen them, the white stark against her irises. Her muscles go rigid, jaw clenching, panic overtaking her as she peers at me like I'm a monster here to do her harm. Not a man who would do anything to keep her safe.

I drop my hold, giving her breathing room. "Sorry, I—"

"What happened back there…," she interrupts, pointing toward the house. "It was extremely unprofessional of me. It's certainly not how I typically conduct myself with clients. I assure you, it will not happen again."

"Londyn…" I step toward her, on the brink of telling her I don't give a damn if I'm supposed to be her client. She should know that's never been the case. That she's always been more than just my interior designer.

Her hand shoots up, stopping me from saying anything further. "All the time we've spent together has caused the lines to become blurred." She swallows hard, her voice wavering slightly. "I think it's best if we go back to the way things should be. Back to our initial agreement."

I cross my arms in front of my chest, an eyebrow cocked. "Initial agreement?"

"Yes. I'll stick to overseeing the design. But I will no longer participate in the remodel with you, other than when necessary to ensure my design is implemented correctly."

"Is that right?"

"Nash is a talented contractor. I have no doubt he'll be able to help you out if need be."

I don't say anything right away, simply rake my analytical gaze over her. She may think she can fool everyone else, but she can't fool me. I know her better than she thinks I do. Than she probably wishes I do. She's on edge, uncertain. Like her heart wants one thing, but her brain is telling her to take a different path.

Or maybe her past is.

"Why are you doing this?"

"I told you. You're my client."

"Bullshit, Londyn." My chest heaving, I close the distance, but don't touch her, remaining just out of reach. "Bull. Shit."

"It's not bullshit," she retorts, her lip curling. "You're my client. End of story."

"That's a lame excuse and you know it. So tell me why you're *really* doing this. I know you feel this connection. You can't deny it. You felt it the second we met in that rainy crosswalk. And it's only grown stronger over these past few months. What happened back there…" I point to the house, just like she did. "It wasn't a fucking mistake. It was incredible. Electric. And just so perfect, Londyn. That's what you are.

You are perfect to me."

She flinches, as if the idea of anyone thinking she's perfect is laughable.

"I'm not," she states evenly. "I can't be."

"You are, dammit! In my eyes, you *are* perfect. God, you are just..."

I dig my hands through my hair, pacing as desperation takes over. I'd finally had a taste of heaven. I can't stomach the notion of letting her walk away without a fight. I didn't fight hard enough for Brooklyn, and in the end, I lost her. I refuse to make the same mistake here.

"I barely know a goddamn thing about you, but I know this." I come to a stop in front of her once more. "I can't let you push me away without a reason." I lick my lips, the humid air causing sweat to dot my brow. "So I'm going to ask you again." I lean toward her. "Why are you doing this?"

She searches my eyes, turmoil covering her expression. She pulls her lip between her teeth to stop her chin from quivering. "Because this will never work, Wes."

"Why?"

"Because it won't!" she exclaims, becoming increasingly frustrated.

"Why?" I ask again, not backing down. "Is it because I'm white and you're black?"

She opens her mouth, as if about to argue it's not, as I expect her to. Instead, she takes the out I've given her.

"Yes." She lifts her chin, but her eyes don't lock on mine, the telltale sign she's still not being honest with me. "It is."

I stare at her, wanting her to crack under my penetrating gaze. But she doesn't, remaining steadfast in her resolve.

Heaving a sigh, I back down, my posture deflating as I scrub a hand over my face, defeated. "I'd stand in the rain with you, ya know," I muse absentmindedly.

"Excuse me?"

I shrug. "Another Gampy pearl of wisdom. Do you know how he knew Meemaw was the woman he wanted to spend the rest of his life with?"

She subtly shakes her head, and I grow hopeful when she

steps closer to me.

"Because she stood in the rain with him. They'd gotten caught in a squall. He offered her his umbrella, but she refused. Said if he was wet, she wanted to be, too."

"How did that help?" she asks, her expression softening into one of curiosity.

"It was at that moment he knew she wouldn't run for shelter from whatever storm they faced."

She blinks, but doesn't say anything.

"You may be a goddamn hurricane, Londyn...," I begin, my voice overcome with passion, "but I will weather any storm with you. If you'd just give me a chance. That's all I'm asking for. Just a chance to prove to you that I *am* a good person. That I *am* worth the risk. That I *am* worthy of your time, your trust."

Her eyes gloss over with unshed tears as she finally looks at me. Then she lowers her head.

"I'm sorry, Wes."

Spinning around, she hurries to the driver's side of her SUV. My throat tightens and stomach clenches as I watch what I almost had slip through my fingers yet again.

"Her name was Brooklyn!" I call out before she has a chance to slide in behind the wheel.

Intrigued, she pauses, stealing a glimpse at me over her shoulder. But she doesn't say a word.

"My ex. The woman Miss Clara heard I was going to marry. Her name was Brooklyn. And she broke my fucking heart, Londyn. Absolutely shattered it."

She blinks, her motions measured as she gradually turns her body to face me, her SUV separating us.

"It's been two years, but in those two years, I've been hesitant to take a risk. To put my heart out there. Especially with you. And not because you're both named after a city, which is just a goddamn cruel twist of fate. But she had a shadow over her..." I pause, then add, "just like you do. I see your darkness, Londyn. I see it. I have since the beginning. Which is why I didn't want this." I gesture between our bodies.

"But then Julia reminded me of something Gampy and

Meemaw always told us. Another one of their pearls of wisdom, so to speak."

"What was it?" she asks softly.

I smile subtly, grateful to hear her voice. "That sometimes the right path isn't the easy one." I shake my head as my muscles tighten. "You aren't easy, Londyn. Nothing about you ever has been. You're frustrating. And stubborn." My voice grows louder and more impassioned with every word I speak. "And there are a million things about you that drive me fucking crazy. So many things about you that scare the shit out of me. But goddammit, you are so fucking right for me. I feel it in my bones. In my heart." I bring my hand to my chest. "In my soul."

She licks her lips, her sad eyes peering at me with a mixture of confusion and denial. "Wes, I—"

"I'll give you the space you need to figure this out. Lord knows, it took me a while to finally realize the truth."

"And what's that?" she asks shakily.

Sensing her defenses lower, I hesitantly step around to the other side of the SUV, stopping a few feet from her.

"That you're worth the risk, Londyn. That if tonight is the only time I'll ever get to feel your lips against mine, it'll still be worth it. Will still be worth any heartache that finds me because for one amazing moment, I felt real. *You* make me real. So you can run away all you want. But I've never felt this before, not even with Brooklyn. And you can be damn sure I won't give up just because you're scared. Because you don't think it'll work out. I know something like this doesn't happen every day. This thing between us is bigger than us. Bigger than your past. Bigger than your fears. I just need you to finally realize that. And I can't do that for you."

I stare at her for several seconds, willing her to respond. To admit this petrifies her, like it does me. *That* I can work with. *That* I can understand.

Instead, she shakes her head. "I can't do this with you anymore, Wes."

I open my mouth to plead my case further, but before I can, she ducks into her SUV, slamming the door and cranking the

123

ignition. Her tires kick up sand and dust as she peels away.

But not before stealing a glance back at me.

And it's that glance that gives me hope.

# CHAPTER SEVENTEEN

LONDYN

Sweat beads on my forehead and trickles down my nape, my arms and legs screaming at me as I spar with Hazel in her garage that she turned into a home gym. In the winter, it's cool and refreshing. In the heat of summer, however, it's stifling, the air thick. But it's what I need to release this pent-up aggression.

Since arriving home last night, I haven't been able to stop thinking about Wes, growing increasingly frustrated with every passing second. Who does he think he is, claiming he could tell I wasn't being completely truthful? So what if I wasn't? That shouldn't matter. He should have accepted my reason, no questions asked. Hell, I shouldn't have had to even give him a reason. Not when he's my client. That should have been reason enough.

Then why can't I erase the taste of his lips from my memory?

Why can't I forget the way my body sprang to life the second he pressed them against mine?

Why do I still crave more of him, having spent the past twenty-four hours fantasizing about how incredible it could be between us?

Because there's no doubt in my mind. That's exactly how it would be. Incredible. Volatile. Wild. At the same time, gentle. Safe. Peaceful.

Groaning in annoyance, I throw quicker and more forceful punches. Hazel adjusts her stance, her inquisitive eyes watching my every movement as I increase my pace, not relenting until my muscles give out and, with a scream, I collapse on a nearby bench.

My chest heaves as I struggle to capture a breath, my entire body trembling from over-exertion.

Sitting beside me, Hazel hands me my water bottle. I grab it with an appreciative nod and take a swig. Once my thirst is momentarily quenched, I lean forward, pouring some water onto my neck to cool myself down.

"So… Want to talk about whatever has you all worked up?" Hazel asks after a beat. "Or perhaps I should say *who*ever has you all worked up."

"I'm not worked up," I insist, although my words lack anything remotely resembling conviction.

"Sure you aren't." She rakes her disbelieving stare over me. "Everything is just hunky-dory. Which is why you're home on a Sunday when you haven't been since you took the job with the hottie in a suit. And why you nearly broke my damn hand sparring just now."

"Hunky-dory? What is this? The 1950s or some shit?"

She rolls her eyes, taking a long drink from her own bottle. "You know what I mean, Lo. You always pretend everything's okay when secretly, I think you're desperate for someone to talk to. So here I am, your friend and neighbor, asking if you're okay. So…" She nudges me. "Are you okay?"

I chew on my lower lip, debating what to tell her. She's the only person in the world who will understand my trepidation about everything. She's been there, too.

"Wes kissed me," I blurt out.

She blinks, my statement obviously taking her by surprise. "And?"

"And I kissed him back."

"And?"

"And what?"

"You know," she urges. "Give me the goods. Don't hold back on me now that y'all have finally locked lips."

"Okay, first of all, don't call it locking lips. Second of all…" I trail off.

"Yes?"

"Well, I don't think there is a second of all."

"Then tell me about the kiss. How was it?"

I crane my head back, my pulse quickening from the memory of the kiss that led to a lot more than just a kiss. How

126

it started soft and tender, soon exploding into this insane connection both of us were powerless to stop, a freight train gaining more and more speed as it careened toward a cliff. That's what scared me to the point that I felt like I had no option but to push him away. I was absolutely powerless. Defenseless. Vulnerable. I vowed years ago to never put myself in that position again.

"Intense." I don't think there's any other word that can possibly describe it. "It got out of hand pretty quickly."

"Out of hand? How do you mean?"

"One second, his mouth hovered over mine in a barely-there kiss. And then…"

"Yes?" She leans toward me, hanging on to my every word.

"Then he was pushing my panties aside and giving me this mind-blowing orgasm with just his fingers."

"Well, halle-*fucking*-lujah!" Hazel exclaims, her voice echoing in the garage. "'Bout time someone got you off."

I roll my eyes. "I've slept with other guys, Haze."

"And then came home and put your vibrator to use because they couldn't get the job done," she reminds me.

I blow out a breath. She's not wrong. Up until Wes, I assumed it was the penance I was forced to pay for my sins all those years ago. But now I know what's possible with him, which only confuses me more. I swore I'd never give up control of my body to any other man again, the men I've slept with in recent years more than happy to let me call the shots in the bedroom. But with Wes, I had absolutely no control.

"So what happened after?" She arches a brow, sensing it didn't end with us flying off into the sunset like Danny and Sandy in *Grease*.

"I freaked out. Pushed him away. Made a pretty big scene of it all."

"Why?"

I shrug noncommittally. "He's my client."

"True." She pinches her lips together. "Or are you using that as an excuse?"

I glance at her. Do I stick to the lame explanation I gave Wes, or do I tell her the truth? After all, if I can't be honest with Hazel…

"Because I'm not sure I can ever be the person he needs or deserves," I admit, my shaky voice giving away my emotions.

"What makes you say that?"

I narrow my eyes, giving her a knowing look. "You know why. Wes has no idea who I really am. What I've done. If he did—"

"For someone who pretends to be such a hard ass, you have shitty self-esteem."

"I don't—"

Before I can finish, she grabs my wrapped hand, tugging me off the bench and toward the wall-to-wall mirror opposite us. With her hands on my biceps, she forces me to peer at my reflection.

"What do you see?"

"Me," I respond flippantly.

"That's not what I'm talking about. So let's try this again. What. Do. You. See?"

I feign annoyance, but eventually relent, taking a moment to consider what I see whenever I stare at myself.

"I see a girl who pretends she has her shit together but, in reality, is barely holding on," I admit through a strained voice. "I see hundreds of dreams that disappeared in the blink of an eye. Dreams I probably shouldn't have had anyway. And I see someone who will never be worthy of love, so why should I even try finding it?"

"Are you done?" Hazel asks with a raised brow.

I nod. I see a lot more, but I'd rather not reveal just how low my self-esteem really is, despite the front I put up.

"Then let me tell you what *I* see."

"Hazel…" I attempt to spin around, not wanting to have to listen to this, but she doesn't let me, her hold on me resolute.

"I see a woman who's scarred, but has somehow found the strength to continue on, even on those days when it would be so fucking easy to throw in the towel."

I squeeze my eyes shut, a lone tear trickling down my cheek.

"I see a woman who had her dreams dashed, but persevered and made new dreams. Better dreams. Brighter dreams.

Despite the constant fear that she may not achieve them, she pushed forward, chasing after those dreams with everything she had. And do you want to know why she did that, even when the odds were stacked against her?"

I swallow hard, remaining silent, unsure I'd be able to speak even if I needed to.

"Because she's fucking fearless."

I shake my head, swiping the tears off my face, the emotions of the past few days catching up to me. From overcoming my fear of heights with Wes. To witnessing him stand up to Grady's derogatory comments. To the snake crawling across me. To the euphoria of his kiss.

For weeks, I've been riding a tumultuous seesaw. I should have known it was only a matter of time until I crashed to the ground with more force than I could endure.

"But mostly, I see a woman who has so much love in her. A woman who deserves to be loved in return. And I guarantee you, Wes sees the same thing I do when he looks at you."

I spin around, peering into Hazel's eyes. "How do you know?"

She shrugs. "I don't. It's a risk you have to take. But if he's half the man you say he is, he'll focus on your strengths, your perseverance. Not things that may be lurking in your past."

"And if he doesn't?" I ask, although I already have a feeling that's not the case, especially after his heartfelt plea last night.

Hazel wraps her arms around me, hugging me tightly. "Then he never deserved you in the first place."

# CHAPTER EIGHTEEN

WESTON

"You still haven't heard from her?" Julia asks from over the rim of her coffee mug as we sit at a table in the corner of her bakery in Buckhead on a Friday.

It's been nearly two weeks since I've seen Londyn. Nearly two weeks since I've spoken to her, too. To say it's driving me crazy is an understatement.

"I have. She sent me an email the other day with options for kitchen appliances."

"Oh, wow!" She feigns excitement. "That's exactly what I'd hope for after I poured my heart out to someone. Questions about kitchen appliances."

I shrug, glancing around her busy bakery, a line out the door, even at two in the afternoon. "It's better than nothing."

"Have you tried talking to her about things? Does she know you haven't been back to the house, either?"

"That's not true," I argue.

"It's not?" She leans back in her chair, giving me a smug look.

"I've been busy. There was that golf tournament on Saturday."

"But you didn't go down on Sunday, either."

"You and Imogene are heading back to Charleston next week. I want to spend more time with you two."

I bring my mug to my mouth and take a sip of coffee, hoping she can't see through my lies, that the mere thought of walking into that house causes a heaviness to settle in my chest. In such a short time, Londyn snuck into my soul and weaved herself around my heart. Now, when I think of Meemaw and Gampy's old house, I don't only think of childhood memories. I think of Londyn. I fear I always will.

"And we'll both be a quick flight away. Or a five-hour

drive. So why don't you tell me the real reason."

I turn my attention out the large windows that make up the front of her bakery. The sidewalks of this trendy area of the city teem with tourists and locals spending their afternoon shopping or grabbing a bite to eat with friends. I still marvel at how much Julia has accomplished in the past several years. Not only has she raised Imogene, sometimes on her own, since her husband travels extensively for his job as a public relations consultant, but she took a home-based business of fulfilling online orders for her sugary concoctions and moved it to an actual brick and mortar store. Now, she has bakeries all over the South.

"Because I'll feel her there, and it hurts," I admit, facing her. "Probably more than it should, considering we've only known each other a few months. And we only kissed once."

Julia gives me a reassuring smile. "But in those few months, you've both shared pieces of yourselves with each other. There's something to be said for getting to know someone like you and Londyn have. And to be honest, after you told me about what happened to her mother, I understand why she'd be hesitant to enter into a relationship. It may have been twenty years ago, but losing someone as tragically as she did never leaves you. Hell, there are days that I still struggle with losing Gampy and Meemaw."

"Me, too."

"So imagine losing your mother because of some whack job with a gun. On top of that, imagine having to live with the knowledge that your father may have been able to save your mother if he hadn't chosen to protect you first. Don't get me wrong," she adds quickly. "He did what any parent would. If someone came in here waving a gun and started shooting, I'd grab Imogene and get her the hell out of here. Let everyone else fend for themselves. I'd miss you and would bawl like crazy if anything happened to you, but I wouldn't hesitate to protect my daughter first."

I smile slightly, briefly covering her hand with mine, squeezing. "Which is why you're such a great mother."

"I couldn't imagine what it must be like to live with that

knowledge, though." She shakes her head. "That's got to fuck with your mind. I may not have had the best birth mother, but she was still my mom, at least when she wasn't high. I was young when she overdosed, but I remember them telling me she was gone. For the longest time, I had trouble getting close to people. I worried they'd leave me, too. It's why it took me so long to finally allow myself to get close to you. But once I realized you'd do everything in your power to always be there for me, I lowered my walls. Maybe that's all Londyn needs right now. To know you'll do everything in your power to be there for her."

"Perhaps." I pinch my chin, unable to shake the feeling there's more to it than that.

"Give her some time. I'm sure she'll come around. And look on the bright side."

"What's that?"

"She kissed you back. That's got to count for something." Smirking, she stands, grabbing my mug and heading toward the bakery counter.

I rise to my feet, about to argue my doubts, when Imogene's excited voice cuts through.

"Daddy!"

I fling my eyes toward the door, watching as a muscular blond wearing a three-piece suit and dark-framed glasses strolls into the bakery. Setting his roll-aboard off to the side, he bends down, allowing Imogene to run into his outstretched arms. As he swings her around, showering her with kisses, I glance at Julia, about to ask if she knew he was coming here. Her confused expression is all the answer I need.

"I assume you didn't know about this, either?"

She jumps at my question, eyes widening before she plasters a smile onto her face. "You assume correctly."

"Are you okay?" I whisper.

"Of course," she responds in a chipper voice. Perhaps too chipper. "Just surprised." With another forced smile, she skirts past me and walks up to Nick. I follow, but give them space to celebrate their reunion.

"What are you doing here?" She crosses her arms in front

of her chest, her stance almost defensive.

"Is that any way to greet your husband after not seeing him all summer?" His response has a teasing quality to it, but I swear I hear a warning mixed in.

"I'm just…surprised. I thought you were still in London."

"I finished with my client early. My flight to Charleston connected out of Atlanta anyway, so I figured I'd surprise my wife. We can spend tomorrow in the city, maybe you can take me down to Meemaw and Gampy's old house and show me around, then we can all drive home together."

"But I'm not scheduled to head back until the end of next week."

Nick frowns, the lines of his chiseled and arguably attractive face falling. Then he puts Imogene down, crouching slightly. "Why don't you go play with Uncle Wes for a minute while I talk to Mama, okay?"

"Okay, Daddy."

Nick straightens, turning his bright blue eyes toward me, extending his hand. "Good to see you, Wes."

"You, too." I shake his hand, my expression even.

Then I meet Julia's gaze, silently asking if she's okay. She subtly nods. I hesitate, but eventually steer Imogene back toward the table, giving her some paper to draw on. I sit, drawing with her, but still keep an ear tuned to Julia and Nick's conversation as best I can with all the ambient chatter and orders being shouted behind the counter.

"I just spent eight hours on a plane after being out of the country for over a month," Nick says in a barely audible voice. "I'd expected a little enthusiasm from my own wife."

"I'm happy to see you," Julia tells him. "Like I said, I'm surprised you're back so soon. That's all."

"Do I need to be concerned?"

"Of course not. I'd just planned to have next week to finish up training the new head pastry chef here. That way, I can be certain she has everything under control while I'm back in Charleston."

"How hard can it be to follow some simple recipes?" he comments snidely.

I hold my breath as I sketch on Imogene's paper. I fully expect to hear one of Julia's notorious comebacks in response to Nick's insinuation that her job isn't difficult. Or at least argue that many of the pastries she makes aren't as easy as following a simple recipe. That she creates works of art. Especially some of the wedding cakes she designs. But she never does.

"I want to make sure everything's perfect. I'm sure you can relate."

Neither of them says a word for what feels like an eternity, my anxiety increasing with every passing second. Finally, Nick speaks, his tone brighter and less accusatory.

"You know me so well. How about this? We spend tomorrow together here. If your new chef manages, you'll know she's ready to handle things without you. She's most likely itching for you to stop being a helicopter boss anyway."

"You're probably right about that."

"I usually am."

The sound of footsteps grows closer, and I refocus my attention on my sketch, not wanting to let on that I've been eavesdropping.

"Come on, MoMo," Nick says as he approaches, helping Imogene out of her chair. "I'll take you to Uncle Wes' house and we can play with that mongrel dog of his." He shifts his gaze to mine. "You don't mind an extra house guest for a few nights, do you?"

"You're family, Nick. You're always welcome."

"Thanks, man." He pats me on the back before glancing at the paper on the table. "Who's that?" he asks, gesturing to my doodles.

I follow his line of sight to see I'd absentmindedly sketched Londyn's likeness.

"That's Miss Londyn," Imogene says proudly.

"Wow," Julia murmurs, sidling up next to me and peering over my shoulder. "That looks a lot like her."

"Miss Londyn?" Nick looks from me to Julia, eyebrows raised expectantly. "Did I miss MoMo's Meet the Teacher night for school? I don't recall a Miss Londyn at the academy."

"Miss Londyn isn't a teacher, Daddy. She's helping Uncle Wes with the house."

"She's my interior designer," I explain.

"I see." He studies my sketch for another beat, then returns his attention to Imogene. "Shall we be on our way, ladybug?"

"Yes."

"Can I have your keys, Jules?" he asks. "I took an Uber from the airport. I need Imogene's booster seat anyway."

Julia's expression falters. "I have some errands to run. Things we need for the bakery. If you want to head back to Charleston this weekend, I—"

"Here." I reach into my pocket and hand her my keys. "You can have my car so Nick can take yours."

"But how are you going to get back to the office?"

"I'll just Uber. It'll be fine."

"Are you sure?"

"Of course. You have things you need to do. My car's just going to sit in the garage all afternoon. You may as well use it."

"See. It all works out," Nick booms. "So... The keys, Jules?"

"Sure." Unclipping the ring of keys from the belt loop at her waist, she unhooks her car key and house key, handing them to him.

"See you at the house. Try not to work too late."

"I won't," Julia responds halfheartedly.

He grabs the handle of his suitcase and rolls it behind him, Imogene's hand clutched tightly in his free one as he walks out of the bakery. Once they round the corner toward the staff parking lot, disappearing from view, Julia blows out a long breath.

"Is everything okay?" I ask, fully facing her. "Are *you* okay?"

"What makes you think I'm not?"

I place my hands on her biceps to stop her from avoiding this conversation. "It's just a feeling. You don't seem like yourself."

"I'm fine, Wes," she replies, pushing away from me and

135

skirting through the growing crowd, picking up crumb-covered dishes and lipstick-stained coffee mugs on her way. "He threw me for a loop. You know how I like to stick to a schedule, especially with Imogene. His being home early messes with my routine."

I follow her behind the counter and into the kitchen in the back. "You're sure that's all?" I narrow my gaze on her as she places the mugs and plates into their appropriate dish racks.

"Eventually, you'll learn how things sometimes change once you get married. After being with the same person for several years, the spark fades. I guess I get so used to doing everything on my own that when Nick comes home, he feels more like an annoyance than my husband and father of my child. It takes me a few days to get used to having someone to answer to."

"Someone to answer to?" I shake my head, brows furrowed. "I don't—"

"Not like that," she interjects quickly. "I'm not explaining it correctly. When it's only Imogene and me, I can do whatever I want without having to take into account anyone else. I see that big brother protectiveness coming out. You have nothing to worry about." She squeezes my arms reassuringly. "Promise."

I study her for a moment, searching for any indication things aren't as she claims. Finding nothing, I relax my posture and nod. "Okay."

"Okay."

"But you'll tell me if something isn't right?" I press.

"You know I will." With a smile, she lifts herself onto her toes and places a soft kiss on my cheek. "Now, get out of here so I can get back to work." She grins, the Julia I've known and loved most of my life returning, softening my unease.

"You got it, boss." I mock salute her, then turn, heading back toward the dining area.

"Hey, Wes?" she calls as I'm about to push through the swinging doors. I pause, glancing over my shoulder. "You're a good brother."

"I love you, Jules."

"Love you, too. Now go. Design your buildings. And think of a way to get through to Londyn."

"I have a feeling designing the most complex building might be an easier feat."

"True." She smirks. "But I've never known you to shy away from a challenge."

# CHAPTER NINETEEN

LONDYN

"It was so good to see you again, Lo," Justine says, giving me a hug as we linger in the lobby of a popular happy hour spot just around the corner from my old office.

I'd almost turned down her invitation to go out and celebrate one of my former co-worker's birthdays, since I no longer work with them. But I needed something to keep my mind off the fact that I'm not spending my Friday with Wes at Meemaw and Gampy's house.

I'd thought doing something that was once a weekly occurrence would help. But nothing did. I saw Wes in every man wearing a dashing suit who walked by the restaurant. I saw him in the group of tourists stopping by for a quick drink. And I saw him in our bartender, the dazzling blue eyes and refined accent nearly identical to his.

"It was great to see you, too."

"I'm glad you finally had time. Sounds like getting fired was the best thing to happen to you."

I thought it was, too. Until I made the mistake of falling for my client. Now I'm not sure which way is up. I keep hearing Hazel's voice telling me to take a risk, to share my fears with Wes. But that would mean telling him all the gritty details of my life I wish I could forget. I'm not sure I'm ready to open the wounds I still don't think have properly healed.

I smile. "I doubt I'll ever want to work for someone else again, other than clients."

After we finish saying our goodbyes, I make my way toward the garage, in no rush to return to my lonely house. As luck would have it, I soon find myself at that same crosswalk where my life changed earlier this summer. But this time, I'm not caught in a torrential downpour, everything slick with rain. The sun peeks through a few scattered clouds as it slowly descends toward the horizon.

The signal changes to WALK, and I step into the crosswalk, a nostalgic smile tugging on my mouth as I stare at the coffee shop. I can't help but wonder what my life would look like if I hadn't given Wes my business card. If I hadn't pressed my luck and tried to make it across the street before the signal changed. If I hadn't been fired.

If I had to do it all over again, would I do anything differently? Do I *wish* I had done anything differently?

Despite the way things played out, I can't say I regret any of it. In my heart, I'd rather have felt what I did with Wes for the brief time we spent together than to never have crossed paths with him at all.

Then why do I keep pushing him away? Why does taking this leap of faith scare me more than heights or snakes?

Lost in the thought of whether I can share the darkest parts of myself with Wes, I don't notice when I come to the end of the crosswalk. My foot catches on the curb, and I stumble directly into a hard, suit-clad body about to cross.

"Whoa. Easy there," a familiar voice croons as an arm wraps around my torso.

I dart my head up, a flush of adrenaline coursing through my veins, my stomach fluttering as I peer into Wes' striking blue eyes.

"What is it with you and this intersection?" he jokes when I don't immediately say anything, too stunned to form a coherent thought.

I blink, unsure how to respond or act around him now. Apart from the occasional email about design choices, I haven't spoken to him since the night of our kiss. But god, it's good to see him again, to feel his warmth, to inhale his scent.

"I think it might be cursed," I finally reply, stepping out of his hold, smoothing a hand over my dress. "And I can't even blame it on heels this time." I gesture to the Egyptian-style sandals laced up my legs.

"I may have to quit my job and man the corner just to keep you safe."

"Probably not a bad idea." I force a smile as an awkward

139

silence descends on us.

I should walk away, thank him for helping me yet again, then hurry home. But I can't manage to put one foot in front of the other, still as drawn to him as I was during our first meeting in this same spot.

"I got your email with the different options for the kitchen," he offers.

"What did you think?" I ask quickly, doing a horrible job of masking the nerves in my voice.

"You choose. I'm sure whatever you decide will be perfect. Whenever I've questioned your ideas, you always ended up being right. I trust you."

"Let's go with the first option. It'll have a vintage feel with a unique fridge and old-style stove, but will still be state-of-the-art."

"Perfect."

"Great."

I stare at him, another awkward silence stretching between us. I feel like I should say something, but what? That I've missed him? That these past few weeks have been torture? That all day, all I wanted was to get into my car and drive to Gampy and Meemaw's like I used to on Fridays. That's when it hits me. He's not there, either.

"Well, I should be on my way," he states.

I tilt my head. "Why aren't you at the house?" I blurt out before he can turn from me.

His mouth opens as he blinks, but his uncertainty only lasts a second before he transforms back into the confident man I've always known him to be. "Julia needed to use my car. Her husband came into town unexpectedly and has her car, so I let her use mine since she has errands she needs to run for the bakery. I'll just go tomorrow instead." His mouth quirks into a small smile, but there's a sadness within.

"Oh. Okay." I fidget with my hands, rocking on my heels. I'm not sure what I wanted him to say. Maybe that the thought of being there without me pains him. But that's ridiculous. Isn't it?

"See ya around, Londyn."

The WALK signal lights up, and Wes continues in the direction he'd been heading, his frame getting smaller and smaller. As he steps up onto the opposite curb, I finally find my voice.

"Wes?" I shout over dozens of heads.

He comes to an abrupt stop, slowly glancing over his shoulder.

I chew on the inside of my cheek, a hundred thoughts fighting for attention in my mind. "Can we... Can we go talk somewhere?"

He smiles slowly, causing my stomach to do backflips. It's only a smile, but it hits me deep in my soul.

Facing me, he's about to step off the curb when I notice a movement out of my peripheral vision. My eyes widen, my heart catapulting into my throat.

"Wes!" I yell. "Car!"

He jumps back onto the sidewalk as a pickup swerves around him, horn blaring. He stares at the crosswalk for a few moments. Then his eyes meet mine, and he shrugs. I blow out a relieved breath, grateful I didn't just witness him becoming roadkill. And without telling him the truth. If I had any hesitation about whether sharing my story is the right thing, it's eviscerated now.

The light feels like it lasts hours instead of minutes, both of us staring at each other from opposite sides of the street as we wait. When the WALK signal lights up again, Wes breaks into a trot, crossing in record time.

"*Now* who needs to guard the corner to keep whom safe?" I joke.

A blush crawls across his face as he runs his fingers through his hair. "Not my finest of moments. Maybe now we can call it even."

"Sounds good to me."

"Want to take a walk?" He nods in the vicinity of Centennial Park.

"I'd love to."

Neither one of us speaks as we make our way to one of Atlanta's most famous landmarks. It's a little after six in the

141

evening, but the sun hasn't yet set, tourists still exploring the area and getting their photos taken in front of the fountains and Olympic rings.

After several minutes pass and I don't think I can take the silence anymore, I finally speak. "You were right."

"About?" He shoves his hands into the pockets of his navy blue suit.

"When you said you didn't believe I pushed you away because I'm black and you're white. You were right."

He forms his lips into a tight line, nodding. "I know." His voice isn't boastful or cocky. More like even and humble.

"The truth is…" I draw in a deep breath, summoning the courage to share my story. "The truth is, I've been married before."

On a sharp inhale, he darts his eyes to mine. "You have?"

I nod, keeping my gaze trained forward. I can't bear to look at him right now or I fear I'll break down. I need to get through this. Need to give him the explanation he deserves. What he does with the information is up to him, although I hope he'll understand.

"I was twenty."

"One of those married young, but later regret it type of things?"

I wish it were that simple. But nothing in my life has ever been simple.

"His name is Sawyer Ross." I pause, waiting to see if there's a flicker of recognition at the name. Thankfully, there isn't. While Wes isn't exactly the type of person who would spend his Sunday morning watching a television preacher, Sawyer's become more than just that in recent years. He's become an outspoken advocate for civil rights, too. It's admirable if you didn't know him. But I do. He'll do anything for fame and notoriety, even throw his own wife under the proverbial bus.

"He survived the shooting that took my mother's life. His father didn't. Saved him by throwing his body over his. Despite him being four years older, we formed a friendship. At least a stronger friendship than we had before."

"I imagine it must have been helpful to have someone who

understood what you were going through. Survivor's guilt and all that."

"I suppose." I smooth a few curls behind my ear, wrinkling my nose. "It definitely changed us, as any traumatic event would. But while I questioned how a God who was supposed to be this loving being could take my mother, Sawyer went in the opposite direction. In his mind, there was a reason God spared him. He saw it as his calling to spread His word."

"Ah," Wes exhales, nodding. "So he became a priest."

I laugh, grateful for the moment of levity. "We're not Catholic, but close. He went to college. Studied divinity with the hope of becoming a pastor of his own church. He has an incredibly charismatic personality. Couple that with being a survivor of a famous church shooting, and he had quite a bit of negotiating power when it came to accepting a post at a church. But he was missing one thing a lot of churches want in a pastor, especially after all the scandals with priests in the Catholic church." I give him a knowing look.

"A wife."

"Bingo."

I steer us off the main path through the park and toward the tree-shrouded garden walk, preferring the semblance of privacy to share the next part of my story.

"Like I mentioned, we became friends, even though we were on somewhat different paths. He volunteered as a youth pastor in high school and during the summers he was home from college. I preferred to spend my free time building furniture or going to the park with my sketch pad. Four years may not sound like a big difference, but when you're a teenager, it's the difference between a shy, awkward fourteen-year-old girl and a mature eighteen-year-old man. That is, until the summer between my freshman and sophomore year of college."

"What happened then?"

I shrug. "I think he finally realized I wasn't just a little girl anymore. That I'd become a woman. He definitely didn't look at me like I was a little girl anymore." My cheeks heat as I steal a glance at Wes. I wasn't sure how he'd react to hearing about my ex, but he seems more intrigued than anything. "We went on a few dates, but nothing serious ever came of it."

"But something serious eventually did come of it, right?"

"I suppose you could say that. After that summer, I went back to school in upstate New York and didn't really think twice about the few dates we'd gone on, if you could even call them dates. I focused on my studies, since I was there on a scholarship. We exchanged the occasional email or text, but nothing with overly romantic tones. Since we didn't have any sort of agreement to be exclusive, I dated a few guys here and there, had even told Sawyer about a few of them, and he didn't seem to care. But when I went home the next summer, things were…different."

"Different?" Wes tilts his head. "How do you mean?"

"Sawyer had interviewed at a bunch of churches, mostly in Virginia. There was one that was extremely interested in him. It was a pretty big deal, too. This wasn't just some small church in the middle of nowhere. It was a large church closer to D.C., one with a great deal of influence. One where he'd *have* a great deal of influence."

"Let me guess. They were hesitant to hire him because he wasn't married yet."

"Yes. I knew all this, too. Heard him talking to my father about it when I was home for spring break. I figured it was their loss if they would pass over someone they were truly interested in just because he wasn't married. Sawyer was barely twenty-four at this point. He'd only been out of college a few years.

"Then one day, my father asked me to come see him at the church after I got off my shift at the local hardware store where I worked during my breaks from school."

"And?"

I stop walking, facing him. With a shrug, I smile half-heartedly. "They had it all planned. I'd marry Sawyer the following month before he went back for his final interview with the board at this other church."

"And you agreed?"

"I honestly didn't think I had a choice. Ever since I lost my mother, I felt compelled to do whatever my father asked of me, for the most part. He chose me instead of her—"

"Something any parent would do," he reminds me.

"I see that now, but because of his sacrifice, I always felt forced to…obey, I suppose. So, instead of a beautiful proposal where the love of my life poured his heart out to me while declaring his unending devotion, I agreed to marry a man much like one would negotiate a car sale. Except in this scenario, I was the car." I sigh. "A few weeks later, I was no longer Londyn Bennett, but Londyn Ross."

"Is that why you pushed me away? Because you used to be married? I don't care about that. I—"

"I wish it were just that. But it's not. I told you all of that so you'd understand this next part. There's more."

He cocks a brow. "More?"

I nod, turning from him and continuing up the winding path. "Despite their arguments to the contrary, I managed to convince my father and Sawyer to let me finish my studies. Told them my agreement to marry Sawyer would be off the table otherwise. So, a few weeks after I married Sawyer, I packed up my things and headed back to college. Of course, part of our agreement was that I could no longer live in the dorms. I got an apartment off campus that was right above this great little coffee shop."

"Like in *Friends*?"

I laugh. "More or less, except this was rural New York. And during my senior year, that coffee shop was where I met Jay."

"Jay?" His voice sounds hesitant, as if able to sense this is where things change.

After everything I endured that year, I often wondered what my life would have been like had I not chosen the apartment above the coffee shop, instead moving into the townhouse that was more spacious but about fifteen minutes away from campus, requiring me to drive and deal with parking. Would I have eventually found my way to The Grind anyway? Would I have been sitting at that table when a man rushed by, his commuter bag swinging on his shoulder, knocking my coffee all over my Greek Art coursework? Would

I have accepted his offer to buy me a fresh cup? And would I have said hello the following day when I saw him again?

"It all started innocently enough."

Spying a bench along the walkway, I head toward it, lowering myself as I prepare to share the next part of my tale.

"I didn't even know he was a professor when we first met. I was just happy to finally have someone mature I could talk to, someone who seemed to understand me. No one else in my classes could really relate to what I was going through. They were all still single without a care in the world. So meeting Jay was exactly what I needed, at least in the beginning."

"Was he one of *your* professors?" Wes asks, sitting beside me.

I quickly shake my head. "No. Nothing like that. I'd never even seen him on campus. He was a newer professor in the English department, taught some upper-level electives. I was an art history major. At first, we didn't talk much, other than the polite hello when we saw each other at the coffee shop. Or a random comment about the weather. Then…" I trail off, chewing on my lower lip, unsure how Wes will react to my next admission, especially knowing I was married.

"What is it?" He drapes his arm along the back of the bench, his thumb gently caressing my shoulder. It's an innocent gesture, but is exactly what I need right now.

"At some point, I started spending all my free time in the coffee shop, hoping he'd be there. It was stupid, since I knew he was married with a baby at home, but he'd become the bright spot in my life. We began sharing parts of ourselves with each other. He told me about the research he was doing on the interplay of the portrayal of women in Greek mythology and their modern counterparts. I shared my love of art, archaeology, and architecture. We didn't have dumbed-down conversations about the latest reality show drama or which celebrity had cheated on whom. Better yet…" I rub my palms along my dress. "Our conversations didn't only revolve around religion, as was often the case with my father and Sawyer."

"You finally felt a real connection to someone," he says in understanding.

"Our conversations were deep. We talked about our fears. Our dreams." I pause, lifting my gaze toward Wes. "Our desires."

He doesn't immediately say anything. Just stares straight ahead, his jaw tight, eyes contemplative.

"I'd been feeling somewhat...frustrated with the way everything happened with Sawyer, with our marriage. A part of me hoped that, with time, I'd feel that connection, that spark you see in movies. That things were tough because we'd spent the majority of our marriage up to that point living in two different states. Then a part of me wondered if it was because I was so...inexperienced."

He arches a brow. "Inexperienced?"

"Sawyer was my first. So I thought maybe he didn't want to sleep with me because I wasn't any good at it.

"I can't quite pinpoint when my conversations with Jay shifted from the development of art and architecture in the Byzantine Empire to conversations about sex. It seems stupid now, but I didn't have girlfriends I could talk to. And I didn't exactly trust *Cosmo* to give me tips on how to make my childhood friend actually want me sexually. So I told Jay all about my feelings of inadequacy in my marriage. And the bedroom. But he..."

Tears dot the corners of my eyes. I feel so stupid that I hadn't seen it before. But I was young and naïve. I truly believed he was doing what any friend would. I didn't realize this was just part of his personality as a master manipulator.

"Yes?" Wes asks with a quiver.

When his hand clutches mine, I grit a smile. No wonder I haven't wanted to share the details of this before now, even with Hazel, who knows more about me than anyone else. Finally sharing the gritty, dark details is excruciating, a vice squeezing my heart, even all these years later.

"He made me feel beautiful. Made me feel like I was enough. Like any man who didn't appreciate me wasn't worth my time."

Wes blinks, his expression even as he processes everything. Then he floats his gaze to mine, his features taut. "Did you have an affair with him?"

I pinch my lips together, eyes brimming with tears. My throat tightens, my vision going blurry. "It depends who you ask."

"I don't follow." He furrows his brow. "You either had an affair or you didn't. I don't see any gray area in this."

"There is if you don't consent."

# CHAPTER TWENTY

WESTON

I stare straight ahead, but barely see the squirrels chasing each other. Or the grass blowing in the breeze. Or the rollerbladers skating by. All I see is red, my heart pounding a thunderous rhythm. My jaw tenses and nostrils flare, every muscle becoming rigid as rage consumes me. It takes everything I possess not to demand the location of this Jay guy right now. All I can do is pray he's already in prison, although something tells me Londyn isn't that lucky.

"What happened?" I ask through pinched lips, my voice coming out harsher than I'd intended.

She fidgets with her hands, her chin dipped close to her chest as she averts her gaze.

"Hey." I touch her cheek, bringing her eyes toward mine. "It's okay. Whatever you're comfortable sharing."

She blinks repeatedly, swallowing hard. "I know. And I appreciate it."

"We can stop. We don't——"

"No." She straightens her posture, vehemently shaking her head. "I need to get this out. Even if you never look at me the same way again, at least you'll finally know the truth."

"I would never look at you any differently, Lo." I swipe my thumb under her eyes, erasing her tears. "You've got to realize that by now."

"I wouldn't make any promises yet, Wes."

I peer at her, my hackles rising. Then I pull away, giving her space. "Okay."

Tilting her head back, she stares at the darkening sky for a beat before looking forward again. "Every year, the College of Arts and Humanities threw an end-of-year masquerade ball at the dean's house for the graduating seniors, their dates, and the faculty. It was this breathtaking Victorian a few blocks from campus. Old wood, and dust, and heavy tapestries."

"Sounds stunning."

"It was. While I hate to admit it, I took quite a bit of care in choosing a mask and dress because I knew Jay would be there."

"Did you ever see each other on campus?"

"No." She pauses. "Well, I guess that's not entirely true. I did occasionally. And the more we discussed…intimate things, the more I began seeing him. He'd walk by my lecture on 20th Century Photographic History. Then I'd notice him lurking in the library near where I was studying with a few of my classmates. Then again when I was in the art studio, working on a project. I liked that I had his attention. But we never crossed that line. Whenever we talked, it would always be in reference to *my* husband or *his* wife. He'd never tell me things he wanted to do to me, or me him. But that night, everything changed."

"What happened?"

I can already tell this guy is bad news. Londyn admitted she felt inadequate and insecure in her marriage. Instead of giving her solid advice, he preyed on a young woman. He manipulated her, stalked her, then God knows what else. I'm not sure I want to know. But I'll listen. For Londyn's sake.

"I was twenty-two, so the champagne was flowing. It didn't help I'd never been a big drinker, at least compared to some of my fellow students. After three or four glasses, I was feeling pretty damn good. When the party ended at midnight, I was wavering a little. At least I'd had the forethought not to drive. So I started walking back to my apartment."

"How far away was it?"

"Not too far. Five or six blocks maybe. But before I could get far, Jay pulled up in his car and offered to drive me. I didn't immediately agree, unsure what people would think if they saw us together."

"Weren't you just at a party with him, though?"

"Not *with* him. Was he at the ball? Yes. But we didn't really talk. We never did when we saw each other on campus. We kept that line drawn. At the coffee shop, we could debate the meaning of life from our separate tables, but on campus, he was a professor, and I was a student."

I pinch the bridge of my nose, still processing this fucked-up relationship she's describing, doing everything to keep my anger in check, something that's becoming increasingly difficult with every second, with every tiny detail I learn about this waste of space.

"Did you get into the car?"

She pauses, then sighs. "I did. He pulled out of the lot and began driving toward my place. Then he asked if I wanted to have our own little afterparty. I was hesitant, for good reason. I mean, this was the first time we were alone together. Everything about it felt different. That should have been enough for the warning bells to go off in my head. Instead, I asked what he had in mind. He revealed a set of keys, told me they were to the Allen House."

I quirk an eyebrow. "The Allen House?"

"It was this historic landmark on campus. A house built in the early 1800s where the founder of what would eventually go on to be the university held his first classes back in 1835. I'd always wanted to see inside, but only a few faculty members had access. I saw this as my one and only opportunity, so I had no qualms about agreeing, although I shouldn't have, considering he must have stolen the keys from the dean's house earlier.

"During the short drive, I could barely contain my excitement. It sounds stupid now, but it was the first nice thing anyone had done for me. Sawyer hardly listened to a word I said. When I'd share my excitement about a piece of art or an amazing old house or a new archaeological find, he wouldn't even look up from his notebook where he was preparing his next sermon. Most of the time, I felt like I was talking to a wall. But Jay... I'd mentioned the Allen House to him once. *Once*," she emphasizes. "And it was months prior. Yet he remembered. He listened when I spoke. At the time, I convinced myself that was all the proof I needed to assure myself he was just a nice guy. But now I know the truth."

"What's that?"

"The reason he took note of those little things about me was so I'd feel comfortable. So I'd be too blind to see the darkness within him."

She takes a minute, closing her eyes as she basks in the wind kicking up around us. The setting sun casts a glow over her, and I see the pain she's been carrying in the lines of her face. What I wouldn't give to know what's going through her mind right now. If she's trying to come to terms with the guilt I sense still plagues her.

"Everything was pitch black when he led me inside," she begins, her voice shaky. She stares into the distance, as if watching a movie of the night and is simply reporting back as a disinterested observer, not someone reliving her trauma. "There was this...charge. I don't know how else to describe it. It was thrilling to be there. To do something I shouldn't. I'd always been a rule follower, always did what was expected of me with little or no argument. So to be somewhere we weren't supposed to be was a rush."

"What was the house like?" I don't know why I ask her that. Maybe to distract her from what she's about to tell me. Or perhaps to prepare myself for it.

"Incredible. It was built in the Italianate style. Low-pitched roof. Symmetrical, rectangular shape. Wide, overhanging eaves. Square cupola on the top. A porch with balustraded balconies. Molded double doors. Roman arches above the windows and doors. And that's just the exterior. But when we stepped inside... It was like stepping back in time. I didn't understand why the college hadn't done anything with the house, why it seemed to be frozen in time of the last day it served a purpose. There was certainly evidence of other people breaking in — beer bottles and used condoms. Other than that, it was like walking through a snapshot of history."

When she falls silent, I squeeze her hand, offering my reassurance that everything will be okay. That no matter what she tells me, I won't think any differently of her.

"For those few minutes we explored the house, I felt...free. Like I could spread my wings and fly." She shifts her gaze to mine. "Like I do whenever I'm with you."

I smile, but don't say anything, giving her the time she needs to work this all out for herself.

"I don't know what came over me. I didn't feel like myself. Within that house, I wasn't who I was. He wasn't who he was. So when we reached the bedroom..." She pauses, drawing in a quivering breath, briefly squeezing her eyes shut. "I kissed him."

I blink, processing this, unsure how to react to her admission. I put myself in her shoes, try to imagine how I would feel if I was more or less forced into marrying someone I didn't love. Normally, I would say there's no excuse for being unfaithful, but she weaves a compelling story. To feel so lonely that you cling to the first person who shows a modicum of interest? I can't help but sympathize with her.

"I never should have kissed him," she mutters, her voice barely audible.

"What happened next?" I press, swallowing hard, my stomach heavy with dread.

"I tore away, finally snapping out of whatever spell the house had cast, realizing what I'd done. I tried to apologize, tell him it was a mistake, and walk away." Her chin trembles, tears now cascading freely down her cheeks. "But he wouldn't let me."

I bite the inside of my cheek, squeezing her hand tighter, much like she did to mine on the Ferris wheel. I need her to ground me when I feel like I'm being torn apart. I can only imagine how Londyn must feel to relive this.

"You don't have to tell me anything else. It's okay."

"I do, Wes," she insists. "I've kept it all inside for so long now, and I am just fucking exhausted from it all."

I inhale several deep breaths through my nose, then nod subtly, indicating for her to go on, even though I'm not sure I'm ready to hear what comes next.

"He had me on my stomach on the hardwood floor. The entire time, he said he wasn't doing anything I didn't want. And for the life of me, I don't remember telling him no. I can remember all the other details about that moment. The chip on the baseboard I stared at the entire time. The leather and citrus scent of his cologne. A dog barking from down the street. But I can't remember ever telling him he was wrong. That it wasn't what I wanted. It was then that I finally understood how Echo felt."

"Echo?"

"It was a story from Greek mythology Jay told me. Echo was a nymph Zeus often consorted with. When his wife, Hera, grew suspicious, she came down from Mount Olympus to catch him in the act. But Echo protected Zeus, as he'd ordered her to do. In response, Hera cursed Echo, took away her ability to speak anything other than the last words spoken to her. She became just an echo, unable to speak her true thoughts or feelings."

"And what were the last words spoken to you?" I manage to ask.

She juts out her chin, summoning the courage to say them out loud. "He'd said, 'Tell me you're mine.' I just wanted it all to be over, so I kept repeating I was his. Thought it would help him…finish quicker."

"Jesus." I scrub a hand over my face, my expression pinched, my teeth digging into my bottom lip, causing it to bleed. I need the pain to distract me before I do something rash.

"Afterward, I couldn't move, in shock. Then he forced me to get up before we were caught. I was in a daze as he dragged me out of the house and toward his car." She laughs slightly, looking up to the sky. "Do you want to know what detail has always stood out in my mind about that night?"

I want to tell her I don't think I can stomach it, but instead, I remain silent.

"He opened the car door for me. My own husband never did that. And here was this man who'd just forced himself on me acting like the perfect fucking gentleman. Like it never happened. I'd wondered if I'd imagined it all."

"You got into the car with him again? Even after—"

"I was scared, Wes. I remember my entire body trembling violently. I worried what he would do if I *didn't*. So I did. And for the first time since we'd met, neither of us spoke a single word to each other. It wasn't until he pulled up in front of my apartment that he finally did."

"What did he say?"

"He knew how much I hated the constant media attention after my mother's death. So he told me if I were to report this, it would turn into a circus. That my photo would be plastered on every news site out there. Then he said no one would buy my story anyway, since he didn't do anything I didn't want. Like the cursed Echo I was, I repeated it back to him. Told him he was right. That I'd wanted it. I was too frightened to disagree."

I hang my head, squeezing my eyes shut, balling my free hand into a fist. I know the statistics about sexual assault on college campuses. Being the overprotective older brother I've always been, I did a ridiculous amount of research on this stuff before Julia went off to college, armed her with more material on the topic than necessary, along with a can of pepper spray and a pocket knife. But as Londyn's story reminds me, it's not the masked man in a dark alley you have to watch out for. It's someone you know. Someone you trust. Someone you let your guard down around.

"Did you report him?"

"Not right away. I thought if I could get through the last month of school, it would be okay. I didn't know if I could sit through all the questions I'd have to answer if I were to report him. I'd stopped going to the coffee shop. Purposefully avoided spending any time outside of my apartment unless necessary. But then..."

"Yes?" I lean toward her, absentmindedly running my thumb along her knuckles.

"Then I missed my period."

I suck in a breath, hanging my head, my lips pinched with tension. "Jesus..."

"That's when I decided to come forward."

"So he was arrested, right?"

She barks out a sarcastic laugh, rolling her eyes. "Don't I wish. My school touted having a sexual assault task force as part of their campus police, which was where I was told to report this because it happened on campus. But when I did, they made *me* feel like I was the one in the wrong. They didn't take me to an office. They took me to a fucking interrogation room. Made me sit there in an uncomfortable chair while I waited for someone to take my statement."

"Why would they do that?"

"I asked myself the same question. Then I figured it out. Do you know what was different about me compared to any of the other students who'd reported that someone had stolen their laptop or their car was keyed?" She gives me a knowing look.

"Oh."

"Because I'm not white. My father warned me about this when I'd applied to this college. Told me the nearby town wasn't exactly diverse. Neither was the student body. But I didn't care. I wanted to go there because they had a great art history program.

"When a supposed sexual assault special officer, who just so happened to be a white man, finally came in to talk to me, he accused me of stealing the keys to the Allen House, threatened to file theft and trespassing charges against me if I insisted on pursuing this. After that, it was justification after justification. He asked what I was wearing, as if that had anything to do with it. Asked if I'd been drinking. Brought up the fact I'd admitted we'd grown close after both being regulars at the same coffee shop. Then that I'd kissed him, insinuating that I should have anticipated something more would happen. Anything to poke holes in my claim."

"That's so fucked up," I choke out.

"I know."

"So…nothing happened? He got away with it?"

She nods. "He did. After all, Jay had a bright future ahead of him," she says in a mocking tone. "If they were to file charges, it would destroy his life, his marriage, all for, and I quote, 'simply a guilty conscience on your part after you'd made the decision to cheat on your husband'. So not only was I fucked by this guy against my will, I was fucked by the system, too. The system that's supposed to be in place to protect me." She pinches her lips together in contemplation. "Then again, that's not entirely true. The system only seems interested in protecting white men. No offense."

"What did you do?"

"The only thing I could. I graduated and headed home. Or at least my *new* home. I actually looked forward to seeing Sawyer, to focusing on our marriage. After everything, I just wanted to feel love. Find some sort of normalcy. But that's the thing they don't tell you after you go through something like this. Life will never be normal again. You can't just return to before. There is no before. There's only after. Putting one foot in front of the other to make it to the next day. Many victims can't even do that. You're stuck. I suppose I still am."

"Did you tell Sawyer what happened?" I ask in a low voice, my tone free of judgment.

"I hadn't planned on it, as horrible as that sounds. After the police didn't believe me, I started to question what really happened myself. So once I was home, I made an appointment at a clinic. Unfortunately, someone from Sawyer's church saw me there and brought it up to him. He asked me why I went there when I had an OB closer to home. I had no choice but to come clean. Tell him everything that happened. And I told him..."

"Yes?"

"That the reason I'd gone to that clinic was to terminate the pregnancy." She shifts her tear-filled eyes to mine. "It wasn't an easy decision. Trust me. I didn't enter into it lightly. I tried to imagine how I would feel if I had to carry that man's baby for nine months. How I would feel every time I looked at the baby and saw his features. And I knew I wasn't strong enough to do that. That I wouldn't survive. So, unlike my father, I chose myself over my baby."

"How did Sawyer take the news?"

She laughs under her breath, her annoyance clear. "He called me every name under the sun. Blamed me. Accused me of lying about the assault altogether. Claimed the baby was the result of a consensual affair and the only reason I confessed was because I was now carrying evidence of the affair. That if

I were telling the truth, the police would have filed charges, which they didn't.

"I couldn't believe it. I thought he'd understand. Sawyer had always been an outspoken advocate for civil rights, especially in matters of national importance. He'd routinely accuse police departments of not believing black victims, but when it came to his own wife, he didn't give a shit. He treated me like I was no one. Like I was the one to blame, when all I'd wanted was for him to hug me and tell me everything was going to be okay. That he would support me and do whatever it took to help me get through this.

"Instead, he insisted I do something to get right with God. That I confess my sins in front of the entire church. Only then would he consider forgiving me for my supposed betrayal."

"And if you refused?"

"Then he'd have no choice but to cut all ties with me. He said he couldn't respect someone who didn't value the sanctity of marriage. Who didn't value human life like they preach in the Bible. He didn't care that the baby was the result of rape. In his mind, I hadn't been assaulted. I'd simply gotten caught being unfaithful. He even turned my father against me. Convinced him it was the only way to save face with his church."

"You didn't do what he asked of you, right?"

"No." She offers me a soft smile. "For the first time in my life, I did what *I* believed to be right, instead of what someone demanded of me. The following Saturday night, while Sawyer was at the church rehearsing his sermon for the following day, I packed a bag and left."

"Where did you go?"

"I called the only person I could think of. The only person I knew would help, no questions asked."

"Who was that?"

"My roommate from my freshman year." She blows out a laugh. "When you think about it, it's kind of depressing. The people you've known all your life are the first to toss you out, but the ones you barely know will help you without judgment. And that's what she did. She offered me her couch in her apartment in Atlanta without a hint of judgment. Just sympathy and compassion. So I jumped in my car and haven't looked back since."

I nod, my chest aching at everything she endured. Not only that night, but in the months to follow. How everyone who was supposed to help her and stand up for her abandoned her. It's no wonder she pushed me away. If I were in her shoes, I probably would have done the same thing, worried I'd hurt her like everyone else in her life.

I slowly face her, struggling to come up with something meaningful to say in response. *I'm sorry* seems too trivial. Too inconsequential. So I do what she wanted all those years ago.

"Can I give you a hug?"

Her shoulders fall as she chokes out a sob, the sound echoing in the still evening air. "I'd really like that."

Releasing my hold on her hand, I wrap my arms around her, pulling her close. I kiss the top of her head, rocking her gently.

"Everything's going to be okay," I murmur.

A new wave of tears washes over her as she melts into me, clutching onto me as if I'm a life preserver, the only thing keeping her afloat.

"Thank you." She nuzzles further into me, inhaling a deep breath before pulling back.

I cup her cheek. "I'm willing to do whatever it takes, Londyn. If you need time to figure things out, to learn to trust me, I'm okay with that. We can take this as slowly as you need. Just, please, don't push me away again. I won't abandon you like everyone else. I swear to you."

"I appreciate that." She smiles warmly at me, then stands, taking a few steps away. She peers into the distance, indecision covering her expression as she crosses a single arm over her stomach. "But I can't ask you to wait for me."

I rise to my feet, eating up the space between us. "But——"

She spins toward me. "It was your kiss that made me realize this."

"My…kiss?"

"Yes." She smiles slyly. "Your kiss." When she clutches the

159

lapels of my jacket, a thrill trickles through me, my pulse increasing. "It made me realize what I want."

"And what's that?"

"Everything." Her gaze locks with mine. Then she drops her hold, stepping back. "But I'm messed up, Wes. For the past several years, I've made it my mission in life to do everything to prevent feeling the absolute helplessness I did that night. That I did for months to come afterward. I took self-defense classes—"

"That explains the boxing photos on your Instagram," I remark.

She playfully pinches her lips together, a single hand on her hip. "You've been stalking my Instagram?"

I rake my fingers through my hair. "Maybe. I've missed you."

"I've missed you, too," she admits, her expression softening for a moment. Then she steps toward me again. "But I need to work on myself. I thought by taking self-defense classes, by having no-strings sex again, I was taking back control. But they were just bandages on a wound that's still festering. For five years now, I've ignored the source of the problem because the idea of allowing myself to be vulnerable again scares me more than snakes or heights combined. So I can't stand here and ask you to wait for me, to be patient while I sort out my shit. That's not fair to you, or to me. Because I don't know if I'll ever sort out my shit. I hope I can. But if I'm to finally heal from this, I can't have any added pressure on me."

"In other words, it's not me, it's you," I say with a slight chuckle.

"Yeah." She chews on her bottom lip. "I suppose this was all just a roundabout way to say that."

I exhale deeply, lifting my eyes toward the sky, trying to think of anything to say to convince her otherwise, convince her it doesn't have to be like this. Then her words from minutes ago replay in my mind. All she wanted back then was someone to support her and do whatever it took to help her through this. So, as much as it pains me, that's exactly what I'm going to do.

"I don't like this, but I promise to stay out of your way while you get on the path to the happiness you deserve, regardless of whether I'm at the end of it."

"This doesn't mean I want you out of my life completely," she adds quickly. "Truthfully, these past few weeks have sucked."

I laugh under my breath. "Yes, they have."

She pulls at the hem of her dress, lowering her gaze. "So, if it's okay with you, I'd like it if things can go back to the way they were before we kissed." She gradually looks up. "If we can work on the house together again."

"I'd really like that, too."

"Good."

"Good," I repeat.

Neither one of us moves as I simply admire her. Her beauty. Her strength. Her resilience. And in this moment, I feel like I'm finally seeing the real Londyn. I've always found her to be absolutely stunning. But now that she's revealed all the dark parts of herself, I can't help but grow even more attracted to her.

"Can I hug you again?" I ask after several protracted moments.

She nods, walking into my arms.

I wrap her in my embrace, bringing her head to my chest. I trace a soothing pattern on her back as the sun sets on the horizon, turning the sky a beautiful pink. Silence surrounds us like a protective cocoon as I do my best to provide comfort and security in a world that's been nothing but cruel and unjust to her most of her life. But I hope I can show her it doesn't have to be that way.

I hope I can show her what she's been deprived of for too long now.

I hope I can show her love.

# CHAPTER TWENTY-ONE

WESTON

"This is infinitely easier than that wallpaper," I comment as I roll paint onto the wall of what used to be Gampy's office but Londyn plans to return to its original purpose — the parlor.

I wasn't sure how today would go, considering it's our first day with things back to normal. Or at least some semblance of normalcy. I'm not sure how normal things will be again. Not after everything Londyn shared yesterday. Her assault. Being made out to be the wrongdoer by the system. Her husband giving her an ultimatum for making a decision any woman in her shoes would.

I've always considered myself a fairly even-tempered person. It takes a lot to piss me off. Gampy always told me that the pen is mightier than the sword, and I suppose his admonition stuck, as I prefer to use my words instead of my fists.

When it comes to Londyn, though, that's no longer the case. I've never felt the urge to hunt someone down and cause permanent damage as much as I do now, knowing this waste of space, this rapist, is presumably still walking the earth, free to cause other women the same harm. It makes me sick that our justice system would allow such a thing. Maybe I've just worn rose-colored glasses for too long, thinking the system would take care of criminals.

But if I learned anything from Gampy, it's that the system is flawed. It's times like these I wish he were still alive. He'd know what to do, what to say to Londyn. Hell, he'd probably go to battle for her, promise to get her the justice she deserves. I wouldn't even know how to do that. All I can do is what I promised. Be her friend while she finally takes back control of her life.

Although every time she flashes me one of those heart-melting smiles, it takes everything I have to not wrap her in my arms. Press my lips to hers. Kiss her like she deserves to be kissed. With respect. With admiration. With hope. Now that I've had a taste of how sweet she is, I'm desperate for another hit.

"Figured I'd take it easy on you today." She climbs down from the ladder, setting her roller on a nearby worktable made from a couple of sawhorses and a piece of plywood. "But don't get too used to it." When she smiles, a lightness envelopes her, as if yesterday never happened. "You'll have your work cut out for you next weekend."

"Oh yeah?" I cross my arms in front of my chest.

When I notice her eyes briefly go to my biceps as they stretch the fabric of my shirt, a flicker of excitement fills me. Maybe not all hope is lost. Maybe there's still a chance, despite her insisting I not wait for her. But what she doesn't understand is that I'd rather wait years for what I feel in my heart is extraordinary than settle for anything less. I've already waited thirty-six years to feel what I do for her. What's a few more when it's right? And nothing has ever felt so right, her past be damned.

"What's next weekend?"

"The kitchen cabinets will be ready to be installed." One of her curls falls in front of her face, and she pushes it behind her ear.

"You got some paint on your face now." I laugh at how adorable she looks, the paint smear the perfect accessory to her outfit of cut-off shorts, white tank top, and work boots. She's a mixture of style and grace, with a dash of don't fuck with me. It's this combination that's drawn me to her from the moment we met.

She grabs a rag off the worktable and wipes at her forehead. "Did I get it?"

My laughter only increases when I see there's now even more paint, thanks to the rag I've used to clean my hands throughout the day.

"Nope. Certainly didn't."

"And you're laughing?" she shoots back, feigning annoyance. "That's no way to treat a lady. And here I thought you were a gentleman." She playfully bats her lashes, playing up the Southern accent in her intonation.

"Oh, I'm a gentleman all right."

A few weeks ago, I would have made another suggestive comment, but I don't want to push my luck with her. Not yet.

"We'll see about that." A mischievous glint in her eyes, she dips a brush into the gray paint we used on the bottom section of the walls, then flicks it at me, causing paint to splatter across my t-shirt.

I freeze, staring in shock for several moments. Then my gaze darkens. "You're going to regret that, Londyn."

I advance toward her, and she squeals, darting around the worktable, as if that will protect her. Grabbing the roller from the paint pan on the floor, I chase after her. She could escape into the hallway, but she doesn't, heading farther into the parlor instead.

Easily reaching her, I run the roller along the back of her tank and the top of her shorts.

"That's it, Bradford. This means war." She briefly glances at the ladder, then the can of touch-up paint perched on the top. It may be small, but it will still do a fair bit of damage.

"You wouldn't," I say, keeping the roller stretched in front of me, like a sword warding off an opponent.

"Oh, no?"

"No," I reply, although I can't quite be certain.

A month ago, I wouldn't have thought she'd do anything to risk ruining her hard work. But something about her right now — the excitement in her eyes, the devilish hint of a smile tugging on her lips, the easy, carefree attitude that's a complete one-eighty from the tension-filled conversation when she shared her past — makes me think anything's possible.

"What makes you say that?" she muses.

"All our hard work. If you do that, we'll have to reprime and repaint the walls."

"That's true..."

She straightens her defensive stance, putting me at ease. Then she takes a few quick steps toward the ladder and tips it, the can on the top tumbling off. Paint splatters all over the room, the bulk of it landing directly on me.

Her infectious laughter echoes against the walls. "Like you said," she struggles to say. "Painting is a lot easier than wallpaper. And look." She nods at the wall behind me. "Only a few drops got on it. I believe the score is now Londyn, one. Wes, zero," she boasts proudly, hands on her hips, head held high. I want to be mad that I'm dripping with paint, but I can't be. Not when I see how happy she is.

"Don't think you'll get away with it so easily, Lo."

She saunters up to me, hips swaying. What I wouldn't give to crush her body to mine, to cover her lips with mine, to drink her in. Today has been a test in self-control. But it's one I'm determined to win.

"But, Wes. I already have."

"Do you know what my gampy used to always tell me about being cocky? Well, technically, arrogant."

She tilts her head. "What's that?"

"Arrogance is a trait only losers possess."

Before she has a chance to answer, I loop my arm around her waist, tugging her flush with me, transferring the paint covering my body onto hers. She fights against me, arms flailing, legs kicking. If I thought this was triggering a painful memory, I'd stop. But as her laughter mixes with mine, I know she's enjoying this as much as I am.

My hands become too slick to keep her in my grasp, and she manages to escape, but I run after her, dodging flinging paint. I grab a brush, doing the same to her, paint flying and laughter echoing.

As she runs through the room, she slips in a puddle of paint, losing her balance. She reaches for something to prevent her fall. Since I'm the only thing close by, she grabs onto my t-shirt. Unable to stop her forward momentum due to all the paint on the plastic, I slip, as well, falling back onto the floor, Londyn landing on top of me with a grunt.

Pain radiates through my spine, but I don't move yet,

although I should probably help Londyn off me so she doesn't realize how turned on I am, despite the ache in my body. Even if my erection weren't straining against my shorts, she could still see the desire flowing through me, my breathing increasing, eyes darkening, heart visibly thundering against my chest.

I remove my hands from her hips, not wanting to do anything to keep her here if she doesn't want to be. But even when she's free to get up, she doesn't, her body remaining on mine, eyes glued to mine. Her chest heaves with her increasingly rapid breathing as she moistens her lips.

"Londyn...," I begin, a slight waver in my voice.

She brings a hand up to my face, pushing a few tendrils of hair out of my eyes. "Why can't I get over you?"

I swallow hard, unsure how to answer. How can one question be filled with so much hope, yet also so much despair?

"Do you want to?"

She pauses, contemplating. It's both the easiest question and the most difficult at the same time.

"I don't think I do," she finally answers.

"Then don't," I murmur. "I'm by your side. Whatever you need, I'm with you."

She closes her eyes, basking in my assurance. When she returns her gaze to mine, there's a heat within. Gone is the despair and anguish from last night. Now I see hope and the promise for a future.

"And I'm with you, Wes."

As she inches her mouth toward mine, I hold my breath. A part of me wants to stop her before she does something she's not ready for. But the other part of me is an addict for her kisses, a craving for another taste erasing all sense of reason.

I close my eyes, bracing to satisfy this unrelenting need, when I make out heavy footsteps on the porch, followed by the front door flinging open.

Sucking in a sharp breath, Londyn scrambles to her feet. I jump up behind her as Imogene and Julia enter.

"Hiya, Uncle Wes. Hiya, Miss Londyn," Imogene says

brightly, oblivious to what she interrupted. And to the fact that Londyn being here is a big deal to begin with. "What happened to all the paint?" She frowns, looking around at the paint splattered on the plastic covering the floor, Londyn, me, and pretty much everything.

"Yeah." Julia levels a stare on me. I can hear the dozens of unspoken questions. Half about how Londyn came to be here. The other half about why we are both covered in paint.

"Miss Londyn and I were just having a bit of fun. You know how when you're baking a cake with your mama and she sometimes pipes frosting onto your face? This was kind of the same thing." I glance around at the disaster we made. "Except we may have gotten a little out of control."

"I'd say," Julia remarks.

"It looks like fun!" Imogene turns to Julia. "Can we play in the paint, too?"

"I don't have a change of clothes for you. Plus, we don't have a lot of time. We have plans with Daddy later on."

"He's not with you?" I ask, a single brow arched.

"Work emergency came up." She looks in Londyn's direction. "Nick works as a public relations consultant."

"I see."

"He's constantly putting out fires." She grits a smile. I can tell she's annoyed with his absence, especially since it was his idea they spend the day together and come here. "But that's okay. It gives us a chance to say a proper goodbye before we head back to Charleston tomorrow."

"So you've decided to go back early?"

"It'll give me time to get everything Imogene needs for the start of school," she responds.

"Just know you're always welcome."

She offers me a sincere smile. "I know."

"How about we call it quits early and go pay Miss Clara a visit?" I suggest. "I'm sure she'd love to see you one last time before you head home." I glance at my niece. "And little Imogene, too."

"Is that the peach cobbler lady we met at the fair?" Imogene asks.

"Yeah, baby," Julia answers.

"Can we have peach cobbler, too?"

"It's the last night I get to spoil you for a while. You can have anything you want." I beam down at her, then shift my gaze to Londyn. "You're more than welcome to join us if you'd like. I understand if you don't," I add quickly, not wanting to pressure her to do anything she's uncomfortable with. I have a feeling this will happen a lot over the next few months as I try to navigate this new dynamic between us. I don't want to push too hard, but damn if it's impossible to not want to include her in every aspect of my life.

"I'd like that." Then she pauses, looking down at her body. "But I'm going to need some time to shower and get all this paint off me."

"You and me both." I laugh. "You shower first. I can always just go for a swim in the lake with Imogene."

My niece's expression lights up. "Can I, Mama?"

"I don't have a suit with me, sweet pea."

"I still have the one you left here a few weeks ago."

Imogene peers up at Julia with pleading eyes.

"Fine," my sister huffs. "Go up to the bedroom and grab it."

"I'll show her where it is," Londyn offers. "I'm heading up there to shower anyway."

"Thank you, Londyn."

With a nod, Londyn places her hand on Imogene's shoulder, steering her past paint cans. My gaze follows her, unable to look away until she disappears from view.

But I still don't face my sister, knowing I'm about to be subjected to an inquisition.

"So...," Julia begins after a beat, her voice bright. "She's back."

I shrug her off, attempting to clean up the mess we made, paint brushes and rollers strewn all over the floor. At least we covered it in plastic. If we hadn't, I doubt Londyn would have flung paint at me, not wanting to ruin the original flooring.

"Yes. She is."

"How did that happen?" Julia follows me.

"By chance, I suppose. I ran into her yesterday."

A smile plays on my lips as I recall the instant I noticed Londyn heading toward me in the crosswalk. I was about to cross the street toward her, but I didn't, even though I had plenty of time to make it. Even though I was supposed to meet a client for dinner. I stood at that intersection, some bigger force keeping me locked in place. Maybe it was fate. Maybe it was divine intervention. I don't care. Because whatever it was brought Londyn back to me.

"Is that right?"

"Yeah."

"And?"

"And we talked. She explained things." I lean toward her, lowering my voice. "Suffice it to say, she's been hurt, Jules. Bad."

"So have you."

I level my gaze on her, my expression severe. "Not like this. Think of the worst possible thing that could happen to someone. That could happen to a woman. That's what happened to her."

She arches a brow, a question in her gaze. "Was she…"

I nod subtly, feeling guilty about saying anything at all. The last thing I want is to betray Londyn's trust, but I need Julia on my side. On *our* side.

"On top of that, imagine how you'd feel if your own family didn't support or believe you afterward."

She wraps her arms around her stomach, staring out the window. "I don't even know what to say." There's a distance in her expression and voice.

"Neither did I."

"So that's why she freaked out. Why she was scared." Her words are more like a statement than a question.

I nod. "More or less."

"So where does this leave you?"

"Where we were before. She's not ready for anything else."

Julia gives me a knowing look. "But when she is, you'll be there. Right?"

"I promised I wouldn't wait around for her."

"And you actually plan to honor that promise?" She smirks.

I laugh to myself, marveling at how well my sister knows me. "What Londyn doesn't know can't hurt her." I grin, then skirt past her when I hear footsteps zooming down the stairs.

"Uncle Wes! I'm ready. Let's go swimming."

"Okay, munchkin." I extend my hand, taking Imogene's tiny one in mine.

As I turn the corner and start down the hallway, Julia's voice stops me.

"Hey, Wes?"

I pause, glancing over my shoulder.

"You're a good man."

"I hope to be."

# CHAPTER TWENTY-TWO

## LONDYN

The aroma of coffee fills my darkened kitchen on a Saturday morning in October. The world outside is quiet. Only an occasional dog barking or car driving along the street finds its way into my solitude. There was a time I hated waking up before the sun. That's no longer the case, a peacefulness enveloping me before the world wakes up.

Once my coffee is prepared the way I like, I sling my duffle bag over my shoulder and make my way out of my condo. A chill envelopes me as I step outside. There's a briskness in the air this morning now that it's technically fall, but once the sun comes out, the temperatures should near seventy, making it the perfect day for some home renovations.

While this project certainly has taken a lot longer than I originally anticipated, I wouldn't change it for anything. Spending all this time working on the house with Wes has given me a creative outlet I didn't realize I'd needed. Plus, it's allowed me to get to know Wes better. We've even begun spending time together outside of our weekends at Gampy and Meemaw's house.

While I do have a few interior design projects for other clients, they're on a smaller scale. A bathroom remodel here. A kitchen renovation there. So it's easy for me to sneak out and meet Wes.

The truth is, even if I had to rearrange my schedule, I'd do it just to spend time with him.

Once I lock the door, I continue down the walkway, stopping abruptly when I see Wes' black Range Rover idling on the street in front of the driveway. The door opens, and he jumps out, heading to the passenger side.

"What are you doing here?" I ask, slowly making my way toward him.

When I'd left him at Meemaw and Gampy's less than six hours ago, I told him I'd be back at eight this morning. I certainly didn't expect to see him at my place a few minutes before seven.

"There's been a change of plans." He crosses his arms in front of his chest as he leans against his car.

If his statement weren't a dead giveaway that we're not working on the house today, his clothing definitely is. Instead of an old t-shirt, paint-covered pants, and work boots, he's dressed in a navy blue Henley, jeans that fall perfectly from his hips, and casual shoes.

"A change of plans?" I repeat, arching a brow.

"Yeah." He pushes off his car. "I think we've both earned a day off, especially after turning that hidden closet into a laundry room yesterday."

"I'm assuming you have an idea for this day off." I smirk.

"You know me so well, don't you?"

"Either that, or maybe you're extremely transparent."

"I'd prefer to believe the former."

When he winks, a warmth rushes through me, my fingers aching to reach out and touch him. To run my hands through his hair. To pull him toward me. To revel in the scruff of his unshaven jaw as he nuzzles the crook of my neck. But I know the power Wes' kisses have over me. I'm not ready to go there with him again. Not yet.

"Okay then, Mr. Bradford. What do you have in mind?"

"It's a surprise." He extends his hand toward me.

I stare at it, hesitant. As he knows by now, I don't like the unexpected. I find safety and comfort in making plans, knowing what I'm walking into ahead of time.

"Come on, Lo," he begins, his voice gentle and deep. "I promise there won't be heights or snakes. Do you trust me?"

I lift my gaze, locking with his. Do I trust him?

For years, I only trusted myself. Refused to even consider the idea of putting my trust in another human. After all, every person who was supposed to support me, help me, *love* me had betrayed that trust.

It wasn't until I met Hazel that I learned I *could* trust

172

someone. It didn't happen overnight, but after I learned her story, I didn't feel so alone in my pain anymore. But it took me over a year to finally trust Hazel. I've only known Wes a total of four months. Can I really trust him after such a short amount of time?

Is length of time the only indicator of trust, though? I knew my father and Sawyer my entire life. I'm not sure I'll ever trust them again. At least not Sawyer. He should have stood by my side. Instead, he used my predicament to his advantage, drawing sympathy from high-ranking members of his church, all while throwing me to the proverbial wolves.

But Wes has stood by my side. And, as promised, he hasn't pressured me to do anything I'm not ready for. He's remained true to his word, despite how difficult it must be for him to spend time with me knowing there may never be anything more between us than what we have now. That has to count for something.

"I do trust you," I admit in a strained voice.

"Good." He blows out a relieved breath, almost as surprised as I am about my admission. "Then let's go."

\* \* \*

"What are we doing here?" I glance around the dirt lot abutting an abandoned drive-in theater about forty-five minutes outside of the city. Then I return my attention to Wes as he puts the Range Rover in park.

"Figured you'd enjoy this." He nods at the open field in the distance, rows upon rows of tables and pop-up tents.

I squint, trying to figure out what's going on. Then I dart my wide eyes back to his. "A flea market?" I shriek excitedly.

"Last week, you'd mentioned how much you missed going to these, since they're only on weekends and you've been spending all your weekends since June with me. So I did some research. Found one with decent reviews, saw it was today, and here we are."

"You researched flea markets?" I ask in disbelief. "For me?"

His lips quirk up into a gentle smile as his fingers flinch, as if wanting to reach out and push away the few curls that always fall in front of my eyes.

"I'd do anything for you, Londyn," he responds, his voice laden with sincerity.

I swallow hard through the heaviness in my throat. As much as I should tell him he can't say stuff like that, not when I'm trying to finally make peace with my past and heal, I'm simply unable to utter those words.

The more he's slipped in the occasional compliment or words of encouragement over the weeks, the more I've begun to crave them. They help me through the bouts of depression that plague me every once in a while. Although, lately, I haven't experienced many instances of depression. Haven't had days where I physically couldn't get out of bed. Haven't felt the need to storm over to Hazel's and spar with her in the gym until my muscles give out under me. Things have been…good. Better than good. And I have a feeling I have the man at my side to thank for that.

"Shall we?" Wes arches a brow, pulling me out of my thoughts.

"Yes."

He jumps down from the car and rushes over to my door as I open it. He touches my elbow, helping me down.

Excitement buzzes inside me as we walk through the lot, immersed in the familiar atmosphere of a weekend flea market. Deal-hunters haggle on price with vendors. Wood chimes jangle in the slight breeze. The smell of musty fabric mixed with spices surrounds me. All familiar sounds and smells, ones I didn't think I'd miss as much as I have.

As I stroll beside Wes down the first row of vendors, sticking to my rule of not buying anything unless I absolutely must have it and it's a bargain, I steal a glance at him, his expression bewildered, eyes darting around, like a stranger in a strange land. For someone like Wes, he probably is.

"I'm guessing you've never been to a flea market before," I remark as we pass a vendor who seems to do exactly what I do — finds crap and up-cycles it to resell at a hefty profit.

"Is it that obvious?"

"A little." I playfully nudge him, skirting a few little boys chasing each other, their mother darting after them.

"Let's put it this way. My mother would consider going to a *discount superstore* beneath her. So a flea market, which in her mind is like a giant yard sale, is certainly out of the question. Lydia Bradford doesn't buy anything used, except for Julia."

I fling my wide gaze to his, jaw dropped, surprised he'd say something like that about the sister he adores more than life itself.

He holds up his hands. "My mother's words. Not mine."

"Jesus. Sounds like she's a real—"

"Bitch?" Wes interjects.

"I would have said pill, but I suppose your word is accurate, too."

"Trust me. It is."

I nod, shoving my hands into my jacket pockets to stop myself from reaching out and holding his hand, an urge that increases with each step we take. Touching him just feels natural, this act of keeping my distance forced and constrained.

"I thought you had a decent relationship with her. At least compared to Julia."

After some thought, he replies, "I do. Or I did."

I lick my lips, stopping to check out a few galvanized buckets I can clean up, re-distress, and use as decorative pieces throughout Gampy and Meemaw's house to keep up with the historic farmhouse style.

"What happened?" I press, making a note of the stall number on my phone before continuing along the row once more.

"Remember the night of the fair?"

"Not sure that's one I'll forget for a long time, if ever. At least I won't soon forget what happened *after* the fair."

"Yeah. I suppose not." An adorable blush covers his cheeks as he recalls that kiss.

I wonder if he's craved another one as much as I have. At first, I questioned whether I did the right thing by keeping him solidly in friend territory. But several other people in the sexual assault support group I've been attending have agreed with my decision, saying it's better I wait until I'm ready to date. That I shouldn't rush into anything until I'm in the right mental state to deal with the emotional rollercoaster of a relationship.

"Do you remember me mentioning my ex-fiancée, Brooklyn?"

"I do." I pull my lip between my teeth, recalling his passionate plea as if it were just yesterday. That this thing is bigger than us. That I'm worth any risk to his heart. "You really do have a thing for girls named after cities, don't you?" I nudge him with my shoulder, hoping to break through the mounting tension.

"I guess you can say that." He smiles sheepishly, his chin dipping slightly. "Brooklyn was the first *real* person I'd dated."

"So… What? Before that, you made up girlfriends or something?"

A laugh vibrates from his throat as he shakes his head. "Do I really look so horrible that I need to make up a girlfriend?"

"No." My cheeks warm from the heat in his gaze as I try to fight against my grin, albeit unsuccessfully. Wes is the first person in years who's made me smile like this. Who's vanquished the guilt and remorse weighing me down.

"When I say real, I mean she was the first woman I'd met who wasn't trying to be someone she wasn't. You've heard Julia talk about what life as a Bradford was like for her."

I nod. "A little."

"It's all a show. People will kiss your ass one second, then turn around and stab you in the back the next."

"How did you meet her? I'm assuming it wasn't at some posh society event."

"No, it wasn't." His eyes shine with a nostalgic gleam. "One day, I had a meeting with a client in the North End of Boston. I was running early, so I ducked into a local Mom and Pop café to grab a coffee. And that's where I first saw her. She was so unassuming. So demure. So gracious. One of those women who's stunning, but they don't see it." He flashes me a smile. "Kind of like you."

I hold his gaze for a moment, a charge buzzing between us. Butterflies flap their relentless wings in my stomach, as they're prone to do whenever I'm around him. But before either of us does anything we'll regret, I quickly avert my eyes.

"So what happened?" I walk toward a booth and examine a pile of wood pieces, even though I have more than enough spare wood from all the renovations than I know what to do with.

"She didn't love me. Not like she needed to in order to be happy."

"And how does your mother fit into all this?"

He rolls his eyes. "She saw our engagement as her opportunity to plan the social event of the year. Didn't care about me finding someone I loved and wanted to spend the rest of my life with. She just wanted her name to be front and center in the society column."

"Is that really a thing?"

"Down here it is. We both had a lot of pressure on us, Brooklyn more so than me. I suppose I'm partly to blame for that. She'd hoped for a long engagement, but instead of listening to her, I tried to keep the peace between my mother and Brooklyn. So we'd set a date for only a few months after we'd gotten engaged, thanks to my mother's insistence. She took complete control, even going so far as to pre-approve dresses for Brooklyn to try on at the local bridal shop, instead of giving her free rein to choose whatever style she wanted. I was so busy with work that I didn't even realize everything that had been going on."

He turns his urgent eyes on mine. "I'm not blaming what happened on my mother. Even if she hadn't meddled, things would have eventually ended. I played a huge part in our ultimate demise. I was always working. Never made Brooklyn a priority, although I kept promising I would. I never carried through on that promise, though, so I can't blame her for walking away. I told her I loved her all the time, yet I failed to actually *show* her I did, not like she needed. I was so used to people equating love with material things, I didn't realize all she wanted was my presence. But after my mother called her

177

a slut and a whore in front of all her uppity friends in an effort to save face—"

"She didn't," I gasp, covering my mouth. This woman sounds like an absolute nightmare. No wonder Julia steers clear of her. I'd do the same if she were my mother.

"She did. I've always been very non-confrontational. Not a pushover," he clarifies. "If I see something wrong, I won't roll over and take it, so to speak. It's probably from having to play the mediator between my mother and Julia for years. I just want everyone to get along. But when I heard my mother call the woman I loved such horrible names, I lost it. Chewed her out for all her friends to witness. Once I got Brooklyn out of there, of course. And the worst part?"

"There's something even worse than her calling the woman you were going to marry a whore?"

"Well, worse for her." He smirks, a devilish glint in his eyes. "She'd invited a photographer from the society column. Let's just say he captured a rather unflattering picture of my mother as I gave her a piece of my mind. She'd made the front page of the society magazine after all."

I can't help but laugh. "Wow."

"I didn't plan it that way. I'm not that vindictive. But I like to think karma finally paid her a visit."

"I'd say."

I don't know why this story touches me like it does. Everyone has a monster-in-law story. I can only imagine that Mrs. Bradford has very high standards for her son, her baby boy, ones no woman will ever live up to, at least in her eyes. But the knowledge that Wes has no problem standing up for people he cares about, even to the woman who gave him life, endears another part of my heart to him.

"So that's the short of it. I still talk to her. We're not at each other's throats like Julia and her tend to be. But I no longer try to keep the peace. No longer bite my tongue when she's acting unreasonable." He laughs under his breath. "Like the last time I saw her earlier in the summer. I was at a golf tournament the company put on, and she was trying to get me to ask out one of her friend's daughters because, and I quote, 'she has good breeding'."

"*Breeding?*" I snort a laugh. "What was she? A fucking horse?"

"To some of these people, that's what picking a wife is. Marry a respectable woman who will bring some sort of clout to the family, regardless of how incompatible you are, then find...satisfaction elsewhere."

"You mean cheat?"

He places his finger over his mouth. "You didn't hear it from me."

"Of course not." I heave a sigh, no longer paying attention to any of the wares being sold, too consumed by Wes and learning more about his world. "I take it that's not what you want."

"What?"

"Good breeding." I wave my hand. "For lack of a better word."

"Certainly not."

"Then tell me what you *do* want, Weston Bradford," I say coyly.

He stops walking, and I do the same, facing him as he smiles at me. "Love. Nothing more. Nothing less." His answer hangs in the air for several seconds.

Then he steps toward me. My mouth grows dry as I inhale his earthy aroma that still has a hint of sawdust, despite the fact we haven't worked on the house today.

"How about you, Londyn? What's your holy grail?"

"Holy grail?"

"Yeah. You know. The one thing in life you'll always pursue."

I focus my gaze past him, considering his question. A dozen possible answers float in my mind. Happiness. Security. Acceptance. Control. But one seems to overpower all the others.

"Love." I meet his eyes. "Nothing more. Nothing less."

He nods, a subtle smile pulling on his full lips. "Nothing less."

# CHAPTER TWENTY-THREE

WESTON

"How do you possibly see all that potential when you pass an old, beat-up dresser?" I remark after listening to Londyn talk about what she plans to do with some of her purchases.

We'd spent the entire morning scouring the flea market for the best finds. I couldn't help but feel like I was seeing a different part of Londyn as I watched her methodically do one pass of the vendors, making notes, only buying something on that first pass if it was something she'd been looking for. Otherwise, she just made a note to return later to buy, often haggling about the price. And this woman could certainly haggle. I have half a mind to hire her to negotiate contracts for me. She'd probably be more effective than the entirety of our current legal department.

In the end, we walked away with a bunch of galvanized buckets, some wooden tool carriers she claimed would make great planters, and a dresser, which she almost didn't get, but I insisted would fit in the back of the Range Rover.

Since neither of us wanted the day to end, we dropped everything off in Londyn's overstuffed garage, then headed to an art museum. Now we're relaxing over sushi.

"Easy." She shrugs, sipping on her sake. "I see potential in everything."

I smile, holding back my remark that I wish she'd see potential in herself. She needs to figure that out on her own. Just like she needs to finally realize what I've tried to show her these past few months as we've not only worked on Gampy and Meemaw's house, but also got together for dinner at mine. Or went to an outdoor concert at the park near her house. Or strolled through the Castleberry Hill Art District. That she *is* ready to be vulnerable with someone again.

"That's incredible. And you do all that stuff right in your garage? You don't have another workspace?"

She picks up a piece of yellowtail with her chopsticks and places it into her mouth. After swallowing, she dabs her lips. "Nope. Just the garage. Although I will admit that I have moved some pieces into the spare room in my house."

"Some of that stuff is kind of big." I shove a piece of the spicy tuna roll into my mouth. "How do you ship it?"

"I use a crate and freight company. They come and pack everything up, then ship it. But if the purchaser is within a few hours from Atlanta and it fits into my SUV, I'll deliver it."

"By yourself?" I cock a brow. "That doesn't sound safe."

"I told you. I know self-defense." She smiles, but I don't waver from my hard stare.

I'd give Julia the same stare if I found out she was taking orders online and hand delivering her stuff. It makes me even more uneasy with Londyn.

"But, if it makes you feel better, I also carry a gun." She pats her purse.

My eyes widen. "Right now?" I hadn't expected to learn she was packing. Hell, I don't know many women who know how to shoot at all, let alone own a gun.

"I have a concealed carry permit. My neighbor, Hazel, encouraged me to get a gun after I told her about my past."

"Hazel was your self-defense instructor, correct?"

She nods. "Yeah. Said it gave her peace of mind after what she went through."

"And what's that?"

"Her ex beat her and her sons. When they tried to leave, he shot their two sons and her before shooting himself. She survived. Her boys didn't."

"Wow. Sorry to hear that."

"Carrying a gun won't bring her boys back, but it gives her peace of mind, even though she knows how to defend herself. Like me. I know how to defend myself now, but at least I have a backup if need be."

"Well then…" I lean back in my chair. "We'll have to go to the range sometime."

She tilts her head as a small smile crawls across her perfect lips. "You shoot?"

"I do. Gampy taught me."

"Then it's a date." She inhales sharply as her words play back for her. "I mean—"

"I know what you mean." I bring my small sake cup to my mouth and sip the warm liquid. "Not a real date."

"Right." She swallows hard. "Not a real date." She pauses, staring into the distance.

I can almost see the wheels spinning in her head. I study her, urging her to admit she wouldn't mind going on an official date. But she doesn't, turning her bright eyes back to mine, the moment of hesitation passing.

"I hope you're prepared to be emasculated, though."

"Why's that?"

She leans toward me, her powdery scent mixing with the smell of ginger that permeates this place. "Because I will shoot you under the table."

"Bring it on, Bennett." I waggle my brows.

"You got it, Bradford."

We continue to enjoy our meal as she tells me how her upcycling business took off almost overnight. How within a few months, she had saved enough to get her master's degree, so she decided to study interior design instead of art history. I tell her about the charity branch of the architectural firm I founded several years ago that helps people who've been displaced from their homes due to natural disaster or circumstance rebuild. She even offers to volunteer her own time in the future. Then our conversation veers toward a discussion about whether we'll be able to finish Gampy and Meemaw's house before Thanksgiving so we can celebrate there.

As we leave the restaurant, I'm so wrapped up in listening to her talk about all the food her mother made every year for Thanksgiving, I barely register someone calling my name. It isn't until Londyn stops talking and nudges me that I look up.

"Wes?" a tall, slender brunette asks, eyes narrowed as she approaches.

It takes me a minute to place her, but once I do, a warmth fills me as memories rush back.

"Sophia? Oh, my god." As if no time has passed since we've seen each other, I wrap her in my arms, kissing her cheek. "It's so good to see you."

"You, too. I wasn't certain it was you, but I took a risk."

I drop my hold on her, feeling like I'm staring at a living, breathing memory of my summer days with Gampy and Meemaw. She was as much a part of their family as Julia and me. That was the type of people my grandparents were. If you touched their lives in some way, you'd always be family.

"I'm glad you did," I offer. "Truly."

"I didn't mean to pull you away from your..." She glances at Londyn. "Wife?"

"No." I shake my head. "Londyn is..."

I hesitate, unsure of what to say. Unsure what Londyn is to me. Unsure what Londyn *wants* me to be to her. Unsure what I can say so she doesn't read too much into it. The last thing I want is to say something wrong and scare her off. So I go with the truth.

"She's my interior designer," I say. "I bought Meemaw and Gampy's old place on the auction block a few months ago, and we're restoring it."

Sophia places her hand over her heart, her eyes gleaming. "That's wonderful."

I turn to Londyn, her expression unreadable. "Sophia was one of the babies Meemaw cuddled at the hospital," I explain. "She stayed in touch with a lot of the families, and they became part of the family, too. Sophia and I practically grew up together. For years, I thought she was actually my sister." I laugh at how naïve I was back then. We were around the same age and always together. What else was a four-year-old supposed to think?

"Nice to meet you." With a smile that seems unusually forced, Londyn extends her hand toward Sophia, and they shake.

"You, too."

"So, what are you up to these days?" I ask, trying to make

polite conversation.

"I'm a lawyer, actually."

I laugh heartily. "Gampy said you'd make a damn good attorney, what with the way you always tried to negotiate for one more cookie after dinner."

She grins. "Well, I'd like to say my negotiation skills have improved slightly. But it was actually your grandfather who inspired me to take this path. And to do some pro bono work with the Innocence Foundation, like your gampy."

I exhale a small breath, amazed at how much my grandparents influenced this young woman's life. "He'd be very proud."

"Just like he was of you," she reminds me, then tears her gaze from mine, looking at Londyn. "Well…," she continues, her voice brightening, "I'll let you get on with your evening. It was lovely to meet you, Londyn."

"You, too." Her voice doesn't sound like the one I've grown accustomed to. It's more contrived and strained.

"And it was really good to see you again, Wes." Sophia's words force my attention away from Londyn. When she raises herself onto her toes, I kiss her cheek. "Maybe we can get together again sometime?" she suggests. "Meet up for a coffee or a drink to catch up and reminisce about Meemaw and Gampy."

"I'd like that."

"Great." She reaches into her purse and grabs a business card and pen, scribbling on the back. "Call me. That's my cell."

"Will do."

She turns, making her way through the dining room and toward the sushi bar where the other thirty-something-year-old women she came in with are now sitting.

"Ready?" Londyn asks in a curt tone.

"Right. Of course." I rush to the door, opening it for her.

A tense silence settles between us as I walk Londyn to my car, then navigate the few miles to her condo. I try to make conversation, but she doesn't seem interested in talking. It's a stark contrast from the lighthearted atmosphere we've enjoyed all day. I have a feeling it has something to do with the fact I introduced her as my interior designer. Maybe I should have said friend, but the truth is, I don't know if we *are* friends. Don't know if she'll keep spending time with me after the renovation is done. And if I'm being honest with myself, that's why I've been dragging it out. Why I took today off. We're probably only a few weeks away from finishing. And the thought of no longer having an excuse to see Londyn guts me.

When I pull up in front of her place, I start to get out of the car to open her door for her, but she beats me to it.

"I can get it myself." She cracks the door open and jumps down before facing me, but she doesn't exactly look at me. "What time tomorrow, boss?"

I wince, officially regretting my decision to introduce her as my interior designer. I should have known better.

"Maybe we can do something else again?" I suggest, hoping she'll take my peace offering. "Maybe go to the SweetWater Brewery or something?"

"I think it's better if we just work on the house. Since I'm your *interior designer*."

"Londyn…" I sigh. "I—"

"No," she cuts me off, holding up her hand. "It's okay. I *am* just your interior designer. And as your interior designer, I'd like to get this project finished so I can move on."

I narrow my eyes, wanting to ask her if that's truly what she wants. Not just to finish the project, but if she really wants to only be my interior designer. But I don't.

"Nine o'clock okay? I can come get you around eight. I'm staying in town tonight and will head down in the morning."

"That's not necessary. I'll drive myself."

My lips part, and I'm on the verge of insisting to the contrary. But I don't want to press my luck. I promised I wouldn't push her. So I don't.

"Okay. Good night, Londyn."

"Good night." She starts to close the door, but stops. "And thanks for today," she adds.

I nod. "Any time."

Her gaze remains locked on mine for a protracted moment, as if she wants to say something more. But in true Londyn fashion, she seems to talk herself out of whatever it is.

Closing the door, she turns from me, hurrying up the walkway. When she disappears into the house without a single glance back, I expel a breath, resting my head on the steering wheel. How did I manage to fuck up what was nearly the perfect day? Will Londyn ever realize she deserves more than what she's afforded herself?

# CHAPTER TWENTY-FOUR

LONDYN

I collapse onto my couch, burying my head in my hands, wondering how today could have gone from being one of the best days I've had in a while to…whatever it was at the end.

I'd been enjoying Wes' presence. So much so that I didn't want our day to end. Then Sophia approached with her lush, brown hair, heart-stopping smile, and gorgeous body. Her gorgeous, *white* body. They looked perfect together. Like a real couple. It didn't help that they share a history and an obvious fondness for one another, even after not having seen each other in quite some time.

I shouldn't have been jealous. I never made any promises to Wes. In fact, I specifically made him promise he wouldn't wait around for me to sort out my shit. That he'd date other women if the opportunity arose.

But now the idea of Wes dating another woman isn't simply the abstract notion it's been the past few months. It *can* happen. I witnessed it myself.

Do I really want him to meet Sophia for coffee or drinks? What if drinks lead to dinner? What if dinner leads to something…more? Am I really willing to stand aside and watch that happen? I thought I was. I thought that was what I wanted.

Now the mere notion of someone else enjoying his kisses is like a vice squeezing my heart.

In the midst of my confusion and misery, my door flings open, as I should have expected. I snap my head up, a part of me wishing it were Wes calling me out on my bullshit. Instead, Hazel flies into my condo, her eyes alight with excitement. I'm assuming she saw him pick me up early this morning, then just drop me off. Or perhaps her husband, Diego, did. It doesn't matter. That's the thing about living next door to someone. They know all your secrets, whether you want them to or not.

"So how was your day?" She sits beside me, practically bouncing in her seat.

"Good," I reply with a smile, before my expression falls. "Then horrible."

She stops bouncing. "What happened? How did it go from good to horrible?"

"Wes surprised me with a trip to the flea market."

"Aww…" She collapses against the cushions, placing her hand over her heart as she feigns swooning. "To most people, I'd say to ditch the schmuck. But knowing you, I'd say that's the perfect day."

"It was," I agree. "Yet another reminder that when I talk, Wes actually listens."

"Trust me. That counts for a lot these days. I can't tell you how many men I've seen out on dates whose faces were buried in their cell phones. If all they wanted to do was look at their phone the entire time, they should have just stayed home."

"I rarely see Wes look at his phone around me," I remark thoughtfully. "Unless it rings and it's work-related, he ignores it. But so did Jay."

"And Wes *isn't* Jay," she admonishes. "Say it."

I roll my eyes. "Wes isn't Jay."

"Try it again. With meaning this time."

"Wes isn't Jay," I repeat, this time louder.

"Good. Now, where did you go after the flea market? As much as you love those, I doubt you spent twelve hours there."

"He took me to the art museum to check out a new exhibit I'd mentioned I wanted to see. Then we grabbed some sushi. Which is where we ran into this gorgeous brunette he was friends with as a kid. When he introduced me, he called me his *interior designer*."

"But isn't that what you are?" she asks in faux confusion, an expression that screams "I told you so" written on her face.

"I—"

"Didn't you specifically tell him that's all you wanted to be?" She crosses her arms in front of her chest.

"Yeah, but—"

"Then what did you expect, Londyn?"

"I don't know." I dig my fingers into my hair, feeling like a pre-teen obsessing over a single word the object of her affection said when passing each other in the hallway. Instead, I'm a twenty-seven-year-old woman obsessing over the man who's become an everyday part of my life labeling me as I insisted he do. "Maybe for him to introduce me as a friend."

"Or maybe you wish you were *more* than a friend."

"That's ridiculous," I retort, avoiding her analytical stare. "Like I told him, I'm not ready for a relationship. Not right now. Maybe not ever."

She remains silent for what seems like an eternity. "Can I be blunt for a moment?"

I snort. "Since when do you ask permission?"

"Figured it would be the polite thing to do. Because I'm calling you out, Lo. This excuse you've been giving him is bull-fucking-shit, and you know it."

"No, it's not. I—"

"It's the same excuse you've given to every other guy you've brought home, but I kept my mouth shut because I could tell whatever was going on in those relationships was one-sided. That you didn't feel that extra oomph you needed. And that's okay. But with this guy? That's not the case at all. You feel it. The spark. The electricity. The all-consuming yearning."

"Despite what you *think* you know about me, I'm not lying when I say I'm still sorting out my shit."

"Jesus Christ, Londyn." Throwing up her hands, she jumps to her feet. "Haven't you figured it out by now? We're all sorting out our shit. There is not one person walking this earth who has their shit together. I don't know what happened to make you think you needed to achieve some sort of idyllic level of perfection before you allowed yourself to be with someone else, but if you wait for that, you're going to be waiting for the rest of your life."

"I'm not waiting for perfection. I'm just trying to not be as broken."

"You are *not* broken." She rushes back to the couch, her

eyes awash with sincerity and empathy as she grips my biceps. "You need to stop letting what happened to you dictate the rest of your life. It sucks. I get it. And I can't even imagine what it must have felt like for your own father and husband to dismiss your claims as lies. But that doesn't mean everyone else is going to toss you out, too. Anyone worth your time will love every part of you. Even the fractured bits. The flawed bits. The dark bits. Because I'll tell you something... Those dark pieces of your soul that you think make you broken and unlovable? That's what's given you the strength to be where you are today. Be *who* you are today."

I swallow hard, unsure how to respond to Hazel's passionate plea. She's always been the one voice of reason in my life. I'm not sure I'm ready to take the last leap of faith I need, knowing how debilitating the fall can be when it doesn't work out.

"Tell me what's really holding you back, Lo."

"This thing with Wes is scary," I admit softly. "Petrifying."

"Now that I can work with." She drops her hold on me, settling back into the couch. "Tell Dr. Garcia," she mimics in a horrific German accent, making me laugh. "What scares you about the prospect of forming a relationship with Weston?"

I throw a pillow at her. "I can't take you seriously when you talk like that."

"Fine." Huffing, she flashes me a smile.

"What scares you about this?" she asks in her normal voice.

"Falling and him not being there when I hit bottom. When I need him the most."

"And I understand that. But let me ask you something. You told him everything that happened with Jay and your ex, and he didn't run for the hills. Did he?"

"No. Just the opposite."

"And these past few months, you've spent a lot of time with Wes, right?"

"Yeah."

"And not just at the house during renovations. You've done

other things, too, correct?"

"Yes."

"What kinds of things?"

I open my mouth to respond, then pause. "I don't see how this is relevant, Haze."

"Trust me. Tell me what things you two do when you get together outside of the house."

"Well, we've gone to the movies. Had dinner, both out and sometimes at his place. Gone to art galleries. You know. Normal stuff."

"Normal *couple* stuff."

I vehemently shake my head. "No. Normal *friend* stuff. Couples kiss and have sex. We don't."

"A relationship is more than just sex, Lo. It's sharing pieces of yourself. Letting the other person see the darkest parts of your soul, hoping they stand by your side while you search for the light. Sex is merely the icing on the cake. It's not the entire relationship. Hell, there are still some people who prefer not to have sex until they're married. Although I'm not one to buy a car without test driving it first, you can't say their relationship is any less valid because they choose to wait. Hell, do you really think people still have sex when they're ninety? I sure don't. But does that mean they're no longer in a relationship? Does that mean they no longer love each other?"

"What are you saying?" I ask hesitantly, unsure I'm ready to hear the answer I fear I've known all along but was happy to ignore.

She squeezes my hands, her eyes focused intently on mine. "I'm saying you and Wes *are* in a relationship. You just refuse to admit it."

"I don't—"

She holds up her hand, cutting me off. "Who helped you get over your fear of heights?"

I look away. "Wes," I mumble.

"And who comforted you after a snake almost killed you, according to you?"

"Wes," I repeat, my voice more aggravated.

"And who's been by your side while you confront your

191

biggest fear?"

"My biggest fear?"

"Yes. Who's been with you every step of the way as you learned to love again? Who showed you it's *okay* to love again?"

I hang my head, a heaviness in my chest at the idea. "I promised myself I'd never lower my walls for anyone again."

"You didn't have to. Because Wes was more than willing to scale those damn walls to possess your heart. And deep down, you know he possesses your heart. You know you love him."

I dart my eyes to hers, my chin trembling.

She wraps her arm around my shoulders, kissing the top of my head. "And I'm certain he loves you. It's why he goes out of his way to put a smile on your face every day. Why he didn't give up on you even when you'd given up on yourself." She pulls back, meeting my eyes. "So you need to ask yourself, Londyn. Are you going to stop letting your past haunt you? Or are you always going to use that as an excuse for not taking a risk?"

I chew on my lower lip, torn. "It's not that easy."

Hazel's brows furrow in contemplation, her mouth formed into a tight line. "Do you remember what you told me when you showed up to the first self-defense class? Your reason for attending?"

I slowly nod. "That I wanted to take back control of the parts of my life *he* took from me."

"Exactly." She beams. "And you've done that. You've taken back control of your professional life. And your sex life…to a certain extent. There's only one part of your life left. One part you've avoided, which is understandable after everything you went through. After I lost the boys, I couldn't even walk into a children's clothing store or pass the toy section in Target without breaking down. It was debilitating. I barely left the house, worried I'd see a child and lose it. I thought I'd never be normal again.

"But now, I'm able to do all those things I couldn't. Because I didn't avoid my fears. I knew I'd never be able to heal if I kept avoiding everything that triggered the memories of what

I lost. What did I always say in class?"

"Healing happens when you're triggered but have the strength to walk through the pain and toward a different path."

"Isn't that what you want? A new path where *he's* nothing more than a speck of dust?"

I look forward, blinking once, twice, my stomach churning at the thought of putting myself out there. Then I expel a long breath and pull myself up from the couch, grabbing my purse and keys off the coffee table.

"Where are you going?"

I shrug. "To take a leap of faith."

Her expression brightens, a wide smile tugging on her lips. "That's my girl."

# CHAPTER TWENTY-FIVE

LONDYN

My heart pounds with the intensity of a thousand drummers when I turn onto Wes' circular drive and park behind his Range Rover. I stare at the stone exterior of the house, faint light coming from a few windows on the second floor, everything picturesque, right down to the autumn wreath I'd made for him out of recycled items a few weeks ago.

Can I really do this? Can I take that final step, one I've avoided for years in order to protect myself from making the same mistake of trusting the wrong person?

But Hazel's right.

Wes didn't care I'd erected walls around myself. He happily scaled them, one frustrating and aggravating brick at a time. And with each brick, he possessed another piece of my heart. Now it's time to let him all the way in. To take that last step and rise above my past. Above my fear. Above everything that's held me back, causing me to repeat the same cycle year after year. It's time I finally take back control. And it starts with Wes.

Expelling a long breath, I shakily step onto the textured pavers, a force bigger than myself taking over, propelling me up the walkway and toward Wes' front door before I lose my nerve.

I bring my hand up to the door, my heart pounding in rhythm with my heavy rapping that echoes in the still night air. I listen for any movement from within, but don't immediately hear anything, apart from a few cars driving down a nearby street and a dog barking.

Then the door swings wide and Wes appears in front of me. I tear my eyes to his, words caught in my throat as I take in his appearance. He ditched the jeans and Henley for a white

194

t-shirt and plaid pajama bottoms that fall sinfully from his hips, his feet bare.

"Londyn," he breathes, pulling my attention back to him. "Are you okay?" Concern oozes from his voice as he steps forward, eyes skating over me.

"Yes. No. I..." Pausing, I lick my lips, smiling nervously. "Can I come in?"

"Of course." He moves aside, gesturing for me to walk ahead of him.

I continue into his mostly dark house, the only light coming from over the sink in the kitchen and the flames flickering in the gas fireplace in the living room.

"Would you like to sit down?" Wes gestures to the couch.

I shake my head. "I think I need to stand for this."

He stops as he's about to sit, straightening himself. "Okay." Widening his stance, his intense stare bores into me as he waits.

I can't imagine what must be going through his mind right now. What's so important that I drove over here to talk to him instead of just waiting until tomorrow? But this couldn't wait. He's waited long enough for me to realize what's been so obvious from the beginning, if I'd just opened my damn eyes. Now they're wide open. And I don't ever want to close them again.

"The thing is, Wes..." I pull my bottom lip between my teeth, trying to make sense out of my jumbled thoughts, everything fighting for attention. I want to say so many things, tell him everything I've kept from him for months. "When you introduced me as your interior designer earlier, it hurt."

His steps eat up the distance between us, eyes narrowed on me in apology. "I'm sorry, Londyn. I know I—"

"Please." I hold up my hand, cutting him off and stopping him from getting any closer. It's difficult enough to form a coherent thought as it is. "I need to get this out."

He blinks, then nods, giving me some space. "Okay."

"Okay." I take a deep breath as I pace in front of him. "I understand why you did that. After all, *I'm* the one who's constantly insisted we keep our relationship strictly

195

professional. Nothing more." I come to a stop, lifting my eyes to meet his, my pulse racing. "But I think we both know that's not true. You've never just been my client, have you?"

"I don't want to be," he answers softly, his tone even. "But I also promised I wouldn't wait for you. That I'd live my life, and you'd live yours."

"That you did." I step toward him. "But we both know you broke that promise."

"What makes you say that?"

"It's just a feeling. Something tells me this was all part of your plan. That you pretty much tricked me into dating you without realizing it."

"And what would you say if I did?" He holds his breath, as if my next statement will decide his fate. In a way, I suppose it does.

I take another step toward him, only a whisper between our bodies. My heart pounds violently, my stomach in knots.

"I'd thank you for making me realize I can have it all. The truth is, I don't want to be just your interior designer. But I don't want to be just your friend, either."

His jaw tightens, shoulders rising and falling with his increasingly unsteady breaths. I notice his fingers flinch, wanting to reach out and touch me. But he doesn't, the heat of him so close driving me to the edge of reason.

"What *do* you want, Londyn?"

"You, Wes," I admit with a quiver. "I want you. Nothing more. Nothing less."

"Nothing less," he repeats as he closes his eyes, pushing out a relieved breath.

When he returns his gaze to mine, it's fiery, yet ardent at the same time. He gradually lifts his hands toward me, giving me a chance to change my mind, to back out. But I'm done running from him. From love. I want to embrace everything he is and never look back.

Our chests heave in unison as he clutches my cheeks, a spark shooting through me.

"Is this okay?" he whispers huskily, just like he did when we first kissed.

And just like that night, I answer, "Yes."

His mouth inches closer, my insides tightening, my veins on fire with anticipation.

"Is this okay?" he asks again.

"Yes."

"And this?" His lips scrape delicately with mine, the barely-there touch making me thirsty for more.

"God, yes," I moan.

"I was hoping you'd say that."

He moves one hand to my waist, tugging me against him. Our kiss is tender at first as we test the connection we've both been missing these past few months. I can tell he's hesitant, not freely kissing me for fear I'll push him away. For fear it's too much, too soon. But I don't want to leave any doubt in his mind that this is what I want. That I choose to face my fears head-on. That I choose him.

Wrapping my arms around him, I curve closer, swiping my tongue along the seam of his mouth, begging for entry. He opens for me, and I deepen our exchange, clutching him tighter as I rub my body against his.

He growls, his grip on me tightening as he kisses me with more passion, more hunger, more intensity.

He pulls back slightly, breathing labored. "Goddamn," he hisses. "What the hell are you doing to me? I've never..." He licks his lips, seemingly at a loss for words. "Tell me you feel this, too. A hunger that you don't think you'll ever be able to satisfy."

"I feel this," I murmur, raising myself onto my toes, touching my lips to his. "But I do have a few ideas about how to satisfy you."

"Is that right?"

"That's right." I grab onto his t-shirt, peppering kisses along his jawline. "It involves a bed and losing these clothes."

His eyes flame as he crushes his mouth to mine in a bruising kiss. Desperate hands are everywhere, roaming, exploring, reacquainting ourselves with each other.

"I need you," I exhale, throwing my head back as he moves from my lips, sucking on that tender place where my earlobe meets my neck.

"I've needed you since the first time I saw you. Was desperate to know if you tasted as good as you smelled."

"Then why don't you find out."

"You don't have to ask me twice."

In one swift motion, he swoops me into his arms in a cradle hold, his determined strides carrying me up the stairs, my infectious laughter ringing through the house.

I try to take in my surroundings as he rushes down the long hallway of the second floor. I've never seen this part of his home before and don't want to miss anything. But Wes is a man on a mission, everything going by in a blur until he stops at the door at the end of the hall.

He pushes it open with his foot and walks inside the darkened bedroom, only a dim light in the reading area near the fireplace in the corner illuminating the space. My feet sink into the plush carpeting as he sets me on the floor beside the king-size bed. A few art pieces adorn the neutral gray walls, the simplicity matching that of the rest of the room.

"One second," Wes says as he steps from me and toward the reading nook. "Come on, Zeus. You're sleeping somewhere else tonight." When he whistles, the dog reluctantly pulls himself away from his bed, glancing at me, yawning as he walks toward the door.

"You're kicking him out?" I absentmindedly wonder how Zeus slept through me knocking when every other dog I've ever known would have been the first at the door, making a ruckus. Then again, Wes' bedroom is on the opposite end of the house. He probably didn't hear it all the way back here.

Closing the door, Wes smiles slyly as he returns to me. "With what we're about to do, I don't want to have any interruptions." He circles his waist against me, his arousal igniting the sparks within.

"And what are we about to do?"

"Jump, Londyn," he says sincerely. "We're about to jump. Do you trust me enough not to let you fall?"

There's not even a question in my mind. "I do." I hoist myself onto my toes, my lips seeking his. But instead of his mouth covering mine, he places a finger on it.

"But I'm going to warn you. If we do this, I won't let you push me away again. I will fight for you, tooth and nail. So unless you're ready to give me your mind..."

He brushes his lips against my temple, his gentle kiss sending a bolt of electricity through me.

"Your body..."

My eyelids flutter closed when he slides a finger across my cheek, along my jaw, and down my throat, before settling his hand over my chest.

"And your heart..."

I snap my eyes open, my gaze locking with his resolute and powerful stare.

"This isn't a passing fling for me. It never has been. So if you're not willing to finally let me in, I won't do this. Won't put myself through this again."

As he makes his plea to me, his voice is laced with pain. I don't know why it surprises me so much. Maybe because I had this vision of him leading the perfect life, able to have any woman he wants. But now that I know the ache he still carries from having his heart broken, I can understand why he'd be hesitant. We've both been hurt by people we once trusted, but in different ways.

Regardless, Wes is ready to jump in feet first, take a risk on something that scares the shit out of him. Just like he helped me forget about my fear of heights on that Ferris wheel, like he soothed me after that snake slithered over me, like he risked his own life when I was seconds away from getting hit by a truck, I know I can face my fears with him at my side.

Placing my hand over his on my chest, I squeeze. "It's yours, Wes. Just... Promise you'll be gentle with it. You don't understand the kind of power you hold over me."

"It's the same power you hold over me. You have my word. I'll keep it safe. Keep *you* safe."

A lone teardrop slides down my cheek. "That's all I need to know."

He covers my lips with his and places a hand on the small of my back, steering me toward the bed and lowering me onto the surface. Wrapping my legs around his waist, I run my fingers up and down his back, reveling in the tautness of his muscles against my hands. He tears away from me, chest heaving as he rips off his t-shirt. He's about to lower himself back to me, but I stop him, pressing my hand to his chest.

"What's wrong?" he asks frantically.

I raise myself to sitting. "I want to look at you."

"Is that right?" He smirks, eyes dancing with delight in the darkness.

Biting my lower lip, I nod.

"Okay then. I'm at your complete disposal." He leans back, kneeling on the mattress.

I adjust my position, scrambling to my knees. When I scrape my fingers down his firm muscles, he releases a hiss.

"God, your touch drives me crazy."

I glance down at his pajama pants. "I see that."

Emboldened, I smooth my hand down the hard planes of his defined abs, my motions slow as I examine his body before landing on his erection. He inhales sharply.

Leaning into him, I take his earlobe between my teeth. "I *feel* that."

Desperation takes over, and he palms my back, yanking me against him, his kiss hot and heavy as his free hand roams my frame. Grasping the hem of my sweater, he pulls out of our kiss long enough to lift it over my head before slamming his mouth back to mine.

I moan, the sensation of flesh against flesh causing the flames inside me to burn hot and impervious. Mouth to mouth. Chest to chest. Heart to heart.

He reaches around me, deftly unhooking my bra. His stare penetrates my skin and pierces my soul as he leisurely lowers the straps down my arms.

He gently cups my face in his hand, the gesture at complete odds with the ferocity with which he just kissed me. I melt into him, closing my eyes, basking in the affection vibrating through him.

"If it's too much at any point, tell me to stop. Okay?"

"Wes," I begin, my chest heaving as desire scorches through

my veins.

"Yes?"

I dig my fingers into his hair, pulling his face toward mine. "Don't stop."

With a groan, he presses his mouth to mine. This kiss is less hungry, but still brimming with need. His hand moves to my back as he lowers me to the mattress once more, settling between my thighs.

He pulls back, his eyes briefly locking with mine before appreciating the rest of my body. His light touch roams my frame. When he ghosts against a nipple, I inhale sharply, the slight grazing of his hand against the sensitive skin scalding me.

"Is this okay?" he murmurs seductively.

"Yes," I exhale, desperation building inside me. I'm not sure how much more of this I can take. It's the sweetest torture. The cruelest oblivion.

With slow movements, he lowers his mouth to my chest, teasing my nipple.

"Is this okay?" he repeats.

"God, yes." I melt into the mattress, savoring this temporary bliss. But the warmth of his mouth on my breast only increases my craving to feel him on other parts of me. "More."

When he bares his teeth, scrapping slightly, I yelp, then moan, digging my nails into his back. He arches into me, his breathing ragged.

"I need to taste you. Can I do that?"

"You don't need to ask. I'm yours."

He treats me to another impassioned kiss. "Mine."

"Yours."

"Mine," he says once more, then meets my gaze. "But for the record. I will *always* ask for your permission. *Always*."

"Always," I repeat as he travels from my lips, taking his time to enjoy every inch of me. From the swell of my breasts, to the dip of my belly button, to the curve of my hips, worshipping me as if I'm a goddess and he's come to give thanks at my altar.

As he reaches my waist, he looks up at me, a question drawn on his face.

I nod quickly, raising my hips so he can slide off my jeans and panties. After tossing them onto the floor, he returns to me, caressing my stomach, something in his gaze as he admires me. Something I've seen for a while now but refused to admit. Something so much more potent than respect or veneration, although those things are there, too. It's the same look I saw my father bestow upon my mother. The same look I've always wanted a man to bestow upon me.

This man loves me. He may not have said those words yet, but there's no mistaking it.

"Wes, I…"

His eyes search mine. "Are you okay?"

"I'm okay. Better than okay. I…" I trail off, steeling myself for what I'm about to do. But just like with the Ferris wheel and snake, I know Wes will be by my side while I confront this last fear. "I… I love you."

He stills, gaze widening, my declaration ringing out between us.

"You don't have to say it back," I continue quickly. "It's okay if you don't feel the same or aren't ready to say it yet. I just… After months…hell, *years* of keeping all my feelings locked up, I don't want to do that anymore. I'm turning over a new leaf. And I wanted to tell you. Thought you deserved to know."

A smile curves his mouth as he delicately brushes his lips with mine. "Do you really think I would have done everything I have these past few months if I didn't love you?"

I release a nervous laugh. "Probably not."

He pushes a few curls away from my face. "You captivated me the moment I felt you in my arms. I knew you were different. Knew you would be the last woman I'd ever love. So to answer you, I am hopelessly, madly, and completely in love with you, Londyn Bennett."

"Oh, Wes," I exhale as I wrap my legs around him, forcing his lips against mine.

Our exchange turns heated as I circle my hips, his erection

straining against his pajama bottoms causing fire to rush through me when he rubs against me.

"I need you. Don't make me wait any longer."

"Your wish is my command," he replies slyly and snakes down my frame, kissing and caressing as he goes, my legs loosening their grip around his waist. With each inch he travels, the more ragged my breathing, my core tightening with the promise of what's to come.

When he settles between my thighs, he floats his gaze to mine, a devilish glint within. "You have no idea how long I've fantasized about this."

"Is that right?" I smirk.

He slowly nods. "That's right."

"Then what are you waiting for?" I ask breathlessly. "A written invitation?"

"Just prolonging the moment. I don't want this to end any time soon." When his finger skims my center, I moan, sparks shooting through me. "Is this okay?" he asks as he rubs my clit.

"Yes." I struggle to catch my breath, a myriad of sensations filling me. I pulse against him, desperate to feel more of him. To feel all of him.

He inserts a finger inside me, the ache building more and more as I increase my motions.

"Is this okay?"

"Yes," I moan, squirming in anticipation. I peer down at him, his own gaze trained on me as he lowers his mouth toward me. At the first flick of his tongue against my clit, I push out my held breath, muscles relaxing as all the tension that's been building for months rolls off me.

"Is this okay?" he asks one last time.

"God, yes."

"That's my girl." He returns his mouth to me.

His touch is commanding, enticing, intoxicating. Every swipe of his tongue, every plunge of his fingers, every vibration of his moans propels me closer to that point of complete and utter oblivion.

"Your girl," I repeat as I thread my fingers through his hair, moving my hips with the rhythm he sets, euphoria filling me. So profound. So poignant. So powerful.

"That's right, baby." He increases his motions, inserting another finger, stretching and massaging me with a mixture of hunger and benevolence. "Let me feel you."

When his mouth covers me once more, it sends me over the edge. My toes curl. My back arches. My pulse skyrockets. I clench the sheets beneath me, my cries of pleasure reverberating against the walls as I come undone in front of this man. This beautiful, patient man.

As I try to return to earth, I quiver, every inch of me overly sensitive and throbbing.

But I still need more.

"Come here," I order, pulling him up.

With a devious grin, he follows my command, slithering up my body. Craning forward, I slam my lips against his, tasting myself on his tongue.

"God, I want you," he breathes into me.

"And I want you. I need you."

"And I need you." He pulls back. "There's just one problem."

"Problem?"

"Well, I didn't exactly plan for this. I don't have any condoms."

"I'm on the pill," I tell him. "After everything, I—"

He cups my cheek, cutting me off with a kiss. "It's in the past. It doesn't matter. Not here. Not when it's us. Okay?"

"Okay."

"Okay." He captures my mouth with another kiss, circling his hips against me.

I scrape my nails down his back, needing to get rid of the last barrier between us. Finding the waist of his pajama pants, I start to shove them down his legs. He breaks away, kicking them the rest of the way off before returning to me. When his erection rubs against me, I moan, needing more of him. Needing all of him.

Our kiss is reckless, teeth clashing as we take everything we can from each other, nothing extinguishing the flame that's been building since that first meeting. Wes slowly moves against me, tempering my own frantic motions, and I whimper. Our kiss becomes less desperate, more ardent, genuine, heartfelt.

He places a soft kiss on the corner of my lips, then leans back, bringing his erection up to me, spreading my desire around. I close my eyes and lift my hips, silently telling him what I need.

"Open your eyes, Londyn." His tone is a mix between a demand and a plea.

I follow his request.

"I need you to stay with me." He kisses me sweetly. "Need your eyes on me. Okay?"

"Okay." I fight the urge to close my eyes when he rubs himself against my clit, causing another wave of desire to wash over me.

"No going back," he reminds me.

I shake my head. "No going back."

There's something so intimate about our gazes being locked as he eases inside me. My chest heaves, my breathing increasing, this moment more profound than I thought it would be.

"Okay?" he asks.

I nod.

He leans toward me. "I need to hear you say you're okay. I don't want to hurt you."

"You're not. I've done this before," I joke, trying to lighten the mood.

"I'm not talking about physically, Londyn." He brings his hand to my chest, covering my heart. "I'm talking about here. Are you okay here? We don't have to do this if you're not ready."

"I'm ready. I'm okay."

He covers my mouth with his, then pushes the rest of the way in, filling me to the hilt and pausing at the point of absolute bliss, both of us reveling in the sensation as we exhale simultaneously.

He retreats before pushing back into me again, this time

going a little farther. I gasp, an electric shock traveling straight to my core.

"Too much?"

I swallow hard. "Again," I plead.

He groans, burying his head in the crook of my neck, his unshaven jaw causing an ache to build.

"Do you have any idea how good you feel? So warm. So perfect."

I arch into him, signaling with my body what I need.

When he thrusts into me, I exhale, my nails clawing into his back. "Oh god."

"More?"

"Yes."

He withdraws, his motions slow, before driving into me again, my eyes widening at how deep he goes. A shiver rolls through me, my breathing labored. He leans back, a mischievous glint in his eyes as he swipes his tongue against his thumb, then lowers it to my clit, circling it.

"Wes..." I close my eyes, losing myself in the sensation, chasing the euphoria that swells inside me.

"Eyes on me," he reminds me, his voice gruff.

I snap my gaze back to his, my pulse skyrocketing when I see the raw desire within.

He meets my motions, his thrusts becoming less gentle and more frantic. Nothing has ever felt so perfect, so fulfilling, so satisfying. It isn't just the physical connection. It's the emotional. I've never experienced something so strong, so incredible. And it's because I've finally met someone I can be vulnerable around. Someone who knows my scars, my faults, and doesn't judge me because of them. He sees them for what they are. Part of the fabric that makes me who I am. And for the first time, I'm proud of who I am. Of everything I had to overcome to get to this point.

"I won't last much longer," Wes pants, nibbling and tugging on my bottom lip. "You feel too fucking good, Lo."

"Then let go," I murmur.

"Not until you do."

"I don't think—"

"Don't fight it. Let yourself go. Let me feel you clench around me," he growls through his heavy breaths.

His tone mixed with his words is all I need to tip me over the edge. I scream out his name, waves and waves of my orgasm cresting and crashing. When I think I'm about to come down, Wes drives into me with more intensity, pushing me higher once more until he grunts, jerking through his own release, my name on his tongue like an erotic benediction as it echoes in the room.

He collapses on top of me, our hearts crashing against each other in a thunderous rhythm. Our bodies are slick with sweat and sex, but I wouldn't have it any other way. This was raw and real and exactly how it needed to be between us.

"Are you still with me?" he pants.

"I'm still with you."

"Good." He exhales a satisfied sigh. Then he leaves a kiss on my temple. "Don't move." Extracting himself from me, he slides off the bed and makes his way into the bathroom, returning a few seconds later with a towel. I reach for it, but he shakes his head. "Allow me."

I had no problem letting him come inside me, but the idea of him cleaning me up feels so intimate. *Too* intimate.

"You don't have to. I can——"

"I know you can. But I want to take care of you. Let me take care of you. Please?"

I swallow hard at the desperation in his tone. I nod, keeping my gaze trained on his as he brings the towel between my thighs and wipes away the evidence of what we've just done. After cleaning himself off, he joins me on the bed, draping an arm around my waist and dragging me to him, my back to his front.

"You okay?"

I laugh. "You keep asking that."

"And I'll keep asking. I don't want you to have a single regret when it comes to me."

Turning in his embrace, I brush my lips against his. "*Non. Je ne regrette rien*, as the great Edith Piaf would say. Or sing, as it were."

"I didn't know you spoke French."

"I was an art history major. It was highly recommended we study a variety of classical languages. Spanish. Italian. French."

"And you're fluent?"

"I know the important phrases."

"Like what?"

"*Je t'aime.*"

He sighs into me. "*Je t'aime*," he repeats in an unrefined French accent mixed with his smooth Southern.

Unlike my professor, who would have scolded him for his bastardization of the beautiful language, I don't care about the inflection. That's not important. The meaning behind the words is the only thing that is.

"I love you, Londyn."

"And I love you, Wes. Hopelessly. Madly. Completely."

# CHAPTER TWENTY-SIX

WESTON

A scratching sound stirs me and I open my eyes, a pair of dark orbs staring back at me instead of the normal emptiness that greets me when I wake up in the morning.

"Were you watching me sleep?" I ask, hooking a leg over Londyn's waist and bringing her closer. The dim sunlight streams along her delicate features, making her appear ethereal.

She settles against my chest, toying with a few tufts of hair. "Maybe."

"Any reason for that?"

"I like watching you sleep. You look so…peaceful."

She has no idea how true her words are. I can't remember the last time I've slept through the night without waking up every few hours. But last night, I didn't wake up once. If Zeus hadn't scratched on the door, needing to go out, I'd probably still be asleep.

"I feel at peace," I exhale. Pinching her chin, I tilt her head back. "Like I'm finally where I'm supposed to be. Like *you're* exactly where I'm supposed to be."

She feathers her lips against mine, her kiss sweet and tender, yet just as toe-curling and soul-fulfilling as the way she kissed me last night.

"You're exactly where I'm supposed to be, too," she murmurs as Zeus paws at the door again, this time followed by a whimper. "But right now, I think you need to let your dog out."

"I think you're right," I groan, burying my head in her hair, hating the idea of leaving her, even for a minute. "But what I wouldn't give to stay in this bed with you." I circle my hips against her.

"Down boy." She pinches my side. "How about this. You

go let Zeus outside before he ruins your carpet. Then we can spend the rest of today in this bed… Clothing optional." She winks.

"I like the sound of clothing optional." Running my hand along the contours of her frame, I cup her ass and squeeze. "I like the *feel* of clothing optional."

"I knew you would. Now go." She playfully swats me away.

"Yes, ma'am." I leave her with a deep kiss, then slide out of bed.

As I pull on my pajama bottoms, she rolls onto her side, propping her head in her hand, shamelessly watching me. I can't help but smile at how comfortable she seems in my bed, the duvet draped casually along her waistline. She doesn't even try to cover her exposed chest. Which only makes it even more difficult to leave her. But I'd rather not waste a single second of today by cleaning up after Zeus.

Returning to her, I lean down and place one last kiss on her nose before walking out of the room, Zeus excitedly following and barking as I make my way downstairs. He all but knocks me to the floor when I open the sliding glass door, darting through my legs and into the freshly mowed back yard, causing the few birds perched on the top of the portico to disperse.

"Dopey dog," I muse. It's what I get for bringing home a stray dog that had been frequenting one of my firm's construction sites after I first moved back to Atlanta.

I never fancied myself a dog person, my life normally too busy and hectic to take care of one. But he kept following me around, something drawing him to me. After I brought him to the vet and learned he had a nasty case of heartworm that would kill him if left untreated, I knew I couldn't let the poor guy suffer. So I paid for his treatment, left him at the vet for a few days, then brought him home. It's almost like he knew we needed each other. He needed someone to take care of him. And I needed someone to help me get over losing Brooklyn.

While Zeus does his business, I pad into the kitchen and start a cup of coffee. A buzz sounds, and I unplug my phone from the charger on the counter, unlocking the screen. The first thing I usually do in the morning is answer the myriad of emails waiting for me. But not today. I deserve a day off. A *real* day off when I don't even think about work. I haven't taken one of those in years.

Instead, I open up my latest text exchange with Julia and type out a new message to her.

**Wes:** Mission accomplished, Jules.

Her reply comes almost instantly.

**Julia:** Mission accomplished? As in the thing you've been working on for the past few months? And not Gampy and Meemaw's house?

**Wes:** Yes. Londyn is here. In my bed, to be exact.

**Julia:** Then why the hell are you texting me? Go spend time with her.

**Wes:** I plan on it. I had to let the dog out and am making her coffee, but I wanted to update you.

**Julia:** I'm happy for you. Just don't fuck it up. Better yet, don't let Lydia fuck it up.

**Wes:** I'll do my best. I'll call you later.

**Julia:** Sounds good. Love you.

**Wes:** Love you, too. Give Imogene lots of hugs and kisses from me. And from Zeus.

**Julia:** You got it.

I set my phone back down and start making the second cup of coffee. Spotting Zeus standing by the back door, I let him in, then pour some kibble into his bowl.

As I'm preparing Londyn's coffee the way I noticed she orders it when we're together, there's a knock on my front door. I straighten, wondering who'd be here at ten o'clock on a Sunday morning.

"Weston, darling," my mother's shrill voice sounds. "It's me."

I expel a breath, pinching the bridge of my nose. She's the absolute *last* person I want to see, even more so than usual, considering Londyn's upstairs.

"I know you're home, Weston," she continues when I don't immediately respond. "Your car's out front."

"So is another," I mutter under my breath, which is probably the reason my mother chose to stop by today when I haven't seen her in months.

These days, I tend to avoid her at all costs. I put on a smile and remain cordial in public, but the rift she caused after her treatment of Brooklyn in front of my friends and family — in front of *Brooklyn's* friends and family — isn't one I think will ever be repaired. Not unless she finally admits she was wrong and apologizes, something she'll never do.

Wanting to get this over with sooner rather than later, I trudge to the front door and pull it back.

"Well, it's about time," she huffs, pushing past me and into my house as if she owns it, dressed in a navy blue skirt suit reminiscent of Jackie O.

I tower over her by nearly a foot, but I'd learned appearances can be deceiving. She may be petite with perfectly coifed, dyed blonde hair and kind blue eyes, but she's as vindictive as they come.

"And is that how you answer the door?" Her analytical gaze scans my frame that's clad only in a pair of pajama pants. "It's indecent, Weston. I raised you better than this."

Zeus chooses this moment to take a break from eating, growling and barring his teeth. He's usually a gentle, loving dog, one that can't even kill a lizard when he's lucky enough to catch one. The only person he hates is my mother. Then again, I've always found dogs to be rather astute judges of character.

"Zeus, stop," I admonish.

He looks at me, as if asking if I'm serious. Even he doesn't think my mother deserves my attention.

"And as far as your concerns about the way I dress, this is *my* home. If I want to walk around naked, I have the freedom to do that. So why don't you tell me why you're here so we can get this over with." I cross my arms in front of my chest, leaning against the large kitchen island.

"I was on my way to brunch with a few of the ladies from church. I noticed your car was in the driveway, like I said, and decided to stop by, since you haven't been around much lately. I suppose you find it more important to spend your Sundays at that old shack as opposed to attending church like the good Christian I raised you to be."

The one benefit from growing up around someone as phony and pretentious as my mother is she taught me how to fake it like the best of them. So, instead of rolling my eyes so hard they practically pop out of their sockets at her insinuation of being anywhere near a devout woman, I simply smile.

"Is that the only reason? To say hi and berate me on my lackluster church attendance when I've never exactly been a big believer?"

"I can't stop by to see my son?"

"I've been around long enough to know you don't do anything that doesn't benefit you. So why are you really here?"

She opens her mouth, feigning indignation, then quickly snaps her jaw shut. "As it turns out, Caroline de la Roche is home for the weekend. She's recently divorced. It's not ideal, but I suppose when you get up there in age, as you are, you can't be as choosy as you once were. She's coming to brunch with her mother. I thought it would be beneficial for you to attend, as well."

"I'll tell you the same thing I have every time you've tried to set me up with another one of your friend's daughters. I'm not interested." I turn from her, hoping she takes the hint and ends the conversation. But I should know better than that. She's almost as stubborn as I am. But what makes it worse is she's also extremely narcissistic.

"When *are* you going to be interested, Weston? People are

213

talking. It's not right for a man of your age with your upbringing to still be single. Some say you're gay. Others claim you're in love with Julia because of how close you are."

I whirl around, my eyes on fire. "She's my *sister*. Who the hell are you hearing this stuff from anyway?"

"That's not even the worst of them," she continues, relentless in her search for the truth.

"Oh really? What's next?" I gesture down to the dog. "That I'm in love with Zeus here? Because, while we do share a bed on occasion, his rank morning breath doesn't do it for me." I give her a sarcastic smile.

"Don't be ridiculous, Weston," she chides.

I lean toward her. "What's ridiculous is your friends and their unusual occupation with my social life. It's completely normal for a man over the age of thirty to be single. Hell, I don't know if I even want to be married."

She looks at me, aghast. "Why wouldn't you want to get married?"

"Because you and Dad are *so* happy?" I shoot back. "Sorry to be the one to tell you this, but the two of you never exactly set a shining example of a happy marriage. You're more like a walking advertisement for why you *shouldn't* get married."

She blinks repeatedly, incensed at the idea of anyone questioning her. "That's not the point."

"Then what *is* the point?"

She hesitates, pinching her thin, pink lips together, debating her next statement. "Well, if you must know, Helena Beaumont said something this morning that caught my attention."

"I'm sure this will be life-changing."

"She mentioned she saw you at the art museum yesterday."

My face heats, my expression falling. I have a feeling I know where this conversation is headed, and I don't like it. "That sounds right," I respond evenly. "I was there."

She edges closer, her voice low. "She also said you were with a woman. A negro."

I narrow my gaze on her, my stare turning icy. "Mother, I'm fairly certain that term went out of style four or five decades ago. And that *negro*, as you put it, is a wonderful woman named Londyn. I'd appreciate it if you used her name."

Her eyes widen, face blanching. "So you're not denying it then?"

"Denying what?" I lean against the island, acting as cavalier as possible, knowing it will piss her off even more.

"Are you carrying on with her?" she whispers, as if the mere idea makes it difficult for her to speak.

With a smirk, I grab one of the coffee mugs and bring it to my lips. "Define carrying on."

"Did you get lost?" a soft voice interrupts.

My mother and I simultaneously dart our attention toward the hallway, the padding of delicate footsteps growing closer.

"We were supposed to spend all day in bed together. You're really cutting into our naked—"

As Londyn rounds the corner and sees I'm not alone, she comes to an abrupt stop, inhaling sharply. At least she had the wherewithal to grab one of my button-down shirts and slipped it on. Otherwise, this probably would have been more awkward than it already is. But I don't care about making my mother comfortable. I'm no longer interested in putting her happiness above my own. That ship has sailed.

Giving Londyn a reassuring smile, I grab her coffee and hand it to her. A dozen questions swirl in her eyes, but the last thing I want is for her to doubt the promises I made last night.

I place a kiss on her forehead, then wrap an arm around her and pull her close, much to my mother's astonishment.

"Mother, I'd like to introduce you to Miss Londyn Bennett. She's the interior designer I hired to restore Gampy and Meemaw's 'shack', as you call it, although I'd be hard-pressed to call the place of so many wonderful memories a 'shack'. She's also my girlfriend."

I take a sip of coffee, gauging both Londyn's and my mother's reaction. I'm more concerned with Londyn's, though, considering we haven't exactly discussed any labels.

"Your...girlfriend?" My mother grimaces, as if the word leaves a sour taste on her tongue.

"Yes. Although, if I'm being honest, the term feels woefully inadequate to properly convey what Londyn has become to me." I smile down at her, ignoring the heated stare coming from a few feet away.

"But what will people think, Weston?" my mother hisses, forcing my attention back to her. "Think about the firm."

"The firm?" I ask, unsure I heard her correctly.

"What will some of our clients think if they learned you're dating a…a…"

Muscles tensing, I tighten my grip on Londyn when she attempts to slink away. I knew I'd eventually have to face this. After all, the family my mother married into has never exactly been accepting of anyone who isn't white. Some of them probably wouldn't object if we re-instituted slavery. But I'd hoped she would wait to voice her ill-placed concerns until we were in private. Then again, nothing should surprise me with her anymore.

"A what, Mother? A beautiful, smart, kind, compassionate, amazing woman?"

"You know what I'm talking about," she states, treating Londyn with disinterest, acting as if she isn't even in the room. "You're more than aware that some of the firm's longest and highest paying clients have certain…predispositions."

"I am. And if they take issue with the fact that I'm in love with someone who's not white, then they're not the type of people I want to be associated with in the first place. Not the type of people I want the firm associated with."

She balks, peering at me as if I just sprouted another head. "In love?" she mocks. "You can't be serious, Weston."

"Oh, I'm *very* serious." I maintain eye contact with her, making it more than apparent I won't back down. Not this time. Not when it comes to Londyn. "So if there's nothing more you need, I suggest you leave before you say something you'll regret."

"Is this any way to treat your mother?" she retorts. "I raised you to treat people with respect."

"Actually, Gampy and Meemaw raised me, since you were usually too busy getting your hair done or gossiping with your catty friends. And do you know what they taught me? That respect must be earned. I'm sorry to disappoint you, Mother, but you haven't earned my respect in years. I'm not sure you ever have. So until you treat everyone in my life with respect, including Londyn and Julia, I won't bestow that honor on you." I glower at her.

"I..." She blinks repeatedly, struggling to come up with some sort of argument in response, something to make her appear deserving of respect.

I doubt she's done anything out of the kindness of her heart in years, preferring to trample over people in order to feel superior. That's just who she is. She uses people as stepping stones to get what she wants. She doesn't form close bonds. In her eyes, everyone's disposable, including her own parents. It's a wonder she's still married to my father. Then again, his bank account is reason enough for her.

"If there's nothing else you need," I say when she doesn't make a move, "please leave. I have no tolerance for your lack of compassion."

She pins me with a glare, the seconds stretching. Finally, she spins around, storming out of my house and slamming the door behind her, causing the wine glasses hanging below the cabinets to rattle.

I blow out a breath, setting my mug onto the counter. Facing Londyn, I run my hands down her arms. "I'm sorry about that. I shouldn't have answered the door. I should—"

Before I can complete my thought, she grips the back of my head, the harshness of her hold cutting me off. "Shut up and kiss me." She yanks my mouth toward hers.

"You don't have to ask me twice." I crash my lips against hers, our tongues tangling as I pull her closer. My hands roam her frame, something about her in my clothes turning me on more than I thought it would. When my hand disappears under the shirt and I discover she's not wearing any panties, I harden.

Gripping her ass, I hoist her onto the counter, her kiss scalding and intoxicating as I pulse against her. I tear away from her, peppering kisses along the length of her throat, her skin salty and sweet.

"No one's ever stood up for me like that," she exhales huskily, losing herself in my touch. "It's such a fucking turn-on."

With an animalistic desire, she returns her blazing eyes to mine and reaches for my waist, shoving my bottoms down my hips.

My pulse skyrockets, everything about this completely unexpected. Then again, Londyn is the most unexpected thing I've ever experienced.

I never intended to fall for her, just like she never intended to fall for me. But we fell. Now, I never want to return from this sweet place of exhilaration where all the problems we're sure to face will never find us.

Like we just got a taste of with my mother, this won't be easy. Despite it being the twenty-first century, there will be people who won't like the idea of us together, especially in my typical social circles. We've made it this far, though. And as long as we're together, I have faith we'll get through anything life throws at us.

Our chests heave in unison as I bring my erection up to her center, rubbing her desire around. She keeps her eyes trained on me, just like I asked her to last night. Her pupils dilate, need radiating from her.

I'm about to ease inside her when she places her hand on my chest, stopping me.

"What's wrong?" I ask.

A sly smile quirks on her lips. "Don't be gentle this time."

I swallow hard. "Are you sure?"

"Wes, I'm not this delicate piece of glass you'll break if you exert too much pressure. Maybe I used to feel like I was broken, but I don't anymore. I've never been with someone I felt comfortable enough around to explore my sexuality. Sawyer always made me feel like there was something wrong with me if I wanted to change things up or try something new. But now I know what sex can be like. And last night was incredible. Better than incredible. I want to explore everything we're capable of. I'm finally with someone I trust. Who will never hurt me. Who loves me. So, please…"

Her gaze resolute, she slowly unbuttons her shirt, her motions drawn out. With each button she unfastens, my hunger grows to the point I don't think I'll make it inside her before I lose my head. It's not the fact she's baring her body to me that has my desire ratcheting up to its breaking point. It's that she's baring her soul to me.

Curving toward me, she nibbles on my lower lip. "Be free with me." She shrugs the shirt off her shoulders, allowing it to pool behind her on the counter. Then she spreads her thighs wider, leaning back on her hands, giving me permission to do whatever my heart desires.

"If it's too much, tell me. Don't think you have to do this for me."

"I don't. For the first time in my life, I want to do this. For me." She hooks her legs around me, erasing any space separating us. Then she wraps her fingers around my erection, stroking it as she brings it toward her entrance. She thrusts her hips at the same time as she tightens her legs, urging me inside in one quick motion.

"Fuck," I hiss, a jolt of desire striking me deep in my core.

"That's the point, Wes." She digs her nails into my back, and I briefly close my eyes, savoring the combination of pleasure and pain shooting through me. "I want you to fuck me."

My chest rises and falls with my uneven breaths. I fight the urge to ask if she's sure. I don't have to. I see it in the hard determination in her eyes.

Cupping her cheeks, I draw her lips to mine, plunging my tongue into her mouth as I move inside her, slowly at first. I worry if I don't take my time, this will be over in a heartbeat. And I don't want this moment to end.

"I love you," I murmur against her lips as I withdraw, then drive into her.

Her breathing grows ragged, her grip on my back becoming harsher. I repeat the motion, going even deeper as I whisper the same incantations of love.

"Again," she begs against my throat.

"I love you," I say once more, driving into her again. But this time, I don't draw it out, thrusting into her in a punishing rhythm.

"Oh god," she moans, wrapping her legs tighter around me, meeting me thrust for thrust.

My nostrils flare, my muscles clench, my mind a haze as I'm driven by one thing and one thing alone. This incredible, remarkable woman whose path crossed mine. I don't know how or what I did to have luck finally turn in my favor, but I'll forever be grateful.

"Come on, honeybee." I nibble on her neck, addicted to the taste of her flesh.

My legs ache, but nothing will make me stop this now. Any lingering soreness will be worth it when I feel her clench around me. And I can sense she's fighting it, wanting this to last.

"Let me have it. Let me feel what I do to you." I bring my lips back to hers, our breath intermingling. "Be free with me."

"Wes," she whimpers as her orgasm takes over, causing her to writhe and quiver, her cries echoing against the tall ceilings of my home. It's all I need to set me off. I release inside her with a strangled groan, crashing my mouth against hers.

I slow my motions, our kiss transitioning from one of desperation and hunger to respect and veneration. Then she giggles.

Pulling back, I tilt my head. "What's that for?"

She smirks. "Honeybee?"

"Sorry." I run a hand through my hair. "I've been wanting to call you that since our first kiss. I'll stop if you don't like it."

"I think it's sweet. Just wondering if there's a story behind it."

I rest my forehead on hers. "Because your nectar is sweeter than honey…honeybee."

# CHAPTER TWENTY-SEVEN

LONDYN

"As much as I'm kind of digging this blindfold," Wes says as I keep his hands in mine, leading him from his Range Rover and toward Gampy and Meemaw's house, fallen leaves crunching under our feet, "I'd rather you be the one blindfolded." He smiles slyly.

I laugh. I may not be able to see his eyes, but I can picture them heating.

"Plus, I helped with the remodel," he continues. "I know what it looks like inside. This is completely unnecessary if you ask me."

I stop walking as we approach the front porch. "Maybe I just wanted to put a blindfold on you."

"Is that right?" He curves toward me, seeking my lips, but I remain just out of reach, taunting and teasing.

"It was part of my plan so I can have my wicked way with you." I trail a finger down his chest, stopping just shy of his belt. "And while you did help with the remodel, I banished you earlier this month while I put all the finishing touches on everything. Trust me. This house looks nothing like it did the last time you saw it. Now, watch your step coming up the porch."

I help him up the short flight of stairs, through the door, and into the foyer, positioning him beside Julia and Imogene, who wear blindfolds of their own.

While I'd hoped to have an extra week to do the big reveal around Thanksgiving, when I learned they were coming into town early so Julia could help with the large amount of holiday orders at her Atlanta bakery, I pulled several all-nighters to get the house finished before they arrived. I still can't believe it hasn't even been three months since I've last seen them. Or that Wes and I have only been together a little more than a month. It seems like it's been so much longer. Probably because, for all intents and purposes, we started dating back during the summer. I just hadn't admitted it.

"Okay." I clap my hands together, bouncing on the balls of my feet, nervous and excited to see what they think of all my hard work over the last several months, especially these past few weeks. "You can remove your blindfolds."

Imogene rips hers off, Wes and Julia following suit. I simply stand back and soak in their reaction.

"Oh, my god...," Julia breathes, looking up at the high ceiling of the entryway where a lantern-style chandelier now hangs, welcoming everyone who enters. "Is this even the same house?" Her chin trembles as she soaks in Gampy and Meemaw's remodeled home.

"Let's start in the living room." I walk from the foyer and through a pair of open French doors leading to the hallway, a touch I'd seen in many other Southern homes of this style.

"Is this...," Julia interrupts.

I stop, grinning when I see her gaze fixated on the scattered frames I'd hung in the hallway. "I repurposed some of the trim we ripped out. Made them into frames." I gesture to the matting. "And I was able to save some of the original wallpaper."

"And the photos?" Her voice catches.

"Wes helped." I flash him a smile, nothing but admiration and pride in his gaze as he finally sees what I did with the photos I'd asked him to find. It's a wall of memories. Some of Meemaw and Gampy. Some of Wes and Julia during their childhood. Hazel helped, her incredible photo editing skills giving each of them a historic look, fitting in with the overall vibe of the house.

"This is..." Julia shakes her head, speechless. Then she flings her arms around me. "Perfect, Londyn." She pulls back, holding me at arm's length. "It's perfect."

I laugh. "You've only seen the hallway so far. Come on."

With a grin, I turn into the living room, their eyes widening as they take in the space. Natural light streams in through the windows, two comfortable couches sitting across from each other. Besides the kitchen, this is probably the most modern room, although I did keep the fireplace, even if it's purely decorative.

"Is that the original light fixture?" Wes points to the chandelier hanging from the ceiling.

"It is." I grin. "It just needed a little TLC."

He shakes his head and drapes an arm around my shoulders. "This is incredible. I would have put money on that thing being yet another casualty of the house."

"Well, you underestimate my skills, Mr. Bradford." I pinch my lips together. "Because you'll see I was able to salvage a lot of this home's history. Including my *second* favorite thing about this house." I walk toward the doors leading from the living room and into the dining room. "The pocket doors." I slide them open and bring everyone into the formal dining room.

Julia walks to the cherrywood table in the center of the room beneath yet another chandelier I managed to restore, her fingers tracing the place settings.

"Look familiar?" I ask.

"My grandparents got this china as a wedding gift." She gingerly picks up one of the plates and flips it over. "December 1955," she reads the date etched on the back of each of the dishes.

"I found them in the storage unit," Wes explains. "Thought it would be nice to have them here."

They share a look, Julia's eyes brimming with tears. It doesn't matter that they're not technically related by blood. The love they have for each other is more powerful than any other siblings I've met.

"Give you a piece of Meemaw and Gampy to keep."

She wraps her arms around him, hugging him tightly. "Thank you."

"Mama," Imogene says as she tugs on Julia's shirt. "When do I get to see my room?"

"Soon, baby," Julia replies through her tears, wiping her cheeks as she pulls away from Wes.

"Better get on with the tour then." I wink at Imogene. "Don't want to keep you waiting."

I show them through the rest of the house, pointing out pieces I was able to save, including the clawfoot tub in the ensuite bathroom of the master bedroom. The house is a mixture of modern amenities and historic charm, thanks to the occasional accent of original door handles, stained glass, or light fixtures.

"You ready, Imogene?" I ask, stopping in front of the door to the final room of our tour, the one leading to what will be her bedroom whenever she visits.

"Yes!" She's practically bursting at the seams.

"Here you go." I pause before turning the knob, excited to not only see her reaction, but also Julia's and Wes'. I never shared my plans for this room. It was something I wanted to do for them. And Imogene. My way of thanking them for welcoming me into their family. For giving me a place to call home.

"Oh, Londyn...," Julia exhales, walking over the threshold.

"Is this really my room?" Imogene squeals, her frantic gaze darting everywhere, starting at the five-foot-tall dollhouse by the far wall, shifting to the reading nook in the corner, stopping at the luxurious bed in the center, sheer curtains hanging from the ceiling draping around it.

"Do you like it?" I crouch down to her level.

"I love it! Thank you, Miss Londyn." She wraps her arms around my neck, squeezing me before darting away and exploring all the toys I couldn't help but buy for her.

I sense a warmth approach and glance over my shoulder to see Wes looking down at me, his eyes overflowing with affection. He drapes an arm around me, and I melt into him, my heart bursting as I watch Imogene drag Julia throughout the space, picking up a toy to play with, only to find something else that catches her attention seconds later.

"The house looks incredible. And I'm not only saying that because I barely saw you this week and really need to get laid."

I playfully swat him, and he chuckles, causing the butterflies to erupt in my stomach. It doesn't matter how often I hear him laugh or taste his kisses. The butterflies don't seem to tire of him. I doubt they ever will.

"I mean it." He turns me so I'm facing him, linking his fingers together at the small of my back. "You're incredible." He brings his lips toward mine. "And I'll forever be grateful that one day, you made the horrible decision to try to cross the street wearing fuck-me heels during a downpour."

I brush my mouth against his. "And I'll forever be grateful that one day, you braved a torrential downpour to peel my ass off the pavement. Then asked for my number in a very busy coffee shop."

"Best decision of my life."

"*You're* the best decision of *my* life," I sigh, touching my lips to his.

When he pulls back, he holds his hand out toward me. "Come on. There's something I want to show you."

I scrunch my brows. "What is it?"

"Patience, honeybee. All will be revealed in due time." He grins, hand still extended.

Unable to reel in my smile, I place my hand in his. I half expect him to drag me into the master bedroom for a quickie before dinner. Instead, he leads me downstairs and out to the back porch that's now a welcoming space for entertaining, complete with wet bar and built-in gas grill.

"Where are we going?" I ask as he tugs me down the steps and along the dirt path lined with pebbles.

"I told you. You'll find out soon." He beams down at me as we meander around the lake, making our way out to the old horse pasture. A breeze picks up, the chilly fall air refreshing as I inhale a deep breath.

Finally, we come to a stop outside the stables. Wes turns to me, his hand on the door handle. "Ready for your surprise?"

"I'm not sure. I have no idea what this could be."

"Trust me. You'll love it." He places a kiss on my temple, then pushes the door open. A light automatically flicks on, illuminating the huge space.

What was once home to a dozen horse stalls is now one large area, all evidence it was once a stable nowhere to be found. In its place is what I can only describe as a workshop on steroids. The walls are lined with storage cabinets similar to the ones I had installed in the kitchen, the countertops of poured cement in front of a pegboard backsplash.

"I had no idea what kind of stuff you'd want here, so I asked Nash to construct the type of workshop that would give him wet dreams, and he rolled with it."

"Pretty sure this is the workshop of *my* wet dreams, too." I choke out a laugh through my amazement, still taken aback by my surroundings.

This place is easily ten times the size of my current workspace in my garage. I can only imagine the kind of restorations I'll be able to do now that I'll no longer be limited by space.

"I don't think I know what half these saws do, but I can't wait to find out."

"You're a brilliant woman." He pulls me into his embrace. "I'm sure you'll figure it out."

I shake my head, peering into his vivid azure eyes that are alight with excitement as he studies my reaction. "How did you do this? *When* did you do this?"

"It was easier than I thought, actually. You know that week you were busy doing that kitchen remodel back in the city?"

I nod.

"We did it then. You were distracted working on that, so you didn't even notice when we didn't get together for coffee or lunch. Do you like it?"

"Like it?" I clutch his cheeks in my hands. "I love it." I cover his mouth with mine, that same charge shooting through me that did the very first time I felt his lips. One I have a feeling I'll always experience whenever we kiss.

"I love you," he murmurs. "So much."

"So much," I repeat as he steers me back against one of the large workbenches in the middle of the space. When he grabs my ass and places me on the surface in one swift move, I gasp. "And what do you think you're doing, Mr. Bradford?" I ask coyly, batting my lashes.

His eyes flame as he reaches for my blouse, slowly unbuttoning it. "What I've fantasized about since Nash told me this workbench could take a beating and still be standing.

I guess I want to test out his claim. You know. Strictly for research purposes."

"Is that right?" I chew on my lower lip as my blouse falls open, exposing the white, lacy bra underneath. Wes inhales a sharp breath.

"Oh, honeybee." He traces a line along my face, causing my teeth to chatter. Then he treats me to a soft kiss that leaves me desperate for more. "That's so right. *You* are so right."

He hooks an arm around my waist, lowering my back flush against the workbench. With a devilish glint in his eyes, he unzips each of my knee-high boots and tosses them onto the floor before reaching for the button on my jeans. My breathing increases as he unfastens it, then lowers the zipper, inching them down my legs.

"Now for something I've been wanting to do for a long time." He reaches into the back pocket of his jeans, withdrawing the black eye mask I'd used as a blindfold on him earlier. My gaze widens as I stare at it, my pulse skyrocketing. "If you're okay with it."

After what I went through all those years ago, I didn't think I'd ever like the idea of being blindfolded or restrained, the loss of control enough to cause a panic attack. But as Wes and I have explored this undeniable connection over the past several weeks, I've learned I can trust him. With my body. With my fears. With my heart.

All I ever wanted out of my first marriage was someone I connected with, someone with whom I could explore these cravings and desires without being judged. Now I finally have that. If these past several months have taught me anything, it's that Wes will do anything for me. That he'll never hurt me.

Grabbing a fistful of his shirt, I pull him toward me, wrapping my legs around his midsection.

"Put it on," I order huskily.

"Yes, ma'am."

He slips it over my head, shrouding my world in darkness. With the loss of my sight, all my other senses are heightened.

My sense of hearing, the sound of my racing heart seeming to thunder all around us.

My sense of smell, Wes' spicy and earthy scent overwhelming me.

My sense of touch, Wes pushing my panties aside, his mouth covering my center.

"Oh god," I moan, my body fusing to the surface below me.

One thing is certain. We will definitely be putting this blindfold to more use in the future.

# CHAPTER TWENTY-EIGHT

WESTON

Excited conversation echoes against the high ceilings as I glance around the dining room of Meemaw and Gampy's house, the chairs filled with friends and family, both old and new. It's surreal to celebrate Thanksgiving in this house again after all these years. I didn't think I'd ever do this again, thought all I'd have to cling to were memories from the past. But now I get to make new memories in this house. Memories with my new family.

Julia rushes back into the dining room from the kitchen and rearranges a few of the dishes, setting the last bowl on the table. "I always forget the cranberry sauce," she remarks breathily, plopping down onto her chair beside Imogene.

"Everything looks great, Jules," I say with a smile. "You didn't have to do all of this. I told you we could just keep things simple."

She narrows her gaze on me. "And in the spirit of Meemaw, I *did* keep things simple." She waves at the table that's filled with nearly a dozen different types of food. "At least according to her."

We laugh at the inside joke. Meemaw's idea of a simple meal would feed a small army for days afterward. She loved cooking for anyone who walked through the doors of this house. I'm thrilled her favorite room, the kitchen, is now put back to good use whenever we're here.

"I suppose you did." I smile, then look at everyone assembled around the table, Londyn at my side. She'd invited her neighbors, Hazel and Diego, to join our Thanksgiving celebration, as well, and I'm grateful they made the trip out here from the city. We're a mishmash of people from all different walks of life — white, black, Hispanic. Exactly how Gampy and Meemaw celebrated the holidays. The only person missing is Julia's husband, Nick, who got stuck in a snowstorm up north, where he'd been for work. But he's hoping to get here before the end of the weekend.

Clearing my throat, I grab my wine glass and rise to my feet, feeling almost like an imposter as I stand at the head of the table where Gampy once did during large holiday meals.

"Over the years, my sister, Julia, and I have started a tradition, thanks to our gampy. Whenever we'd sit down to a big meal, he'd always start with a toast. Now, whenever Julia and I get together, we do the same thing, although thanks to our competitive natures, it's become a bit of a contest to see who can come up with the best one." I wink. "So, Jules, on this very special first Thanksgiving back here, I yield the floor to you."

I return to my seat, brushing my fingers along Londyn's thigh. It's impossible to keep my hands off her, even more so tonight since she's wearing a wrap dress that falls to her mid-thigh paired with her knee-high boots. I've already told her I have plans for her tonight, and they include her in those boots. And nothing else.

Julia stands, looking at our guests. "I debated what to toast to today, since I feel like I have so much to be thankful for this year. Not only is my daughter turning into such a kind and compassionate little lady…" She glances to her side, meeting Imogene's smile before returning her attention to the rest of the table, "but I'm also able to celebrate my favorite holiday in this house of so many memories with not only the woman my brother loves more than I think he's ever loved anyone, but also with *her* family." She gestures to Hazel and Diego, who share a look. "And that's the thing I've learned over the years." She brings her eyes to mine. "Blood doesn't make you family. Love. Devotion. Commitment. That's what binds you together. And I'm blessed to call all of you my family. So, in the spirit of family, here's one of Gampy's favorite toasts."

She raises her glass. "May the roof above these friends never fall in, and the friends below this roof never fall out."

"I'll drink to that," Hazel says, about to bring her glass to her lips, but Londyn places her hand on her arm, stopping her.

"Not yet. There are a few more, including one I think you'll like."

"Do you want to go next, honeybee?" I ask. "I'd prefer to go last, if you don't mind."

"Of course not."

Smiling, she pushes back from her chair and stands, raising her glass. She closes her eyes and clears her throat before refocusing her attention on everyone. "A drink to those who do and those who don't," Londyn begins.

Hazel bursts out laughing. I assume it's an inside joke between the two of them. She jumps up, standing beside Londyn, her glass also raised.

"But not to those who say they will but later decide they won't," Hazel continues, then glances at her husband, who happily stands, as well.

"For the ones I'll toast from the dawning of the day to the darkness of the night," Diego states before looking back to Londyn.

"Are the ones who say I never have...," she finishes, returning her attention to me. "But for you, I just might."

Retaking her chair, she curves toward me, her mouth brushing mine, sending a shiver through me. I might be misreading the signs, but I can't shake the feeling this is Londyn's way of declaring in front of all the important people in her life that she's finally made peace with her past. That she's finally willing to only look forward to a future...with me.

"For you, I just might," I repeat, momentarily forgetting we're not alone as I swipe my tongue against the seam of her lips, begging for a quick taste of her.

"You two kiss a lot," Imogene comments, breaking through our moment.

We reluctantly pull away from each other, and Londyn averts her eyes, as she always does when embarrassed.

"You go, girl," Hazel remarks, nudging her.

"It's what two people do when they're in love," Julia tells Imogene.

She frowns. "Then why don't you kiss Daddy?"

Julia swallows hard, darting her nervous gaze to me, as if worried about how I'll respond to this news. But I won't press. I've been through relationship troubles myself. I hope they can work out whatever they're going through. For Imogene's sake.

"We do, sweet pea." She smiles, but it wavers.

"Okay then," Londyn interjects, obviously sensing Julia's unease. "I believe we have one toast left."

I lift myself to my feet once more. "I'll admit, I took some artistic license with one of Gampy's favorite toasts. Made it more fitting for the occasion."

Drawing in a deep breath, I raise my glass. This time, everyone joins me, knowing this will be the final toast of the evening. Then I shift my attention to Londyn, as if speaking only to her. In a way, I am.

"Here's to roses and lilies in bloom. You in my arms and me in your room. A door that is locked, a key that is lost. Honeybees, and Ferris wheels, and a bed that is tossed. Smiles, and laughter, and a place to get away. And a love that lasts forever and a day."

I allow my words to sink in for a moment, unshed tears glistening in her eyes. Then I turn my attention back to the rest of the guests.

"Here's to a wonderful meal amongst good friends. Memories made together that time transcends. A bottomless glass and a cup that runs over. Hearts filled with love that never sobers. Smiles, and laughter, and a place to get away. And friendships that last forever and a day."

"I'll drink to that," Julia says as we all clink glasses.

When I lower myself back to my chair, Londyn squeezes my thigh. I look at her, and she lifts her lips to meet mine.

"I love you. Forever and a day."

"Promise?" I murmur in a low voice so no one can hear.

"Absolutely."

"Good. I'm going to hold you to it. Because I love you. Forever and a day."

She kisses me sweetly before pulling back and scanning over the ridiculous amount of food she and my sister had busied themselves preparing the past few days. Turkey. Baked ham.

Cornbread dressing. Mashed potatoes. Buttermilk biscuits. Sautéed green beans with mushrooms. Fried okra. Sweet potato casserole. Deviled eggs. Homemade cranberry sauce. Macaroni and cheese, which Julia claimed she made for Imogene. But I notice her steal a healthy portion of it.

"I have to say," Julia begins once everyone has filled every inch of their plates with food. "That may be your best toast yet, dear brother. You should have saved it for the masquerade ball on New Year's Eve. Your midnight toast there is always epic."

I feel Londyn tense beside me, and I give her a smile that's a mixture of reassuring and apologetic.

"True." I push my food around my plate, not looking directly at Julia. "But I won't be attending this year."

She scrunches her brow, taken aback by this news. "Why not?"

I'd intended to wait until after the holiday to share this with her and ask her to fill in for me, considering she's on the board of my Homes for the Homeless charity. We've both been so busy — her with an offer to expand her bakery chain to the West Coast, as well as preparing for Thanksgiving, and me with breaking ground on a new hotel in Miami the firm is overseeing — I haven't had time to bring it up.

I reach beside me, squeezing Londyn's thigh, wordlessly telling her it's okay. "The last thing I want to do is spend my first New Year's Eve with Londyn at a masquerade ball."

"You didn't mind taking Brooklyn," she reminds me. "Hell, we even moved it up to Boston that year."

"This year's different," I respond firmly, hoping she picks up on my tone. But thanks to all the wine she drank while cooking today, she doesn't, turning her attention to Londyn.

"You'd love it. And when I say that, I don't do so lightly. I usually avoid these kinds of things like the plague. But the New Year's Eve Masquerade Ball is the one social function I actually look forward to attending. Not to mention it's a huge money-maker for the charity. We easily get over half our yearly donations at it."

"That's true. But like I said, I won't be attending this year.

233

I'm sure you'll be a much more charming host than I've been anyway. With you being the Master of Ceremonies, I think we'll raise even more money, since you're much prettier to look at than I am."

"Well, I certainly can't argue with that." She shrugs, then focuses her attention on Diego.

"So, Londyn tells me you're a firefighter."

"Yes, ma'am," he responds in a thick New York accent. "In Atlanta."

"Fascinating," she exhales, no longer concerned about the masquerade ball.

But I can tell Londyn is.

\* \* \*

"Is it true?" Londyn asks later that night when I step out of the ensuite bathroom and walk toward the bed where she lies on her side.

"What? That I'm about to do very naughty things to you?" I crawl under the duvet, snaking an arm around her waist and tugging her close, peppering kisses along her jawline.

"No." She swats at me, her giggles echoing in the stillness.

Imogene went to sleep hours ago, and I'm pretty sure Julia is passed out after all the wine she drank, leaving just Londyn and me.

"Well, yes. I *am* looking forward to all the naughty things you're about to do, but that's not what I mean."

I slither down her body, easing her t-shirt up, revealing her torso. "Then what do you mean, honeybee?" I ask, circling my tongue around her belly button.

She moans, and I glance up, watching as her chest rises and falls in a quicker rhythm.

"I mean…" She licks her lips, seeming to struggle to form a sentence, especially when I lick a line down to the waist of her panties. "About New Year's Eve. That it's a big money-maker for your charity."

I pause, not moving for several moments. Then I meet her eyes. "And if it is?"

234

"Wes...," she sighs, her voice almost like a warning.

After I told Julia I wouldn't be going, I'd hoped it would be the end of the discussion. I should have known Londyn would want to talk about it. Although there's nothing to talk about. The second she'd told me what happened after the masked ball she went to in college, my mind was made up. There's no way I'm going to force her to attend something that will trigger too many horrible memories.

Expelling a breath, I return to her, propping my head in my hand as I trace a circle on the smooth flesh of her hip with the other one. "What is it?"

Her dark eyes shine in the dim lighting of the room, a thousand emotions swirling within. Every time I look at her, I find something new. Like the tiny flecks of gold in her eyes as she admires me. Like the adorable smattering of freckles below her ear that only those lucky enough to kiss her there can see. Like the vein in her forehead that becomes more noticeable whenever she has something important to say.

Like it is now.

"I don't want you to have to sacrifice anything to be with me."

"I'm not sacrificing anything."

"You're sacrificing your relationship with your mother," she reminds me.

"I don't care about that. If you're trying to get rid of me, you need better material than my mother's approval."

A shadow of a smile plays on her lips, but it vanishes just as quickly as it appeared. She's about to respond with yet another argument, but before she can, I press my mouth to hers, silencing any further protest.

"You can list every reason under the sun, and I'll tell you the same thing every time. I don't care. Don't care what my mother thinks. Don't care that we come from two different worlds. Don't care that this relationship won't always be easy. Because for every reason you can come up with for why we shouldn't be together, there's one even more important reason we should."

"And what's that?"

"That I love you. That I'll do whatever it takes to make you happy, no questions asked. That's why missing the ball wasn't a difficult decision. Hell, it wasn't even a decision."

"You would really do that for me? Miss this huge fundraiser? I know how important your charity work is to you."

"But you're more important," I assure her, cupping her cheek. "When I was with Brooklyn, I lost sight of what was important. I tried to do it all. Run the firm. Raise funds for the charity. Be the man she deserved. But along the way, I stopped focusing on her. Instead, every decision I made was with the business in mind. Not her. Not her well-being. Not what she needed or deserved. I won't do that with you. I won't allow a single day to go by where you have to question my devotion to you."

"I don't know what I've done to deserve you, but I'm not going to question it anymore." She crushes her lips to mine, her grip on me tightening as she hooks a leg over my waist. When I feel her warmth against me, I groan, hardening beneath her. "But I have one request," she says after tearing out of our kiss.

"That I give you an orgasm nightly? No problem."

She rolls her eyes. "Is sex all you think about?"

"Not all. But on a daily basis, sex is on my mind at least twenty-three hours of the day."

"Perv." She playfully swats me as I squeeze her ass. "But seriously. One request."

"Whatever it is, it's yours."

"Okay. Go to the New Year's Eve Masquerade Ball."

"I already told you. I'm not spending New Year's Eve away from you. There's no way in hell I'm going to be anywhere you're not at midnight."

She runs a hand along my torso. "And you won't be. I'll be there with you."

I narrow my gaze on her. "Londyn, I appreciate the gesture more than you can imagine, but *you're* my priority. As is your emotional well-being." I shake my head, my brows furrowed. "Do you really want to do this?"

She swallows hard. "I won't lie and say the mere thought doesn't make me anxious. But if there's anyone who can help me through this, it's you." She treats me to a ghost of a kiss, which only makes me want more of her. "You've already helped me face so many of my fears. And because of that, I'm stronger. Because of *you*, I'm stronger. So I want to do this. I want to wear a ridiculously extravagant gown with an equally extravagant mask. I want my mouth to grow dry when I see you in your tux for the first time."

Resting a hand on my chest, she applies pressure, forcing me onto my back and crawling on top of me, straddling my waist. Her mouth is warm as she trails kisses along my jawline, hovering over my lips.

"Then I want you to find me at midnight and kiss me in a way that may border on indecent."

My hand moves to her hair and I grip it, locking her in place as I smash my lips to hers in a tumultuous kiss.

"I want people to look at us and only see two people madly in love. Not our past. Not our differences. Only us. Only love."

"God, I love you," I murmur as I flip her onto her back. When she runs her hands through my hair, her fingers digging into my scalp, I arch into her touch.

"So is that a yes?"

I bring my mouth back to hers. "You should know by now…"

"What's that?" She smirks.

"I will never deny you what you…desire."

"Is that right?" she retorts, a devilish glint in her eyes.

"That's right, honeybee." I move from her lips, kissing my way to her chest.

"Well then, do you want to know what I desire right now?"

"I'm on pins and needles."

"Your mouth," she heaves through labored breaths as I circle her belly button with my tongue. "On me."

With a mischievous smile, I hook my fingers into her panties and slide them down her legs. "As always, your wish is my command."

# CHAPTER TWENTY-NINE

LONDYN

I slide the ridiculously expensive nude pumps onto my feet, then step back, admiring my reflection in the full-length mirror in the bedroom of the downtown Atlanta hotel suite Wes booked.

While I've been apprehensive about tonight, Wes has done everything to put me at ease. From spoiling me with a stunning gown. To booking an afternoon at the spa, complete with massage, manicure, and pedicure. To reserving this beautiful suite in the hotel where the New Year's Eve Masquerade Ball is being held, in case I need to disappear for any reason. He thought of everything to make this as trauma-free as possible.

I study my appearance, feeling like I'm staring back at a different woman. In a way, I suppose I am, thanks to Wes. The version of Londyn he first met all those months ago is gone, replaced by a stronger Londyn. A more open Londyn. A Londyn who finally feels valued again.

I turn to my side, taking in the rose gold gown. It's fitted through the bodice with a deep V at my chest and an exposed back before flowing out at the waist into layers of sparkling glitter fabric with a small train. I've never felt so glamorous, even on my wedding day. Then again, I didn't really get a true wedding out of the deal. Didn't get to go dress shopping or plan the wedding of my dreams. Instead, I wore a simple white dress I found at a thrift shop, and my father married us in his church mere weeks after Sawyer made his proposition to me. No bridal shower. No bachelorette party. Nothing. Maybe that's why the marriage never felt real to me.

Shaking off the memory, I return my attention to the mirror, doing one last check of my appearance. Once I'm content the subtle makeup the beautician applied doesn't need any touching up and the rose gold mask with glittering diamonds is securely in place, I turn from the mirror, heading toward the bedroom door.

The second I step into the living room and my eyes fall on Wes standing in front of the floor-to-ceiling windows overlooking downtown Atlanta, his stance exuding power and dominance, my pulse increases, my mouth growing dry. Able to sense my presence, he turns toward me, his lips parting as he takes in my appearance.

Over the past half-year that Wes has been a client, then a friend, then more than a friend, I've been treated to a variety of looks. From the dashing businessman who had no problem running into the rain to help a woman in need. To the dingy jeans and t-shirt wearing handyman who made a tool belt look absolutely sinful. To the casual man wearing shorts and flip flops as we hung out, talking about everything and nothing at once.

And I love every single one of those looks.

But Wes in a tuxedo with a simple black mask is on a different level altogether. He's like a really hot Zorro. Or a dressed-up Dread Pirate Roberts.

"Wow," I exhale.

"Wow," Wes murmurs at the same time, his eyes wide with wonder as he drinks me in. With determined strides, he walks toward me. Heat fills his gaze. But I also see appreciation.

Taking my hand in his, he twirls me around to get a better look at my dress before yanking me into his embrace.

"You're stunning, Londyn," he croons.

"You're not so bad yourself." I reach for his bowtie and adjust it, lifting myself onto my toes. "And I have plans for this later on."

"Oh really?" He waggles his brows.

I slowly nod. "Sure do." I brush my lips against his. "And it involves you keeping this mask on."

"I think that can be arranged." His mouth covers mine, our tongues swiping before he pulls back. "Speaking of masks, I hope you don't mind, but I took the liberty of getting you a different one. One that may be more appropriate than this one." He walks behind me and carefully unties my current mask, taking care not to mess up my hair.

"More appropriate?"

"Yes." His eyes dance with delight as he strides toward the coffee table, a black, shirt-sized box sitting on it. Lifting it, he returns to me, holding it out.

I take the box from him, carefully lifting the lid. When I pull back the tissue, I gasp as I peer at a striking gold mask with intricate detailing throughout, the shade a perfect accent to the gold flecks in my gown. But that's not what makes it so perfect. As I take a closer look, I notice tiny snakes framing the mask, like the hair of Medusa.

"May I?" Wes asks smoothly.

I nod, still speechless.

With a smile, he takes the box from me, removing the mask. Shifting me toward the mirror over the couch, I watch our reflection as he stands behind me and secures the mask to my face.

"Do you know the story of Medusa?"

"More or less," I answer, not wanting to tell Wes that *he* spoke of Medusa often. Jay has no place here tonight. He has no place anywhere at anytime.

"She was the only mortal among the Gorgon sisters, who were all monsters," he explains, his fingers careful and deft as they tie the dark ribbon into a knot behind my head. "While Medusa was stunning, her greatest charm and what attracted all men to her was her golden hair. One such man was Poseidon." Content with his work, he lowers his lips to my neck, feathering it with soft kisses.

"I know that part of the story. How Poseidon couldn't resist the temptation and forced himself on her in Athena's temple."

"True." He pulls back, stepping in front of me. "I won't deny what happened to her is a tragedy. How instead of punishing Poseidon, Goddess Athena blamed Medusa and turned her into a monster, snakes taking the place of her once beautiful hair, eyes so petrifying the mere sight of her turned men to stone." He takes my hands in his, brushing my knuckles in a reassuring manner.

"That's why I felt this mask was fitting. Not because your story may have similarities to Medusa's, but to remind you just how powerful you are. That you have the ability to turn all men to stone." Bringing a hand to my chin, he tilts my head back, forcing my eyes to his. "You turned *me* to stone. I'd rather be crushed to dust than go another minute without you by my side."

My heart expanding in my chest, I clutch his cheeks and drag his lips toward mine, coaxing his mouth open. It's not a lust-filled exchange that leaves me panting and gasping for air. But it still makes me feel more desired than any other man's kiss ever has.

After my mother died, several of the ladies at the church took me under their wing to help raise me, especially when I was a teenager and dealing with all the unique struggles teenage girls face that my father was grossly unprepared to address. One of them, Miss Tania, always told me never to settle for just good enough. To hold on to my heart until I met someone who could see my darkness and not only chooses to stay, but helps show me the light within. That's exactly what Wes has done. He's shown me the light within.

"What do you say, honeybee?" Wes says once our kiss comes to an end. "Shall we go ring in the new year?" He holds his elbow out for me.

I hook my arm through his. "We shall."

\* \* \*

Crystal chandeliers sparkle overhead as white-gloved waitstaff circle the large ballroom, trays of champagne and hors d'oeuvres balanced on their fingertips. Women wear gowns designed by all the big names in fashion, while the men have donned formal tuxedos. Everything about tonight exudes money and class. It's certainly not even remotely close to how I typically spend New Year's Eve, which is usually over at Hazel and Diego's condo, dressed in yoga pants, watching as many Christmas movies as we can before the holiday season is officially over.

As we make our way through the ballroom, Wes stops to talk to everyone who calls his name or approaches. I can tell this is his Weston Bradford persona, not the Wes I've gotten to know. When he introduces me as his girlfriend, he doesn't hesitate or bat an eye. A few people, especially those he mentions are old friends of his parents, look at me with disapproval. But that only makes Wes hold me tighter, leaving no question in anyone's mind I'm not going anywhere. At least his parents aren't here, having spent the holidays in Aspen, probably because his mother wasn't on the guest list to begin with, according to Wes.

"There you are," a familiar voice says as Wes accepts congratulations from another acquaintance about his latest contract, something about a deal to design and build twelve new hotels in Hawaii.

I turn just as Julia sidles up to us. Her shimmery green dress sparkles with her every movement. It's slim throughout her body, only flowing out near the bottom in a traditional mermaid style. To complete the look, her green mask has seashell and pearl detailing.

"Julia…" I wrap my arms around her, as if I haven't seen her in ages, instead of just a few hours, since we'd been at the spa together. But it's comforting to see a familiar face. Well, as much of it as I can see anyway.

To my surprise, being surrounded by people wearing masks hasn't been nearly as anxiety-inducing as I thought it would be. Like I told Wes, it's time I replace all my negative memories with good ones. That's why tonight is so important. It may be the last day of the year, but for me, it's the final page in this chapter. I'm turning the page on my past and never looking back.

"You look beautiful. I like the mermaid vibe."

"You look gorgeous, too. Good thing Wes got you that Medusa mask." She scans my frame. "With a dress like that, you'll need the ability to turn men to stone."

"Hey, Jules," Wes greets, kissing his sister's cheek before wrapping an arm around me, pulling me close. "And don't you worry. I have absolutely no intention of letting her out of my sight for a second. Why would I want to when I have such a beautiful view?" The intensity in his gaze causes a thrill to trickle through me.

"Think you'll make it to midnight? Or will you need to retire early?" Julia jests.

"No promises." He winks, delicately caressing my exposed back, sending another jolt of want through me. Then he scans the ballroom. "Did Nick make it in all right?"

She briefly chews on her lower lip. "Actually, he had a last-minute meeting with some publisher up in New York. An opportunity arose that he couldn't pass up. At least according to him."

"Publisher?" I furrow my brows. "I thought you said he's a PR consultant."

"He is." Julia swipes a champagne glass off a tray as a server makes his rounds. "But his degree is in English literature. He used to teach, but since he wasn't tenured, he had to pretty much start the job hunt over again every year."

"God, I'd hate that."

"Yeah. Me, too. Not to mention, it was difficult for me to get my business off the ground because of the uncertainty of his. So about five years ago, he took a job with a PR firm and discovered he was damn good at it. He's extremely persuasive, and a great writer. He can take a story that paints someone in a bad light and put one hell of a spin on it. But when that firm faced some public relations issues of their own, he decided to branch out and become a freelance consultant since he had such high demand from his former clients to keep them on."

"Sounds like it's a good fit," I comment.

"It is. Plus, it keeps him in one place, apart from having to travel a lot to deal with clients. But I can tell he misses the analytical side of teaching, so for the past few years, he's been working on a book. Earlier this year, a publisher picked it up."

"What kind of book?" I ask, making conversation.

Julia sips her champagne, looking to the ceiling. "Something about how all humans are predisposed to live out the underlying themes found in various myths. Heroism. Fate. Pride. Justice. Revenge. He's obsessed with Greek mythology.

Taught several classes about it."

I choke on my champagne, the effervescent liquid burning my throat and nose as I struggle to breathe.

"Are you okay?" Wes asks, fixating his eyes on mine, patting my back.

I blink as I cough, momentarily stunned speechless. Who cares if Jay studied literature and was also obsessed with Greek mythology? That he was also extremely persuasive and a good writer? The idea is completely irrational. There are hundreds, even thousands of men who fit that description. Plus, Julia's husband's name is Nicholas Prescott. Not Domenic Jaskulski, or Professor Jay around campus.

I shake it off, blaming the ridiculous notion on my surroundings, and offer Wes a reassuring smile, clearing my throat. "Of course."

"Good. Then why don't we dance."

"Dance?"

"You don't expect to look as gorgeous as you do and me not want to show you off, do you?"

"Always the charmer, aren't you?"

He leans toward me, feathering a kiss against my cheek. "Always." He lingers there for a moment before addressing Julia. "Will you be okay for a bit?"

She lifts her glass. "There's an open bar and overflowing champagne. I'll be *more* than okay."

"I knew I could count on you, Jules." He laughs as he steers me toward the center of the dance floor, the familiar Sinatra tune the band had been playing coming to an end.

When the pianist plays the opening lines of "La Vie en Rose", memories of my mother singing this song flash before me.

"Care to dance?" Wes murmurs into my ear, the heat of his breath warming my neck.

I face him, placing my hand in his. And just like earlier in the suite, he twirls me around before pulling me against his chest. He places a hand on my hip, the other one still entwined with mine, and begins moving in time with the lazy, rhythmic beat of the classic French tune.

"My mother used to sing this," I reminisce as I drape my free arm along his shoulder, toying with the few tendrils of hair falling over his collar. "One night, when I couldn't have been more than five or six, I'd gotten out of bed to get a glass of water. As I walked past the living room, I saw my parents dancing. My mother was singing this song. In that moment, I could physically feel how much they loved each other. It was so beautiful. After she died, I would always listen to this song, clinging to the memory of her singing it. Clinging to the man my father was when she was still alive." I swallow hard, my heart squeezing at everything I lost when that gunman burst into the church.

"Do you know what the lyrics mean?" Wes asks in an effort to distract me.

"It's about seeing the world through rose-colored glasses now that she's found the love of her life." I sigh as Wes pulls me even closer. "All he has to do is take her in his arms, speak words of love, and she's home. Happy. Secure."

I tilt my head back, no longer sure if I'm talking about the story in the song, or my own with Wes.

"You for me, me for you, for the rest of my life," I murmur.

"I knew I liked this song for a reason," he whispers as he buries his head in my neck, inhaling deeply as we sway to the tune.

When the singer starts the second chorus, Wes attempts to sing along with her, completely butchering the French language. But I don't care. It makes me laugh, reminding me how easy it was to fall in love with him. I fought it, did everything to keep my distance. Somewhere along the way, though, I fell. It wasn't a quick descent into madness as you often read about or see in the movies. This wasn't love at first sight. Our journey to this point was gradual, each day causing me to sever another tie binding me to my past until I barely remember any of it.

"That's the mark of true love," I say through my laughter as the song fades.

"What's that?"

"That even though you can't speak French worth a lick and

245

eviscerated a song very near and dear to my heart, I still love you."

"You for me, me for you, for the rest of our lives, honeybee."

"You for me, me for you, Wes," I reply as he treats me to a kiss I feel deep in my soul.

The next few hours pass with much less pomp and circumstance as the ball shifts from being formal to more celebratory, the copious amounts of alcohol available causing people to let down their guard. The masks seem to help, too. It certainly helps me.

At some point, a DJ replaced the band, the music no longer jazz standards but more modern songs. And since Julia has a night when she doesn't have to worry about Imogene, having left her with their nanny in Charleston, she has no problem letting loose on the dance floor. Being the good friend I am, I join her. Or maybe I just can't help myself when the DJ starts playing "Uptown Funk". Then again, neither can Julia.

"I'm going to have to start hiring the two of you to come to more of these things," Wes laughs as Julia and I make our way off the dance floor, needing a minute to catch our breath. "Y'all make it infinitely more entertaining."

"If you can't let loose on New Year's Eve, when can you?" Julia shoots back, joining him at a high-top table near the bar. She takes Wes' scotch from his hand and throws back a healthy gulp.

"I suppose you're right." He smiles at me before turning his attention to Julia. "Don't forget we have a speech to make."

"I haven't. If we didn't have that speech, I would have been doing shots all night instead of sticking to champagne."

"Aren't you just the picture of responsibility?" He chuckles, taking his scotch back from her.

"When you have kids of your own, you'll understand what a rare treat a night without a child truly is."

"I'll take your word."

Wes brings his scotch to his lips, about to sip, when he stops, squinting into the distance. "Nick?"

Hearing her husband's name, Julia stiffens, her eyes

following Wes as he excuses himself and walks toward a man dressed like every other man here — dashing tuxedo and black masquerade mask. But I don't pay too much attention to him, too worried about Julia's nervous reaction.

"Are you okay?" I whisper, my hand covering hers.

"Yeah. Just surprised." She forces a smile, but she seems jittery.

"Julia said you got caught up in New York," I hear Wes remark over the music.

"I couldn't miss kissing my lovely wife at midnight," Nick replies. "Plus, it's about time I meet this girlfriend of yours."

"Come on over then." Wes leads him toward the table. "Nick, this is my girlfriend, Miss Londyn Bennett."

I tear my gaze away from Julia, unable to shake the premonition in my stomach that something is seriously wrong. When my eyes skate over the tall man in a tuxedo, his blond hair slicked back, it's no longer just a premonition. Something *is* seriously wrong.

"Londyn," Wes continues, oblivious to the panic racing through me, "meet Julia's husband, Domenic Jaskulski. But he tends to go by Nick."

# CHAPTER THIRTY

LONDYN

It's ironic, really. I'm wearing a Medusa mask, yet I'm the one turned to stone, unable to move, to think, to breathe. For years, I'd imagined what I would do if I ever saw him again. Now that he's mere feet away, I'm frozen.

Truth be told, I never expected to see him again. I certainly didn't expect to run into him here of all places. And I never could have imagined he'd be married to the woman who's become like a sister to me. That he'd be the father of one of the most precious little girls I've ever met.

*Imogene...*

The reality hits me hard. The pictures he proudly showed me of his little girl all those years ago. It was Imogene. The man Imogene looks up to, loves, cherishes is the same man who destroyed my life.

I want to pinch myself, wake up in Wes' arms, learn this is all a nightmare. But if this were just a nightmare, I wouldn't smell his familiar cologne of leather and citrus. Wouldn't feel a tingle of apprehension trickle down my spine. Wouldn't hear his voice with such striking clarity as he addresses me, a sly smirk curling his lips.

"It's a pleasure to finally put a face to the name," he says with the same smooth demeanor he had all those years ago when he first introduced himself as Jay. "Or as much of the face as is allowed tonight." He extends his hand.

I somehow manage to float my eyes toward it, my stomach churning at the idea of his skin touching mine.

Sensing Wes' curious stare on me, I put on the same act I have the past five years and extend my hand, allowing him to take it.

"Nice to meet you... *Nick*," I emphasize.

I struggle to breathe as he doesn't simply shake my hand,

but brings it to his lips and brushes a soft kiss on my knuckles. I do everything to keep myself still, not wanting to raise any questions from Wes or Julia. When I can't stand it any longer, I tear my hand from his, settling deeper into the crook of Wes' arm. I've never been more happy to feel his protective grip on my hip than I do now.

Looking at Julia, I force a smile. "You two don't have the same last name?"

She parts her lips to respond, but before she can, Nick drapes an arm along her shoulders, pulling her against him. I notice her wince slightly.

"I married a bit of a feminist. She insisted on keeping her birth mother's last name. Hopefully she'll reconsider one of these days so she'll finally have the same last name as her own daughter."

If I didn't know him, I wouldn't have picked up on it, but he appears emasculated at the notion of Julia not taking his last name. Good. I wouldn't want that attached to me, either.

"I'm sorry to interrupt, Mr. Bradford," a petite brunette in a smart skirt suit says, tapping Wes on the shoulder. He drops his hold on me, facing the woman. "It's time for your and Ms. Prescott's speech."

"Of course. We'll be right up." He dismisses her, then turns back to me. "Duty calls. You okay?"

It's a question he's asked repeatedly tonight. And repeatedly, I'd assured him I was. But that was before… Before my world was turned upside down. Now I'm so far from okay, it's laughable.

"I'll take good care of her in your absence," Nick says from behind me.

I keep my gaze even, doing my best not to react, although the idea of being alone with him has me wanting to scream, to run away and hide. But I refuse to do that. I didn't spend the past several years reinventing myself just to become the scared little girl I was back then.

Wes turns his attention to Nick, scrutinizing him for a moment. Hope builds inside me that he'll notice something's amiss. But he doesn't, offering Nick an appreciate smile before leaning toward me and feathering a kiss on my cheek.

"I'll only be a few minutes. Then I'm coming for my midnight kiss."

"I'll be waiting." I force my lips to curve up into something resembling a smile, but I have a feeling I fail horribly.

With a nod, Wes turns, placing his hand on Julia's back, steering her toward the stage. But after only a few steps, he spins around, tacking several determined strides back toward me.

"Wes. What are you—"

Hooking an arm around my waist, he pulls me against him. "How about a sneak preview before I go?"

This isn't the first time Wes has kissed me in front of hundreds of people. He's stolen kisses all night. Most appropriate, some not so appropriate. But this time, when his lips descend toward mine, all I can feel is the heat of Jay's...Nick's possessive stare scalding my skin.

"I love you, honeybee," Wes murmurs.

I sigh, basking in his affection. It's exactly what I need right now. A reminder of how deep his devotion goes.

"I love you, too. Now go. Make your speech. Then come back and kiss me in a way that is utterly indecent."

"Indecent?" He waggles his brows.

"Shockingly so."

That's all the motivation he needs. Leaving me with one more kiss, he spins, following Julia onto the stage. I don't move. Simply keep my eyes focused solely on him. In my mind, if I keep him in my sights, nothing else matters. Only him. Only us. Only this love neither one of us thought we'd ever find, but that we somehow managed to experience.

"I must say, your mask is quite stunning," Nick whispers from behind me as the music fades and the woman in the suit strolls to the center of the stage. "The detailing is exceptional."

"You would think that, wouldn't you?" Facing him, I plaster on my best fake smile. "I'm sure you get off on the story of Poseidon and Medusa. Hell, it's probably why you love Greek mythology so much. It's all very..." I trail off, looking for the correct description. But there's only one that fits.

Glowering, I finish, "It's all very rapey."

He belts out a pompous laugh, my words seeming to have little effect on him. When I first met him, I thought him to be so sophisticated, so worldly. I looked up to and admired the man who seemed so out of my league. He fascinated me, enthralled me. But it was all part of his game.

"That's an analysis I haven't had the pleasure of examining. At least in those terms. But as I've said time and again, everything that happens in mythology is important for the hero's journey. Just like everything you've endured was important for *your* journey."

I cross an arm over my stomach, turning my attention back to the stage as Wes takes the microphone, thanking the crowd for attending and their generosity in raising several million dollars in the span of one night.

Lifting a shaky hand to my mouth, I sip on my champagne to distract myself from my current reality. "You always did seem to gravitate to the heroism encapsulated in the tales, didn't you?" I return my gaze to his, venom swirling within. "I always found a different theme infinitely more intriguing."

He narrows his eyes on me. "And what's that?"

Immediately following his assault, I probably would have backed up. Flinched. Cowered. But no more.

"Revenge." I allow my response to linger in the space between us, making my meaning crystal clear.

"Ouch," he muses coolly as if he doesn't have a care in the world. As if he's free of blame or fault. Based on what I've determined of him, he doesn't believe he did anything wrong. "Seems the kitten's grown some claws." He brings his glass to his lips and takes a sip of what I assume to be a ridiculously expensive scotch.

"I had no choice," I snarl, shifting my gaze forward once more, my brain barely registering the numbers Wes rattles off of the hundreds of people who are no longer living out of their cars or fighting for space in homeless shelters because of his initiative. "Thanks to you."

"And therein lies the rub," Nick counters. "It *is* thanks to me."

I rip my head in his direction, jaw dropping. I knew he was self-centered and egotistical, a man insistent on exerting power and dominion over everyone and everything. That was the reputation he had all over campus, something I never saw for myself until it was too late. But this is on a completely different level.

He angles toward me, his eyes on fire. "Before me, you were this meek little thing who couldn't even stand up for herself. You were Persephone, stolen by Hades and forced into marriage to a man you didn't love, with no one to come and save you from the fiery pits of hell."

I bark out a laugh. "I stood up for myself. You make it sound like I didn't have a say in the matter."

"Did you?"

My lips part as I mentally rewind to the day my father called me into his office and Sawyer was sitting there. Admittedly, the entire thing felt wrong on so many levels, like I was simply a pawn to get Sawyer what he'd worked for. But what about everything I'd been working for?

Refusing to show Nick a hint of weakness, I straighten my spine. "I was able to finish my education because I stood up for myself. Made it part of the deal to marry Sawyer."

"Not sure I'd call that standing up," he remarks nonchalantly. "You agreed to marry some schmuck who couldn't even satisfy you." He pauses as applause rings out around us. Then he inches toward me, his breath like knives against my skin. "But I did, Londyn Jade."

Inhaling quickly, I dart my wide eyes to his, speechless by his insinuation. When he inclines closer to me this time, I back up, the look in his gaze one I'd seen before. One I'd blamed on my overconsumption of alcohol, not seeing it for what it truly was. A warning. A caution to run.

"You can deny it all you want, but you enjoyed it." His voice is low and heated as his fingers brush my hair over my shoulder.

I jump back, leveling my fierce stare on him. "No, I didn't."

"I know you did. I *felt* that you did." He takes a satisfying gulp of his drink. "But if you need to convince yourself otherwise so you don't feel guilty, that's fine. Regardless, you can't ignore that I made you into the woman you are today. If I hadn't shown you what was possible, would you have escaped that empty life you'd been living? Would you have spread your wings? Learned to fly? Become this independent woman who turns heads whenever she walks into a room?"

"I—"

"No," he says vehemently. "The answer is no. You'd still be sitting in the front pew of that church every Sunday, listening to the husband you'll never love droll on about whatever wrong he felt compelled to right that day. I freed you."

I shake my head, adamantly refusing to agree with his assessment.

"Take your darling Medusa. She would have been nothing without Poseidon. Before he became infatuated with her, she was this inconsequential mortal who, while beautiful, was completely ordinary. Poseidon *made* her extraordinary."

"One could argue that was Athena."

"But had it not been for Poseidon taking her in the virgin goddess' sacred temple, Athena wouldn't have had cause to punish Medusa. So yes, while Athena turned her into a monster, it was because of Poseidon's actions. Do you think we'd be reading about an ordinary mortal who lived a wholesome, albeit sheltered life? There's no drama," he declares excitedly. "No passion. That's what I gave you. I gave you passion."

I faintly hear the crowd begin counting down from ten, but it doesn't register we're seconds away from the start of the new year, my mind clouded.

"Like I did for Julia," he adds.

"What did you say?" I hiss, my eyes wide as my brain swirls with dozens of questions. Did he do the same thing to Julia? Did he assault her, too, getting her pregnant, and that's why she stayed with him? Or does he mean something else entirely?

"Hope you took good care of my girl," Wes cuts through, pulling me to him.

"I certainly did," Nick remarks, draping an arm around

253

Julia's shoulders.

I should look away from him, focus solely on Wes, but I can't. Instead, I continue to study his expression for any hint of what he meant by his last statement. But as was always the case, it doesn't falter. An impenetrable fortress.

When that proves futile, I shift my attention to Julia, an awkwardness in her stature as she stands beside her husband, as if his touch sickens her. Or maybe I just *want* to see it. I don't know what to believe anymore, my own eyes feeling like they're betraying me in the cloud of alcohol and masks.

"Come on, honeybee," Wes croons as he grips my chin, forcing my eyes back to his. "Let's ring in the new year."

I stare into his brilliant blue orbs, urging them to provide me the peace and serenity they have since the beginning. Since he carried me out of that crosswalk and to safety. But they can't. The safety and security I thought I'd found has been eviscerated.

"Five... Four...," he says, joining the countdown.

I try to find my voice, but I'm unable, too scared about what this new year will bring. I want to rewind the clock to when Wes and I danced. Want to live life in that moment, and that moment only. I fear what we shared then is gone forever.

"Three... Two... One... Happy New Year!" The room erupts in cheers over the opening measures of "Auld Lang Syne", confetti and streamers falling from the ceiling, covering everyone.

"Happy New Year," Wes murmurs, lowering his mouth to mine. "I have a feeling this will be the best year yet."

I smile, wishing I could share his enthusiasm. But a premonition deep inside tells me everything's about to change.

"Happy New Year," I respond, drawing him to me, our lips meeting in a desperate kiss.

For the past few months, Wes has become the calm in the storm of my life, a magic elixir that could chase away the darkness.

I don't think anything can do that now.

# CHAPTER THIRTY-ONE

LONDYN

"This can't wait until tomorrow?" Wes asks the following afternoon as I step into my living room, dressed in a wrap dress and my knee-high boots.

All night, I'd tossed and turned, unable to sleep for more than a few minutes at a time. Whenever I heard a sound outside our suite, my heart leapt into my throat, panic overtaking me at the idea that Nick had somehow sweet-talked his way into getting a key and was about to break in. But that never happened. Still, I needed to get out of that hotel. Needed to go where I felt safe. And that was no longer at either of Wes' homes. I needed *my* condo. So after we ordered an extravagant room service breakfast, I lied and told him something work-related came up and I needed to get home.

"They wanted someone to look at the place today," I respond, looking to where he's lounging on the couch with his tablet in front of him, fixing a few designs his team sent him earlier in the week.

I hate that I'm lying to him, but I need to talk to Julia without Wes knowing until I have some answers. Or at least more information. So instead of telling him of my plan to pop in to visit Julia at her bakery this afternoon, I told him I had to meet a potential client for a historic home renovation.

"I'll be as quick as I can," I assure him with a smile.

Not wanting him to read too much into my anxious demeanor, I saunter toward him and take the tablet from his grip, straddling him.

"Then when I get back, we'll have some fun." I whisper my lips along his jawline, a bit of scruff starting to grow back.

"Is that right?"

I nod. "Why, yes, it is, Mr. Bradford."

"And what kind of fun did you have in mind?" he asks,

squeezing my ass as he moves against me, making it clear how much he wants me.

"Use your imagination. I'm sure you'll come up with something." I hover my lips just over his, pausing there a moment before pushing off him.

"You're really going to leave me like this?" he groans, making no move to cover up his obvious arousal.

"I sure am. But don't worry. I'll be back soon."

I turn from him, heading toward the foyer and grabbing my purse off the entryway table.

"Hey, Londyn?" Wes calls just as I'm about to disappear out the door.

I pause, glancing over my shoulder and meeting his eyes.

"I love you."

I sigh, tension momentarily leaving my body. He tells me he loves me several times a day. But something about this one feels...different. I can't quite explain it. But I don't care. It's exactly what I need right now.

"And I love you. You for me, me for you. For the rest of our lives."

"You for me, me for you. For the rest of our lives," he repeats.

I hold his gaze for a beat, then turn, leaving him behind so I can run my...errand.

As I make my way to my car, I pray Julia isn't too hungover and shows up at the bakery to catch up on paperwork, as she mentioned she planned to do this afternoon. I debated texting or calling her, but didn't want to clue Nick in. The last thing I need is for him to figure out what I'm planning and get to Julia before I can.

The fifteen-minute drive from my house to Julia's bakery in Buckhead seems to take an eternity, my nerves kicking up with every light I'm forced to stop at and wait. I have no idea what I'm even going to say to her. How do you tell someone her husband is a rapist? Worse, how do you ask if he ever did the same thing to her? How do you convince someone it's okay to come forward? That she doesn't have to hide anymore?

When I pull into the parking lot closest to the bakery, my

stomach churns, a flash of anxiety pulsing through my veins. I debate turning around, unsure whether this is the right thing to do. But I refuse to remain the cursed Echo I was all those years ago. I need to do this. For me. For Julia.

Slinging my purse over my shoulder, I head toward the rear service entrance, assuming the front door is most likely locked since the bakery is closed for the holiday. When I turn the corner and see Julia's SUV parked there, I expel a relieved breath. Approaching the back door to the bakery, I pause, running my sweaty palms over my dress before knocking.

"Julia?" I call out. "It's Londyn. Are you here?"

I press my ear to the door, listening for any motion from within. Not immediately hearing anything, I knock again, calling out once more.

"Jules?" I try the handle, expecting it to be locked. Instead, it turns, the door giving way.

I don't do anything right away. This is the point in scary movies when I usually scream at the woman not to go in. That it's a trap. But this isn't a scary movie. This is Julia's bakery. And she told me she'd be here. I have no reason to believe otherwise. She probably just has her earbuds in, her music drowning out everything else.

"Julia?" I crack the door open, a loud groan echoing from the hinges. I step inside, timidly making my way through the storage area and into the kitchen.

Normally, this place is a beehive of activity, every surface covered with flour and trays upon trays of cookies, cakes, and pastries. But today, it's devoid of life, florescent lights reflecting off shiny aluminum surfaces.

"Jules, are you here? It's Londyn. There's something I need to speak to you about. It's kind of important."

The heels of my boots click on the tile flooring as I head toward her office at the far end of the kitchen, dropping my purse on one of the metal prep tables. When I peek my head in and see she's not here, either, my shoulders slump. She was here at some point. What looks like purchase orders sit on her desk, the door to the safe open. Plus, I saw her car out back.

"Julia's not here."

The deep voice causes the hair on my nape to stand on end. I whirl around, inhaling a sharp breath when my eyes fall on Nick's intimidating frame. For the past several years, I pictured him in the attire he wore the night he assaulted me. The same attire he wore last night. Dark suit. Dark tie. Dark mask. Dark, dark, and more dark, his blond hair the only lightness he possessed.

But now, he's dressed in a pair of jeans, cream sweater, and loafers, just like he was during the months we forged our friendship. The months we bonded over art, literature, and marriage struggles. It almost makes me soften my resolve. But I don't. I know the truth. That Nick is a wolf in sheep's clothing.

"And whatever you came here to tell her better not be about me."

"Where is she?" I ask, flashing a brief look at my purse just a few feet away.

"At the hotel. She can't handle her liquor all that well. And being the compassionate, doting husband I am, I came to get the paperwork and bank deposits she'd wanted to go over."

I stare at him. Should I believe him? Or is there another reason Julia wasn't able to make it here?

"So, is it?" he asks when I don't immediately respond.

"Is it what?"

"What you came here to discuss with Julia. Is it about me?"

I cross my arms in front of my chest, widening my stance. "And if it is?"

"Oh, Londyn, Londyn, Londyn," he retorts slyly, advancing toward me. But with each inch he gains, I take a step backward in retreat, my pulse quickening. "When will you learn? I don't play to lose. I only play to win. Do you honestly think she'll believe you over me? I'm her husband. You're just some bitch her brother's fucking for the time being. Plus, she already knows about you."

I blink, my expression falling. "She does?" My breathing increases as even more questions circle in my head. If she knows, why would she remain married to him?

"She doesn't know it was *you*, per se, but she knows the truth you agreed to. That I developed a friendship with an undergrad student who was going through a difficult time. That said undergrad student attended the same masquerade party I did. That said undergrad student drank too much. And being the charitable man I am, I offered to escort her home." He smirks. "College campuses aren't safe at night, especially for a beautiful young woman in a tight little dress." He lasciviously licks his lips, his gaze darkening as he continues toward me. "She knows I was stressed with the new baby. And when said undergrad student kissed me, I was weak and couldn't resist. All of which is absolutely true."

"It was a mistake. I realized that immediately afterward."

"I don't think you thought it was a mistake, Londyn. I think your upbringing says you shouldn't have wanted me like you did. You may have fought me physically, but mentally, you wanted me."

When my back hits the wall, I peer over his shoulder for a potential escape route. My muscles tighten, limbs shaking. But I do everything to give off the impression that he doesn't scare me. He gets off on fear. And I refuse to give it to him.

He rests his forearm on the wall beside me, effectively caging me in. "Which is why I was able to make you come, Londyn. Don't forget that. Don't forget I was the first man to ever make you feel like that. So you can call it assault. Call it rape. Call it whatever. But we both know the truth. You wanted me."

His sinister stare rakes down my frame as he smothers my body with his, his arousal prominent against my abdomen.

"And I think you still do."

"You're fucking delusional," I spit out. "It's only a matter of time until Julia realizes just who she married. You're right. She may not believe me. She may take your side. But Wes believes me. He knows everything that happened. The *true* version of events. The only thing I left out was who, but that can be rectified. You may be her husband, but he's her brother. She'll do anything for him. You?" I pinch my lips into a tight line. "Not so much, especially if what you did to me strikes a chord with her. If it sounds a little too familiar to something she's also experienced."

His jaw tightens, eyes widening for a moment. Apparently, I hit a sore spot.

He drops his arms, no longer trapping me against the wall, giving me a chance to breathe. "Maybe I was wrong about you."

"How so?"

"Maybe you're not Medusa. Maybe you're more like Ovid's Philomela. Are you familiar with that story?" He cocks a brow.

"It rings a bell," I say, despite the voice in my head telling me to take this opportunity to run, to flee. But like that night all those years ago, I don't listen, allowing him to pull me into his chess match once more.

"Tereus was a king who married a woman named Procne," he begins, pacing in front of me, as if lecturing a class of eager students. "After a while, Procne missed her sister, Philomela, so she asked Tereus to bring her to their home. He agreed and set out on the journey. When he saw Philomela, he fell in deep, deep lust."

His voice turns into a growl as he stalks toward me like an animal prowling after its prey. My chest heaves as I remain glued in place, detached from reality, like I'm just watching a movie, not living through this.

"He couldn't shake it. He tried. Reminded himself he was married to her sister." He presses his hips back against mine, circling them.

A whimper escapes my throat, my body seeming to betray me like it did that night. I squeeze my eyes shut as tears escape and slide down my skin.

"He knew he'd never be satisfied until he had her." He leans toward me, dragging his tongue up my cheek, licking my tears.

A tingle rushes through me, partly out of desire, partly out of fear. I think that's what confused me so much about what happened, made me think perhaps I was to blame. It wasn't until I attended a sexual assault survivor's meeting that I learned it's completely normal, that a small percentage of women who are assaulted do feel pleasure. It doesn't mean they enjoyed it. It's still a brutal act. For some, there's simply a disconnect between the pleasure receptors and the brain.

"So, just before they reached his kingdom, he had her in the woods. When she threatened to go public with it, he had no choice but to cut out her tongue."

My stomach roils at the brutality of it all. I shouldn't be surprised. Greek myths are notoriously barbaric and violent. Which is probably why Nick seems drawn to them. They feed his addiction.

"I can't blame him," he says nonchalantly. "He did whatever he needed to protect the kingdom he built. The *life* he built. Just like I'm willing to do."

He makes a move to cage me in, but I'm ready for him and quickly duck away, darting toward the door. But what is normally only a dozen or so feet away now feels like the length of a football field. I only make it a few feet before he wraps an arm around my arms and chest, using his strength to lock me in place. His strong grip makes it impossible to fight him off.

"But don't forget," I pant, hoping to distract him.

"What's that?" he growls.

"Philomela still found a way to tell her sister of Tereus' crimes." I swallow hard against the pain as he tightens his grip on me. "Wove a tapestry. And let's not forget Shakespeare's Lavinia from *Titus Andronicus*. They cut off her tongue *and* hands, yet she refused to stay silent, holding a pencil or quill with her mouth to write out her abusers' names. You can attempt to silence me all you want, but the truth will eventually get out. It always does."

He momentarily loosens his grasp on me, and I take advantage of it, leaning forward to throw him off balance. He stumbles and I quickly spin around, using an upper strike of my open palm in the hopes of breaking his nose. But he moves at the last second, avoiding the blow.

"Kitten really did grow some claws. And learned to fight, too," he remarks breathlessly.

Refusing to engage him any further, I rush toward the exit once more. And once more, Nick catches me, grabbing my bicep and yanking me toward him. His eyes wild with fury and excitement, he reels back, landing a hard slap to my cheek. The blow knocks me off balance, causing me to trip and fall to the floor.

Disoriented, I struggle to stand, but before I can, he's on top of me, keeping me pressed to the floor, a wrist bound in each hand as he straddles my back. It's the same position he used all those years ago. I do everything to swallow down the memories, trying to buck him off, but it only seems to encourage him, his arousal hardening against me.

"You know, I love a woman with some fight in her. There's something incredibly intoxicating about something off-limits." He drags his tongue from my earlobe to that place where my neck meets my shoulder. "Something forbidden."

Despite wanting to panic, I try to stay in control, something I didn't know how to do the last time he had me like this. But instead of zoning out, I focus on any possible escape routes. I have two. Make another dash toward the door and hope to be able to outrun him onto the street and flag down someone to help. Or I help myself and go for the gun in my purse, which is only a few feet away.

"Do you have any idea how often I've thought of you over the years… What was it Wes called you last night?"

I stiffen, holding my breath.

"Oh, that's right." He takes my earlobe between his teeth, biting hard. I yelp, kicking against him, but I'm on my stomach and unable to push up enough to make any difference. "Honeybee."

Bile rises in my throat as Wes' term of endearment rolls off Nick's tongue with such ease. I hate that he's destroyed that, just like he's destroyed everything else.

"And lucky me that you happen to be wearing a dress. If you ask me, I think you *hoped* you'd run into me here."

He adjusts, taking both my wrists in one hand now, trailing a path along my side, lifting up the hem of my dress and ghosting his finger against my panties.

"You were so easy to fuck back then. So ready. So eager." His breathing becomes more ragged as he pushes my panties to the side. "Just like you are now."

"If that's what you need to believe, be my guest. But don't kid yourself. You're just a lie parading around as the truth."

Taking advantage of his weakening restraint on my wrists, I wiggle one away, throwing an elbow back in one swift move and hitting his nose. There's no audible crack, but it's enough to force him to loosen his hold on me.

"You bitch," he bellows, holding his nose to stop the blood from flowing.

I clamber to my feet, my heart pounding with more intensity than it ever has. I'm no longer thinking of anything other than reaching my purse and gun, all my effort focused on that. Nothing else.

The seconds feel drawn-out immeasurably as my fingers fumble for the zipper of my purse and slide it open, barely able to maintain a hold on it. Reaching inside, I say a silent prayer when I feel the cool metal handle of the revolver, pulling it out of my bag.

I'm about to spin around and aim it at Nick when it's knocked out of my hands. I watch as it skids across the floor and toward the back door, frustration building inside me. But I refuse to give up. I can't. Not now. It's either him or me. This time, I won't go down without a fight.

Using every ounce of stamina I possess, I dart after the weapon, but Nick tackles me, a sharp pain radiating through my hip when we hit the floor.

I scream as I reach for the gun, both of us grabbing onto it at the same time. I summon all the strength I can to aim the barrel away from me and at Nick, but I'm beyond the point of exhaustion, my shaky muscles ready to give out. The last thing I remember seeing before the percussive pop fills the space is Nick's cold, malicious eyes peering at me.

I've always been fascinated with history. From the stories various cultures and generations told through their art. To the way we've evolved as a society since the dawn of time.

But one of the most intriguing subjects I studied was the American Revolution. Most of my classmates never found it that remarkable. After all, it's shoved down our throats, from the midnight ride of Paul Revere to the "shot heard 'round the world".

And it's the "shot heard 'round the world" that always fascinated me. How a skirmish between the Minutemen soldiers and the Redcoats on the Lexington Green changed the face of this country. The altercation itself isn't too exciting. Confrontations between opposing sides are what wars and battles are made of. What I found so significant about it is that to this day, over two hundred years later, no one knows which side fired that initial shot.

One single shot fired on the village green.

Yet it changed the course of history as we know it.

Just like this one shot is about to change *my* history.

## TO BE CONTINUED...

# ATONEMENT

***Coming Soon...***
***The epic conclusion to the Possession Duet.***

Londyn Bennett entered my world like a hurricane, one I was grossly unprepared for. But in the short time we've known each other, she's opened my eyes to things I never expected. She taught me about acceptance. Compassion. Love.

Because of her, I've also been forced to learn about prejudice. Cruelty. Hate.

We may come from two different worlds, but the second we met, our hearts beat as one, nothing able to sever our connection.

Or so I thought.

When the bubble we've been living in bursts, will our love be strong enough to weather the hurricane-force winds threatening to upend everything? Or is hate too powerful to overcome?

A wise person once told me that the right path isn't always the easy one.

I never realized just how treacherous the right path could be.

www.tkleighauthor.com/atonement

# PLAYLIST

*The Butterfly Effect* - Before You Exit
*Forgive Myself* - Griff
*Fire* - Jordy Searcy
*Lovestruck* - Neisha Grace, featuring Natalie Weiss
*Letting Go* - Tristan Prettyman
*In the Silence* - JP Cooper
*Using* - RITUAL with Emily Warren
*Rewrite the Stars* - Zac Efron, Zendaya
*Call it a Night* - Wild Rivers
*Sin in your Skin* - Aiden Martin
*Perfect for Me* - Justin Timberlake
*Not Losing You* - Maddie Poppe
*Moment* - Noah Guthrie
*Been a Long Day* - Rosi Golan
*This is on Me* - Ben Abraham, Sara Bareilles
*Grace* - Rachel Platten
*Orpheus* - Sara Bareilles
*Rainbow* - Josh Rabenold
*Power over Me* - Demot Kennedy
*Promising Promises* - Jon McLaughlin
*I Don't Look Like Her* - Daisy Clark
*Love Song* - Emily Bear
*Something in the Rain* - Rachael Yamagata
*Let Me Down Easy* - Andrea von Kampen
*Colour Me In* - Damien Rice
*Masterpiece* - JP Cooper
*Heaven* - Julia Michaels
*Suddenly* - Jason Walker
*Enemies* - Jason Walker
*La Vie en Rose* - Madeleine Peyroux
*Uptown Funk* - Bruno Mars
*Need You Tonight* - Welshly Arms
*In the Air Tonight* - Judith Hill

*Uninvited* - BELLSAINT
*Something I Can Never Have* - Nine Inch Nails
*Holding Out for a Hero* - Nothing But Thieves
*Bang* - Moda Spira

# ACKNOWLEDGMENTS

I know I tend to say this about all of my books, but this time I mean it. Writing the first half of Wes and Londyn's story has been the most challenging part of my author career. I've written twenty-something books at this point (I think 27?), and it never gets easier. I know how to write a love story. But the story contained in these pages is so much more than a love story.

There were quite a few scenes I literally had to get up and step away from my laptop because it physically hurt my heart. I'm lucky to have grown up in a very welcoming and accepting family. I never really learned what hate was or was exposed to it in any way. Like Julia teaches young Imogene, my parents taught me to treat everyone I encountered with respect, regardless of race, national origin, or sexual orientation. And these were all lessons I carried with me into my adulthood, and during my time working in the criminal justice system.

So on that note, I must first thank all my incredible sensitivity readers for taking the time to read this and offer me feedback on what it's like being black in America — Renita, Curtis, Crystal, and Keeana. You all rock my world. I promise to have Atonement to y'all very soon. And thank you for supporting this project with everything you have.

A big thank you to my husband, Stan, for never complaining when inspiration strikes and I ramble restlessly, talking out plot points for you to help with. I couldn't do this without you.

Thanks to my little Harper Leigh. You make me want to be a better person. It's my hope that you never have to know hate.

To my amazing editor, Kim Young. Thanks for working your magic on these pages. I can't tell you how much I appreciate all you do to fit me into your schedule.

To my incredible PA, Melissa Crump. You rock my world. Thanks for keeping me organized. I couldn't do any of this without you. I know. I tried. And I was ready to pull my hair out. Love you.

To my BFF, A.D. Justice. Thanks for always being a quick message away whenever I need you to talk sense into me. This business would suck if I didn't have you on my side.

To my beta team. Thank you for dropping everything to read and offer feedback for me! Joelle, Lin, Stacy, and Vicky. You guys rock my world. #BurnhamBitchesForLife

To my admin team — Melissa, Joelle, Lin, Vicky, and Lea. Thanks for keeping my social media and reader group running smoothly when I'm locked in the cave. I'm so incredibly grateful for all you do for me.

To my fantastic promo team! Thanks for always helping to share my books with the world. I can't tell you how much I appreciate everything you do for me.

To my review team — thanks for taking the time to review each and every one of my books, regardless of the subject matter. I appreciate each and every one of you!

To my reader group. Thanks for giving me a fun space to disappear to when I need a laugh.

And last but not least, thank you to YOU! Thanks for picking up this book. Whether it's your first T.K. Leigh book or your twenty-something, I appreciate each and every one of you. Sorry about the cliffy. I promise to get Atonement to you as soon as possible!

Love & Peace,

~ T.K.

# ABOUT THE AUTHOR

T.K. Leigh is the *USA Today* Bestselling author of the Beautiful Mess series, in addition to several other works, ranging from fun and flirty to sexy and suspenseful. Originally from New England, she now resides in sunny Southern California with her husband, beautiful daughter, rescued special needs dog, and three cats. When she's not planted in front of her computer, writing away, she can be found training for her next marathon (of which she has run over twenty fulls and far too many halfs to recall) or chasing her daughter around the house.

T.K. Leigh is represented by Jane Dystel of Dystel, Goderich & Bourret Literary Management. All publishing inquiries, including audio, foreign, and film rights, should be directed to her.